This book is dedicated to parents who have quietly helped their children to love - no matter what.

Thank you Mum. Thank you Dad.

MARK JAMES BIRKETT

FINDING FRED

MJ Birkett Publishing: Salisbury, UK

mark@mjbirkett.com

Illustrations & Cover by MJ Birkett Publishing

mark@mjbirkett.com

Contents

PART I
Leaving
2008

CHAPTER 1: Home

Fred loved Fridays. They allowed him to feel a temporary escape from the terrible decision to become a teacher. He told himself that he was saving the world but most days he just felt like a knackered baby-sitter who had probably made his students worse. Fred fantasised about teaching in the way he did most things: he imagined it would involve climbing onto desks, slamming fists into the air, and inspiring a generation of poets and artists – Robin Williams in the Dead Poet's society. But his reality had more in common with a prison guard: they both dealt with dangerous people. The days demanded discipline, the discipline to stop cowering behind a desk and the discipline to stop the children climbing underneath them. As to the aspiration to inspire poets and artists, he would settle for students who tolerated punctuation. To Fred, teaching was a giant red pen of crap. He hated it.

At 25, he was becoming cynical. His days of high idealism and champagne socialism were fizzling away. Austere grim managers insisted on routine and regularity; they drained his dreams like some anti-flood trawler sucking moisture from the ground. They demanded reality when he yearned for fantasy: *8b are not capable of live performance and dramatic recreation* – the facts of his superiors drifted through his head.

"Line them up in silence, make them write the date and title in silence, and then get them to start a simple task in silence," his mentor, Sasha, told him, again.

"They're not learning anything though. It's trivial; meaningless. About obedience and patriarchy." Fred bemoaned.

Sasha smiled at him, "It's just to settle them. Trust me." She pulled a folder from her bag. "Here, use these." She handed him a pile of resources to use. "Now, come-on, let's talk about something more interesting. Who's the special man this weekend?"

Fred melted. The armour he wore for professional jousting came off. He was an open book when it came to his personal life. His thoughts and feelings poured out like Niagara Falls. "He's a lawyer or something fancy like that," Fred said, "Can't quite remember, but we're going to meet in London…"

"Naughty," Sasha said, placing her stationary back into her pencil-case.

"Carpe Diem, Sash," he said, his tongue slightly poking, slightly resting, across several teeth to the side of his mouth.

"Perhaps for you, Fred. The rest of us have to get our kicks from the soothing respite of a well-deserved free-period." She nodded toward the clock on the wall of the staffroom, a pale blue that hadn't felt fresh paint in decades. "While you enjoy last period of this glorious Friday afternoon with 8b, I'll delight in a nice cup of tea and get my papers marked. How's that for Carpe Diem?" The rain pelted the greenhouse-like windows, and it made them appear as if they would just give-in and shatter at any moment; it didn't help that the school bell pounded the frames like an invisible psychiatrist applying electro-convulsive-therapy.

"You are so mean," Fred said.

Sasha lifted her bag from the grimy desk and walked over to the comfy chairs. She buried herself in a set of essays, and without looking up, she reminded Fred to use the starter tasks: "You'll thank me later," she said as a wicked smile stretched across her face.

Sheets of paper, broken crayons and glue sticks ricocheted across the floor and desks. The students had departed when the real authority of the school, the bell, had sounded for the last time of the week. Fred loved these moments. 3.00pm Friday afternoons were the peaks of happiness: every minute after was a minute closer to a Monday morning. Carpe Diem, he thought whilst closing the door, leaving the state of his classroom behind him. Pam, the cleaner, wished him a good weekend as he passed her in the corridor.

As Fred entered the staffroom, Sasha remained in the same comfy chair minus 20 essays. "Coming to the pub, Sash?" He asked her, collapsing into a chair opposite. "You've marked all that already?" He stared at her pile slightly horrified, slightly awe stuck.

"I'll meet you there in half hour, shouldn't take me much longer to finish these."

"Oh, come on Sash. It's Friday."

Before she could tell him to sod off and let her finish, a group of other teachers flooded the room. "Come-on Freddie, first rounds on you, you tight bastard!" Sasha waved goodbye to him without removing her eyes from the script on which she was scribbling comments. The teachers collected bags and coats from the staffroom and departed – Fred included.

Fred squeezed into the back of a red Micra, between a well-built PE teacher whose dream had always been to play Rugby for England, and a 6-foot Maths teacher who he loathed – *Obnoxious Nick*, he thought to himself in the confined space of that poor car, which was repeatedly attempting to ignite. Heeta, a fellow English teacher of Fred's, twisted the key again and again, each time pressing her brown fingers a little tighter around them as if the keys could absorb her optimism and hope. She slammed her hand on the wheel as if smacking a pony in a state of joy. "Yes girl!" Her voice boomed, deep and strong, in opposition to her delicate physical appearance. The car's passengers erupted into a chorus of cheering and roaring as the poor window wipers frantically knocked away the rain. The head of RE, sitting beside Heeta reached into her bag and passed several cans of lager back to the boys.

"Cheers!" She said to them sipping the froth of her own open can. The car rattled through the school gates, over the speed bump, and within half a minute Eliot High dissolved into the grey clouds. Bea, the Head of RE, had already guzzled half her can of lager while Tom, that aspirant Rugby star, had finished his. Fred noticed and finished the rest of his can in one go so that he could jibe *Obnoxious Nick*. "Come on, Nick, you've barely touched yours. It's Friday!"

"I don't need to drink to enjoy myself, Fred. Why don't you have another can though – you clearly seem to enjoy it so much." Laughter erupted into the car and attention turned to Fred, who deep down, didn't like, nor could handle, as much drink as he made out. Bea handed another two cans into the back of the car. Fred and Tom took one each. Tom in earnest opened his and took another large gulp. Fred, rather foolishly backed into a uncomfortable situation of his own making, also opened his and pretended to enjoy a large gulp. He'd rather suffer the displeasure of the bubbles and risk premature intoxication than become an obvious hypocrite, and in short, a twat.

"Personally, I'd take it a little easy though," said Nick, "wouldn't want to get into the same state as last week, would you Fred?" Laughter spluttered into the car again.

"What are you talking about?" said Fred.

"Oh, calm down you pair of queens," said Bea. There was no malice in her words for Tom and Fred were both prone to dramatics in their own ways. "You just need to fuck each other and then all the sexual tension will be resolved." She finished her can of lager and continued to speak whilst reaching into her bag to open another. "Consider yourselves lucky. I haven't had anybody in years. It's not quite as easy when you're past a certain age." There was no pity in her voice. She was declaring a fact.

"Ah, come on Bea, you always know I'll give you one if you need it." Tom said in earnest.

"Thanks Tom. Perhaps if you were twenty years older, I'd take you up on that offer, but I need a proper man." Again there was no offence to her words, just another declaration of fact.

"Well, you know where I am, Bea." Tom said taking another large sip. A comfortable silence emerged for a few minutes as the car darted across Nuneaton's mini roundabouts, fish and chip shops and avenues of semi-detached houses. "Your tits are great." Tom added matter of fact.

"What about mine?" Heeta jibed. Bea and the boys laughed as Tom failed to contain his verbal incontinence. She released him from his suffering, "Oh shut-up Tom. We're here. You can buy me a drink as an apology."

The light from within the pub's frosty windows bulbed outward onto the heath's otherwise blackening grass. The recent smoking ban had forced half the pub's population to huddle together in plumes of smoke beside the entrance. Heeta, Tom and Nick waded through while Fred and Bea promised to meet them inside after a quick cigarette. Bea took herself a Marlborough light and left the packet open as an invitation for Fred to take one. After putting the packet away, she also proceeded to use her lighter to get them both going. They uttered greetings as more school colleagues turned-up and filtered into the pub.

"How'd you find Kieran De…" but before Fred could finish, Bea answered him.

"A little bastard."

They took long drags on their cigarettes and stood in silence as the nicotine kicked into their systems. Fred continued, "Can he read, do you think?"

"Probably not," Bea declared in her usual factual tone.

"But how has he got to 12, 13 and not learnt to read?" Fred asked Bea, who merely shrugged her camel-like shoulders humped either side of her freshly cut bob. Fred continued. "It's not right. And it makes our job impossible. How're we supposed to meaningfully help them when they can't read properly?" Bea nodded along, the red embers of her cigarette burning themselves down to ash.

"Alright Bea?" Big Dave asked, stopping to give her full attention. Bea tilted her head causing her blond hair to swoosh across each leather shoulder pad. Her neat white teeth popped-out temporarily, and quite unnaturally, like some horse-pony attempting to smile.

"Yeah, good, Dave." She re-opened her packet of cigarettes, lit herself another and offered him one. He slid his manly fingers into the packet, and felt around at the remaining few, then slowly pulled himself one out, the whole time his eyes locked onto hers.

Fred flicked his butt onto the floor and squashed it with his brown adult-school shoes. "I'll see you in there, Bea," he said whilst walking into the porch.

The place was packed already. Streams of men and women clustered into small groups and hovered between the bar's countertops and tables. The slightly sticky feel of the wooden floor promised more of what was to come: gentle bumps and spillages of beer as people became looser and increasingly comfortable in their instability, until eventually they have that one drink too many and switch into a kaleidoscopic state of deep regret and ecstasy. Well for Fred, anyway. He sifted through the crowds to join his.

"Chug. Chug. Chug." Tom boomed at Heeta, who lifted a full pint of brown ale to her gorgeous little lips, and let it slide down her deceptively powerful throat, into her deceptively tiny body. She slammed the empty glass onto the countertop and told the white boy, Fred to get another round in.

"Yeah Freddie," Tom said lifting his own half-finished glass and pointing at it with his other hand just in case his intention hadn't been made clear. Fred approached the bar and folded his arms once he'd fought for a bit of space to wait-in and eventually be served. Nick stood at the countertop opposite. *Jesus Christ,* thought Fred. They both stared at anything but each other to avoid conversation.

"What can I get for you, love?" the barmaid asked Nick.

"Pint of Newkie Brown, three pints of fosters, and a double Gin and Tonic, please." Fred heard Nick's order. He was clearly buying a round and so he could no longer pretend to ignore him.

"Is that for us?" Fred asked across the bar.

"No, it's all for me." Nick replied.

"I was getting a round-in", Fred said, although the truth was that he hadn't thought about buying Nick or Bea a drink.

"Well, I guess you can get the next one." Nick said as he took the fresh pint of Newkie Brown Ale and sipped a little while the barmaid prepared the rest of his order. Fred wiggled out of his position at the counter and walked around so that he could help Nick carry the drinks.

Nick handed Fred the Gin and Tonic and one of the pints of lager. He pocketed a few coins of change from a £20 note and wedged the three pints together so that he could carry them himself.

"Fucking hell, Freddie, you'll do anything to get out of buying a pint!" Tom said eliciting laughter at Fred.

"Bea, not come-in yet?" Fred asked, hoarding his and Bea's drink while Nick handed the others out.

"Cheers, Nick." Tom and Heeta said, which caused Fred to flush a little.

"Yeah, cheers, Nick." Fred mumbled before changing the topic, "How'd you find Kieran Deel…" but again before he could finish his full name, the others interrupted.

"Fucking arsehole," said Tom,

"Wanker," said Heeta.

"Bit of a plonker," said Nick.

"Yeah, but do you think it's just because he can't read?" Fred responded attempting to muster to the defence of a little shit that he detested and who made his working life a misery.

"He can't read because he's a tosser," said Heeta. "You need to be firm with him and not take any of his crap."

"Yeah, but it must be hard. Going to school every day, sitting in lesson after lesson, not really being able to access it properly." Said Fred.

"He can't access your lessons because they're a pile of shit," said Tom, who laughed at his own comment, and was joined by Heeta and Nick.

"Fuck off. English is difficult. They actually have to think, not like PE," Fred said.

"Ah, well, what is it that you teach again, Heeta? Pretty sure it's English too, and you're not shit." Tom said, continuing to laugh.

"Fred," Heeta said, addressing him firmly before she spoke. "Trust me, don't take his shit. He can read better than you think he can. And if he can't, then he needs to want it a bit more. There's loads of kids that struggle with reading and they're not absolute nob-heads. Don't pander to his crap."

"It also couldn't hurt if you did plan and make your expectations a bit clearer," Nick added. The others could comment, but how dare *Obnoxious Nick. Oh, fuck off,* Fred thought. Bea sauntered into the pub and re-joined them; her unnerving horse-smile had stopped, but a satisfied grin remained. The warm fuzz of several lagers, the thick tar of several cigarettes, and the husky whiff of several big Dave breaths had combined to provoke some internal pleasure. Fred handed her the Gin and Tonic, which she drank nearly in one.

"I'll get us another round," she said and wondered back up to the bar, close to where big Dave stood.

"How long's that been going on?" Nick asked.

"Ain't nothing going on. He just leads her on, promises a bit of knobbing then never follows through. Fucking wanker." Tom said.

"She's a big girl," said Heeta, "and not likely to appreciate you interfering, so leave it alone." Again, her little body contrasted with the absolute authority of her actions. Tom sulked into his pint, which Heeta pushed upward causing it to lift toward his mouth.

Fred took a large gulp of his lager. He was still pissed at their attitude toward his teaching. "So you're telling me, that the system is honestly serving the likes of Kieran Deele…" but again the others cut him off.

"For fuck sake, Freddie, boy. We are the system. And yeah, we ain't the best, but some kids are just little fuckers." Tom said. "You need to stop seeing yourself as a hero." At this, Nick snorted into his Newkie Brown.

"What the fuck are you laughing at?" Fred demanded of him.

Nick, who presented himself with a generally austere but not unwarm or unlikeable personality (to anyone other than Fred) struggled to control himself. The thought of Fred – a hopeless, useless egotistical child (in Nick's perspective) as being a hero, saving others, was simply too ridiculously funny. In his Newcastle accent, he attempted to utter "nothing" several times, but couldn't pronounce the full word without losing himself to further laughter. The others joined-in and this pissed Fred off, even more. He didn't mind people laughing at him; indeed, sometimes he even enjoyed the attention, but he couldn't stand that it was orchestrated by Nick.

"Oh, fuck off, the lot of you. I'm ringing to see where Sasha is." He stormed out to the garden terrace at the back of the pub where clusters of more smokers choked the dark, evening air of the little freshness the overcast day had given it.

Several hours past: ale-pumps piped fresh beer, barmaids poured Gin and Tonics, wooden floors absorbed spillages. Fred was in that delusional state where he believed the entire world was fascinated with his life, that his very existence was akin to the lead role of a live Hollywood movie. The evening only promised excitement, development, drama. A penny splashed into his full pint causing white froth to plop onto his chin and cheek. Everybody sitting around the long table erupted into an Amazonian roar-like cheer as if the pub had become a tribal village hosting a flamboyant wedding-bachelorette ritual. *Fuck,* thought Fred.

Synchronized fists banged the tables and created a chorus of rhythmic thuds. A harmony joined, of 'Down. It. Down. It. Down. It.' Fred looked at his pint, considered the taste of vomit that he sensed brewing at the back of his throat. He closed his eyes, lifted his pint to his reddening lips – a consequence of the several glasses of red wine he'd just finished – and drank the pint in what he imagined to be one gulp, but which in reality was seven or eight gulps of liquid that flowed back and forth between his mouth and the pint glass. At least a quarter of the pint had leaked onto his chin and jumper, but eventually the pint was gone, and nothing, save the penny, remained. The table, although hard to imagine, crescendoed into a louder roar of applause.

Heeta slapped Fred on the back to congratulate him.

"Better get the round in now, Freddie," Tom laughed. But that vomit was on its way. Fred's chair scraped backward, his body wobbling in its otherwise unchanged position. As happens in a state of intoxication, the body tends to react to instructions one at a time, and far slower than one appreciates.

"Hey, Fred, you look like one of 8b," one of the teachers shouted across the table, causing a new pulse of laughter to charge the electric energy among the group.

Now he had pushed his chair away from the table, he had space to lift himself up. Like someone stepping off a rollercoaster, he lingered in the same position for a few seconds, feeling out the floor before he attempted to move. Eventually he removed himself from the group and headed to the toilets, where he locked himself into the cleanest cubicle. It didn't take long for the pork scratchings and salt and vinegar crisps to re-emerge from his stomach. Bits of cheap sausage (which were actually made of chicken) and battery-hen fried-egg were distinguishable in the toilet pan, remnants of his school lunch – and Fridays were the better days to brave Eliot High canteen. The heaving sounds stopped. Sounds of spit hitting the pan promised that the worst was over. Fred unwrapped what little toilet paper was left on the brown cylinder and wiped his chin and lips with it. He tried to keep his lips closed so not to put any vomit back into his mouth. He pushed his feet into the ground to give himself the support needed to get back-up. His palm flattened onto the brick wall and from an upright position, he spat into the bowl a few more times before flushing. He watched the sick spin around and then disappear into the pub's bowels. He flushed the toilet a few more times until eventually the water ran clear and only the pan contained specs of resilient vomit, determined to live out the rest of the night glued to a once white toilet pan. He unfasted the lock and left the cubicle.

Nobody was in the sink area but two of the cubicles were occupied so Fred left quickly before anybody came out and realised it was him that had been throwing up. His empty stomach compelled him to exit the pub. Bea rested against the wall outside the front porch. She took-out her cigarette packet and opened it in Fred's direction as he came out.

"Cheers, Bea." He said as his smelly fingers squished the packet slightly while removing one. Bea grinned. She blew a plume of smoke upward into the now pitch-black air. It looked like mist. She put her cigarette into her mouth, freeing her hand to cover the air around her lighter so that she could ignite it without the wind extinguishing the flame. Fred sucked and the embers took. Nicotine eased the painful feeling of hunger and concealed the potency of vomit in his breath. "Just been sick."

He said in a confessional and simultaneously pleasurable tone as if the knowledge possessed power.

"Yeah, I can smell it." Bea said, again in her declarative, un-emotional manner. Fred leaned against the wall and took several long drags on the cigarette with his eyes closed on the inhale and open on the exhale. It was helping, but the cigarette wasn't enough: he needed to eat.

"I'm going to the chippy. Coming? Or want anything?" He asked Bea, hoping she'd say no.

"No thanks. You coming back though?" She said, showing genuine concern. Bea might have an ultra-liberal demeanour for most of her life, but the moment people tried to leave, a sincere sadness jolted within. "Good. See you in a bit," she added in response to Fred's nod. Luckily, a jolt doesn't linger. The sadness faded as quickly as it emerged. She slumped back against the wall, satisfied, and blew another plume of misty smoke into the air. Fred turned left at the gate and strolled, adjacent to the dark empty heath, toward town.

Ordinarily, that is the times when he has not consumed quantities of alcohol that would make doctors spasm, Fred would be afraid of the dark. His mind would summon the images of murderous horror movie villains – Freddie Kruger, Michael Myers, the guy from the Texas Chain Saw Massacre; but worse than those, it was his tendency to conjure the thought of some creepy, 'ordinary' guy, who kidnaps grown men to torture and mutilate, that truly made him afraid. But in this post-vomit stage of intoxication, his mind was slowed. Calm. Peaceful. He was terribly hungry, but bodily needs didn't bother Fred, half as much as mental ones. He loved this capacity to stroll in the dark alone, unafraid, his mind quiet. It was worth the smell of sick and the morning headache, a now certainty. The state of drunkenness also provides an invisible blanket. Fred did not feel the cold. The winds pillaging Englanders like Viking raiders from the North Sea didn't affect him. He walked between the grand manor houses, and the empty road beside the dark open heath in contentment, a rare and most temporary state for Fred.

It was only a short walk before the open heath transitioned into a commercial strip of property: chippies, Indian restaurants, estate agents, betting shops; the usual delights of modern England. Yellow painted window frames wrapped around a large single pane of glass and a red neon light hung in the centre of it: *Jimmy's*. Fred pushed the door and entered. The smell of damp, vinegared wrapping paper dominated the space. A few plastic tables bordered both sides of the aisle to the counter. Sasha and Nick sat together with bags of chips open in their wrappers.

"Hey." Nick said.

Fred was so happy to be this close to food to be bothered by the sight of Nick. Sasha twisted her neck and looked over her shoulder to see who he had addressed. Realising it was Fred, she moved closer to the wall to make space for him.

"Here you can share mine, I won't be able to eat many more."

"Nah, I'll get my own," he lifted his sleeves to show some of the sick stains, "but thanks." He ordered a bag of chips, a battered sausage and can of coke. Then, joined them at the table.

"I thought you had your date this weekend." Sasha said.

"It's tomorrow." Fred said shovelling three chips into his mouth, overcommitting his delicate stomach to fresh exposure. They lingered in his mouth far longer than he expected; the potato mashed itself over and over on his tongue, as his throat protested at anything else either going up or down it.

"You struggling there." Nick said.

Fred folded his arms on the table and then rested his forehead onto them. "I feel crap." He murmured beneath.

"Should have shared mine," Sasha said regarding her chips. She rubbed Fred's shoulder like an experienced mother able to provide care to a suffering child without sacrificing her role within the adult conversation happening simultaneously. She continued talking to Nick as her palm motioned in a mechanical rhythm up and over Fred's shoulder blade. "So, are you going to go for it?" She asked him.

"I think so." Nick said.

"I hope you do. You'd be really great."

"At what?" Fred said with his face still buried in his arms.

"Head of Year," Sasha said on his behalf. Fred lifted as if struck by a new wave of energy. He shoved a chip into his mouth.

"You?" he said.

Nick didn't react.

"Don't be a dick." Sasha said.

"It's fine. He's just drunk." He stared at Fred, who was gathering some traction with his chips. "Actually, it's not that. I mean, he is drunk, obviously, but that's got nothing to do with it. He just seems to have a problem with me."

"Nick." Sasha sensed an argument and attempted to appeal to Nick's sensibility before it brewed further. She swayed her head sideward to motion her disapproval of further discussion on the matter.

"But you can't be Head of Year... you're well you know." Fred said, continuing to shovel more chips into his mouth. His stomach had won the battle with his throat.

"Ah, I probably won't go for it anyway." Nick said as a way of letting the conversation end.

"Yes, you will." Fred said. "And you'll get it because you're what the system wants." He put another chip into his mouth. "A complete yes-man. You'll do whatever they tell you. And it won't even matter if it's the right thing for the children."

Sasha popped her eyes out at Nick as if to tell him, *I told you*. Nick ignored the comments and imitating Sasha's eye movements, steered the conversation onto a different topic, "anyway, who's still left at the pub?"

Fred picked at the batter around his sausage. He shovelled little pieces into his mouth, in between more chips. "Everyone. I told Bea I'd go back?"

"And are you?" Nick asked.

"Dunno."

"I don't think you should." Sasha said.

Fred looked at the clock hung on the tiled wall behind the metallic countertop. "But it's only eight."

"Come back with us." Sasha said, "We're going to watch a film and just chill."

Fred shrugged. He didn't exactly want to go back to the pub, but he didn't want to just chill or watch a film. *Where can that lead?* He thought to himself. "Nah, it's still early. I'll feel alright after these."

"Well, the offers there." Sasha said, closing the matter, knowing that he wouldn't change his mind. Fred had picked-up a decent pace by now and the chips were depleting quickly. It wasn't long before he started on Sasha's bag, although he never touched any of Nick's.

"Right, we're off," Sasha said, indicating for Fred to get up so that she could get out. "You sure you don't want to come?"

He shook his head and sat back down, "Nah, enjoy your film. I'll see ya Monday."

Sasha and Nick said goodbye and left. Fred glanced over his shoulder to check that they were properly gone and then turned to eat the leftover chips in Nick's bag.

Back at the pub, Bea was still outside smoking on the wall. Heeta was still telling the men to man-up and drink their drinks. And the Amazonian tribe of teachers were still roaring and cheering like an enclosed stadium in which they performed the role of both spectacle and audience. The penny (which upon entering a person's drink bound them to consume that drink without pause) had just landed in Tom's pint, and he was close to needing Fred's bathroom visit. He performed his duty, emptying the pint into his stocky frame, athlete, rugby-player stocky, not fat-stocky. Unlike Fred, he stood with much greater grace, ascending in one motion. He may have felt even more pissed but men like Tom, had some inherent feature that separated their internal expressions from their outward behaviour. This worked as both an advantage and a disadvantage. In times of gross intoxication, like now, it preserved the façade of dignity. It was hard to perceive just how drunk he really was.

He headed toward the toilets, but on his way noticed Bea through the window. He meandered toward her as if she were a smell picked up by a hound. The cold bounced off his manly chest, the alcohol smacking it away. Bea took-out her cigarette packet, her third pack of the evening, and opened it in the direction of Tom.

Although his overall appearance held together, concealing his deeply drunken state, his inability to steady his hand for long enough to place his fingers into the cigarette packet did. He wobbled on the spot attempting to remove one. Bea, helping, took one for him. She placed the cigarette into her own mouth, got it going with her lighter, and then removed it. She held it so that the red maze of burning tar, nicotine and paper faced her. Her thumb and finger clenched the end of the butt, but not so much that Tom's lips couldn't lean in and take the lit cigarette directly into his mouth. His thick lips slightly brushed her thumb and finger as Bea let go.

"Cheers," he said before taking a deep inhale and closing his eyes for just a few seconds. He tilted his neck back, letting it flop toward his back, and exhaled. Then, taking the cigarette into his hand, and pulling his neck back to a normal position, he said, "the stars are fucking awesome."

The clouds must have travelled westward with the sun, revealing the beautiful streams of white specs in the otherwise expansive black night-sky.

Bea exhaled, while looking up. Her cigarette smoke dissipated into the vast space. Tom stretched his arm out so that he could lean on the wall slightly above Bea's right shoulder. He leaned in toward her. "You're fucking beautiful, Bea." He said her name as if he were unsure whether it was going to come out as a gulp of vomit or a word. Luckily, it was a word. Bea, completely unmoved by Tom's advance, remained in her cool resting position on the wall. The only thing she did do was rest her head back onto the wall too, exposing a little more of her neck. Tom leaned in, and pressed his thick, sportsman lips onto it. He rubbed his tongue along her skin, the bristles pressing themselves deeply into pores, naked to the eye. His lips moved around her neck like a gentle face exploring a fresh pillow. His hand did the same to her breast. He moved his body closer and pressed it against hers. He thrust his waist upward imitating the thrusts of intercourse. He removed his lips from her neck, pulled his head back enough to look her directly in the face, and say, "You are fucking beautiful," before sinking his lips into hers, two pillows folding into one another.

Bea lifted her hand and attempted to slide it into the top of his jeans.

"You dirty bastards," Fred said as he returned through the gate. Tom relaxed his pressed body as he twisted his neck over his shoulder.

"Fuck off, Freddie. In-fact, don't fuck off, go and get the round in, you cheap bastard." Tom said smiling at Fred. Bea smiled too. She applied a bit of force to let Tom know to pull off her. He did. She brushed her fingers through her hair as if tidying it, but it hadn't actually become messed up, and said,

"Don't worry Fred. I'll come in with you. It's my round." The three of them re-entered the pub; Tom detoured to the loo on his way. The general pub population had thinned a little but not the tribe of teachers, who merely expanded into the extra space. Bea and Fred re-joined them. The drinking games had moved on. The penny no longer circulated through endless glasses, instead the group chanted some rhythmic mantra between clapping their hands and slapping the table with their palms: clap, clap, thud, thud; hands together, hands together; hands flat, hands flat. Someone repeated a lyric over and over, while random people shouted a number leading to the rhythmic clapping and slapping continuing, or said a number causing it to stop. The chain terminated repeatedly, causing the rowdy crowd to howl and bang on the table each time in the same disorderly manner. They cheered at the misfortune of the one responsible for breaking the rhythm, who consequently, was forced to drink, yet more alcohol, in much the same way as the penny dictated. The bar staff didn't police them for they knew which side their bread was buttered: there was a continual filling of the cash register and flowing of drinks to their tables. Eventually the games stopped. Inebriated conversation became its own entertainment, joyously juvenile drunken chatter.

But like drugs, that wore off at some point. For most, this functioned like the school bell: it told them it was home time. Bea, Tom, Heeta, and Fred didn't like home time. It was perhaps this quality that brought them together as a group within a group. They always seemed to be the ones that remained, the ones that the bar staff had to tell that it was time to go. But where was the question that they needed to answer.

"Nightingales is open," Fred said attempting to conceal his throbbing desire to go. He deemed it a high-risk strategy to reveal his own want in case the others objected. But it was Fred's lucky night: Tom had already found his lady for the evening, so he didn't mind going to a gay club. Bea didn't care as long as everybody went wherever they went together, and Heeta couldn't give a damn as long as they served Tequila. So it was decided.

And the next morning, they suffered. Tom awoke in Bea's bed. His white underpants, a T-shirt and one sock remained on. He lay, mostly, on top of the bed cover. A small pool of drawl gathered on the pillow beneath his mouth, and dirty skid marks showed through his white pants, soiling an otherwise beautiful bottom. Bea lay in her white knickers too, no skid marks though. She hadn't managed to remove her jacket. It covered her upper body like a duvet, leaving only her bottom and legs uncovered. A dull light crept into the room and aroused just enough consciousness in each of them to become aware of terrible, dehydrated headaches. Bea's blond bob flopped as she lifted her left cheek from the pillow and piled her right into it, enough for her to exchange the sight of Tom's squashed, drooling face for the red digits shining on her alarm clock: 8.25am. Her eyelids re-closed and she tried to ignore the pain and pleas for water. It was too far to walk. She would ignore the suffering until it became too much; only when her aching head reached the status of toothache, would she expend the energy required to get-up and fetch water.

Downstairs, Fred lay in much the same manner, and with much the same rationale. His arm flopped off the side of the sofa and he was desperate for water, but his desperation was the lesser evil. There was no way he was getting up. Heeta was the only one with the discipline for basic self-care. The stairs creaked as she made her way to the kitchen for water. Her leather handbag hung over her slender brown arm. It was almost larger than her torso and despite its ridiculousness, suited her. She reached into it, took out a packet of paracetamol, and popped two white pills from the plastic-foil. She placed the packet back into her bag and rested the bag on the kitchen work surface. She positioned one of the tablets onto her tongue and the other on the sink ledge. Water fell into her cupped hands and flowed over almost as quickly. She lifted her hands in that cupped position and drank repeatedly from them, swallowing the pills in the process. Afterward, she filled a glass, drank it in one, and then re-filled it. She carried it through to the living room. She perched her petite yet steel body onto the edge of the sofa and slapped Fred's bottom.

"Here white boy," she said handing him the glass of water and paracetamol. Fred moaned unappreciatively. He turned onto his back and scuttled upward so that his head rested in an upright position on the sofa's arm. "Want a lift home?" Heeta asked.

Fred nodded as he drank small gulps. He lived on the other side of town and the painful thought of walking home outweighed any momentary feeling of hangover. "Give me five minutes," he said, pivoting his legs off the sofa and lifting his back upright, "need to use the loo and have a quick cigarette." Heeta nodded. She turned the television on and lowered the volume. Fred grabbed his jumper from the floor and put it back on while walking upstairs. He peed and then headed to Bea's bedroom to steal a cigarette. The door was open. Fred smirked at the sight of them comatosed on the bed. He stepped as lightly as possible around to Bea's side of the bed, her packet of cigarette's rested on the bedside table. Her eyelid peeled backward as his hand touched the empty packet.

"There's a fresh packet in my bag," she said in a husky, she-bear voice. "Get me one too." Fred turned to search through her bag for the extra packet and a lighter. He removed two cigarettes; lit one, handed it to Bea, and kept the other for himself. Bea rolled over and dragged her body to a more upright position. Her head rested on the bedstead as she took long drags on her cigarette. Fred perched on the end of the bed and lit his.

They blew out several streams of smoke into the bedroom before Bea mustered the energy to speak.

"Heeta giving you a lift." She declared in her factual tone. Fred nodded, "I don't mind dropping you off later," she inhaled and exhaled smoke, "when a bit more of the G&T is out of my system."

"You mean when skid-pants is out of your system?"

"Fuck-off Freddie," Tom moaned into his pillow, "and stop staring at my arse."

Fred and Bea exchanged a warm grin before Fred lifted himself off the bed and waved goodbye. Heeta heard the stairs crunch and so turned-off the television. She put-on her coat and headed to the front door with her disproportionately large handbag. They closed the door and Fred, on autopilot, pulled the handle upward as if to lock it. Fred flicked the cigarette on the pavement at the end of Bea's small garden and extinguished it with his adult school-shoes. Together they strolled the ten-minute walk of shame back to the pub carpark where the warmth of Heeta's red micra – once its engine was provoked into action – awaited them. She dropped Fred back at his student-like flat where they exchanged their usual Saturday morning, 'See-you-Monday,' goodbyes.

Fred checked the message on his mobile phone while standing in his kitchen with another glass of water. '*Hope you're not feeling too rough! Good luck on the date tonight ;) Love Sash xx*'. Fred, instinctually, clicked the button to send his screen into an oblivion of deep black, an expression of desire applicable to his own being. He walked to his bedroom, climbed into the duvet, which was in desperate need of a wash, pulled it over his head and closed his eyes. He folded his thighs into his calves, lowered his chin into his chest, and curved his back as far as it would comfortably allow. In a semi-foetal position, he willed himself to sleep-away his hangover. He dreaded the date and pretended as if it were not going to happen.

But Fred could not spend a Saturday night at home. *Where would that end?* He thought to himself. By mid-afternoon, his intolerable hunger and self-company forced him out of bed. He could not bear to be with his own thoughts under that duvet any longer. He swapped yesterday's clothes for a pair of jogging bottoms and a cheap white t-shirt. Despite unhealthy eating habits, his physique was generally good; not much in terms of muscle, but age gave him the advantage of keeping weight at bay. He grabbed an old hoodie from his computer desk and tossed that on.

The contents of his fridge were embarrassing: rinds of cheese and an almost empty tub of Lurpack. He knew the futility of looking but did it anyway. As he hung on the open door, he contemplated how he would resolve the problem. He closed the fridge door and woke-up his mobile phone. He read another message from Sasha, '*Don't oversleep! This could be the one… ;) Enjoy xx'*. He closed the message and checked the time on the screen: 4.36pm. He grabbed his keys from the work surface and his coat from the hallway, then headed to the chippy.

The sky had successfully guarded against the invasion of clouds that afternoon and so it was still unusually bright; perhaps another 30 entire minutes of daylight remained. Fred scuttled toward the nearest chippy looking like something between a zombie, crack-addict, and football hooligan. In the queue, he attempted to make a list of what he needed to do in preparation for his date, but the smell of grease poked at his hunger and opened the cage of his desire, which his subconscious tried to keep locked away. His mind wandered to intense romantic fantasies of surreal indulgence: luxurious silky curtains blowing sensuously from an elegant Parisian *chambre* into a mosaic tiled private terraced balcony, where dazzling lights shone from the Eiffel tower itself. Barry Manilow's, *When a Man Loves a Women, Can't Take His Mind of Nothing Else'*, rather inappropriately, playing on an omnipresent speaker that resembled his heart. There is no conflict or comedy. It's inexplicably, illogically perfect to Fred. No irony in the lyric is felt. Bliss dominates. He is lost in this seductive fantasy. Fresh white pillows on a super king bed with covers and décor fit only for a palace, flicker into his mind's eye. These three images cycle, over and over: the pillows, the curtains, Barry Manilow's Man loving a woman. No people make it into his Eden; they're not needed. These images are enough.

"What can I get you, love?" the chip shop worker asked with her hands pressed onto the grey paper. Fred ordered a bag of chips and a battered sausage. "Salt and vinegar, love?" She asked once the items were on the open wrapping paper. He nodded.

"Just a little bit of vinegar though please." He added as the woman picked up the plastic bottle of vinegar.

He paid and then walked home with his greasy food, trying to get back into that out-of-body state where his self dissolved; where his being became that Parisian *chambre*. But it was no good. Like an amazing dream that one becomes aware of, and is desperate to return, upon awaking, Fred knew it was futile; that it was gone. He was back in the here and now, conscious of his own egoistic existence, his very hungry, hungover, in-need-of-showering, existence.

Fred's body spasmodically dodged the water falling from the showerhead. He would stretch his arm, from his standing position further down the bathtub, to test whether the temperature had returned to a bearable warm, as opposed to the intermittent scolding and artic modes it sadistically preferred. *For fuck sake,* his teeth chattered each time. The upside-down bottle of imperial leather eventually leaked the most pitiful amount of purple liquid into his hands, which he lathered across as much of his body as it would allow; the most important areas took priority.

He picked-up the damp towel scrunched on the floor and dabbed the bulk of droplets on his body. He darted to the airing cupboard to find a fresh towel. "Bollocks," he said, retaking the damp one from the floor again. He continued to use it until the towel felt like it was making him wetter. He threw it into the corner and darted back to his bedroom.

He opened the ironing board and made a commitment to iron two shirts – one for School. But by the time he'd finished stretching the sleeves and moving the first around and around to achieve only a mediocre job, he abandoned the plan. He pulled the plug from the socket and put-on the semi-ironed shirt. He buttoned-up the black buttons sewn into the deep red, velvet-silk, then, slid his legs into a pair of black chinos.

He left his flat without taking a coat. The lack of clouds that had made the day usually bright for mid-February, was making the evening terrifyingly cold. But Fred didn't like taking a jacket out-out, let alone a coat. He reached the station and squeezed himself onto the train with only seconds left before the doors slammed shut. He plonked himself into one of the dirty stained seats and watched Nuneaton fizzle away.

CHAPTER 2: A silver lining

The city energised Fred. Where paracetamol and day-sleep were damage-limitation – the appeasing of a hangover – the city was a giant spa. It massaged the knots and tension out of his murky mind; the fancy teas and smoothies promised to fill his body with vitalising minerals and antioxidants. He swore to himself as he did most Saturday evenings, that he'd move here properly. He'd stop faking it, pretending he was a local, and be one. He was an adult in the city, a man.

He exited the train station with an external frown, a sour-puss smile that attempted to leak his forced thoughts to the city: *I live here. I share with you the frustration of the daily grind, the rat-race, the dog-eat-dog, restless, competitiveness.* But his bright red shirt and lack of coat gave-away his true identity: *I'm a local country boy infatuated with the allure of the big city, here to find romance, and a happy ever after.*

He peacocked past rows of sandwich and coffee stalls, toilets that you had to pay to use, and tie shops, swerving through the mass of people criss-crossing each other like atoms, and heaven knows how, avoiding nuclear collision. The wind, which the entire way to the station had bitten Fred's cheeks like some horrid rabid flea, had either eased or been denied access to the city. He walked the pavement, although still cold, with a renewed sense of warmth and privilege. He imagined himself a model, striding along a catwalk, the audience noticing the smallest movement of his limbs and concerned, obsessed, with his minutest details. He waited at the crossing for the signal to switch with a bunch of other people. He recognised nobody yet felt completely at home.

He entered a Tesco metro; Nuneaton didn't have fancy metro-supermarkets. It only had the normal supersize ones filled with provincial mums doing the weekly shop for their families. Fred looked around and saw single people everywhere, perhaps even gay ones. Of course, he didn't know if they were actually single (or gay), but Fred's view of the world did not rely on evidence. He was comfortable assuming and willing the world into the shape he needed, and at this moment, Fred needed all those people in Tesco Metro to be sophisticated members of a cosmopolitan urban elite.

The gritty reality was that they were mostly depressed or miserable minimum-wage service-workers picking-up nutritionless ready meals, at a disproportionately high cost of their salary, to eat in dingy flats, with partners of equally hard lives. Fred wasn't having any of that. The city was fabulous, and its people were unequivocally exotic. Whereas Nuneaton and its people were brutish. This was his true home. This is where he belonged. He purchased a packet of Marlborough lights.

"£8.50," the checkout assistant said. Fred jerked as if a wasp had just fired its stinger into the side of his neck. *£8 fucking 50,* he thought before immediately censoring himself. He considered it to be a provincial reaction, not appropriate, and a give-away of his bumkin identity. He entered his credit card into the chip and pin machine, nonchalant, telling himself: *people earn more; things are more expensive; life though is obviously better.* As he tapped his pin code into the machine, he tried to think how much it would have cost him back home, but he couldn't remember. It had been quite a while since he had bought his own packet of cigarettes. He usually just smoked Bea's.

His tube pass cost him another £8.50 and by the time he arrived at the bar, his date hadn't arrived so his Gin and tonic cost him a further £13. *Fucking hell,* he thought, *how do people get pissed here?* He put the thought out of his mind and this created the headspace for him to realise just how nervous he was. From the swivel bar-chair, he looked left and right along the counter to scan the room. From behind, a hand lent forward and gripped his shoulder, a manly hand. Fred's stomach collapsed as if the floor was ten stories beneath where it actually was. His skin tensed and his breath rather awkwardly trapped itself causing his face to look as if he were choking or severely constipated. Luckily he had not yet turned around. He swallowed, which allowed him to regain some inner control via a long series of throat-clearing sounds.

"Hey, Fred, right?" The voice said. Fred still had not turned around. A mirror papered the wall immediately above the drinks and below the glass shelves along the bar opposite. Fred tilted his head and attempted to sneak a look at the guy through the mirror before turning, but the guy lent forward and arched his upper body around Fred so that they could see each other directly, "everything alright?" He asked, squeezing himself onto the barstool beside Fred.

With his throat now clear, Fred said, "Yeah. Nice to meet you," his words came out much faster than usual, "I'm Fred. Sorry about that before; I think my drink went down the wrong hole." He took his drink and poured half it down his throat.

"You're pretty nervous." The guy said, "don't be. I'm Michael. I'm pretty easy going." He held out his palm sideward for a handshake. Fred hadn't really given many handshakes before. Fred offered his hand. Michael gripped it, his manly hands submerged his own, or so it felt. "So, where you from?" Michael asked. He had turned his stool so that most of his body faced Fred rather than the bar.

"Nuneaton," Fred said almost embarrassed, "but I'm thinking of moving here."

The barman interrupted the conversation by asking if they wanted drinks. Fred had finished his. Michael looked at Fred, "What're you drinking?" He asked.

"Gin and Tonic."

"We'll have two more Gin and Tonics," Michael said to the barman, who set about making them immediately. "So, you were saying about moving?" He stared at Fred with his warm, manly luscious lips.

"I'm thinking of..." Fred began.

"Sorry to interrupt, I'm just going to pop to the loo quickly." His stare was mesmerising to Fred. He was so confident with his masculinity, his calmness. He was both assertive, camp, polite, and civilised. Fred's experience was that men were usually one or the other. Confident men were crude brutes like Tom, their assertiveness bound to jibing and joking. Piss-taking. Polite men were nerds or prudes. Stiff. This intense suaveness was utterly new. Of course, he'd seen it in films but not in real life. People didn't interact like this in real life. He nodded unable to withhold an earnest desperately vulnerable smile at Michael. He at least attempted to avert eye contact, but even that came across as naively sweet. Michael definitely looked older than Fred had expected but it didn't matter; he was mesmerised by his charm.

As he left for the loo, he gripped Fred's shoulder just as he had when he arrived. The barman placed one of the Gin and Tonics on the counter. It had a fancy cube of ice within it that took up half the glass; the lemon wedged beneath. Fred took a sip and decided that it would be a better idea to drink this one slower, not because he didn't want to get pissed, but because it would look unsophisticated to Michael.

After another few minutes, the barman placed the other Gin and Tonic on the counter. He brought over a little receipt placed within a flat saucer. He looked at Fred, rolled his eyes and placed the saucer on the part of the counter where Michael was sitting. Once he had walked away, Fred lent over to look at the amount: £26 plus a suggested £2.60 tip. *Nearly £30 for two drinks. Fucking hell,* he thought.

A few more minutes passed, and Fred took a few more sips of his drink. He took his mobile from his pocket to check for messages. None. The time glared in bold red digits: 7.24pm. He put it away and nursed his drink waiting for Michael.

He looked left and right along the bar again scanning the room. The bar was beginning to fill up, so it was more difficult to get a good view of the room and slightly awkward sitting next to what was a visibly empty seat. A few people asked if they could take the stool and Fred had to tell them that it was taken.

It was becoming a bit awkward. The barman had returned a couple of times to take payment. At first, he was sensitive, looking to see whether a card had been placed in the saucer without it being overly obvious to Fred, but by the third time, he made no attempt to be discreet. He fingered the saucer with his index finger, making out that he was checking when he knew full well there was no card in it. Michael wasn't coming back. Fred was not only humiliated but extremely pissed-off that he now had a £26 tab to pick-up. The barman could fuck-off if he thought he was getting that £2.60 tip.

Fred stood in the mostly pedestrianised street and leaned against the glass window of the bar. He lit one of his £8.50 Marlborough lights and smoked the whole thing waiting for a plan to emerge. Nothing. He took another cigarette from his packet and tried the same thing again. Nothing. He was consumed by anti-desires: he didn't want to go home. *Where could that lead,* he thought declaratively. He didn't want to go into a bar alone, *'especially not at £13 a drink… I'd wrack-up a £130 bill within an hour. Fuck.* He couldn't get beyond a feeling of being stuck and so he stood against that glass panel smoking his Marlborough lights waiting for the world to pull him away.

After three cigarettes flooded his system with tar and nicotine, he felt a bit sick and light-headed. *A good enough comprise,* he thought: his body needed him to walk; in its own way that was the world intervening, directing the evening onward.

The street was full of people dressed-up fancy. Couples heading for dinner, friends meeting for pre-drinks and nightclub-dancing. Even the coffeeshops remained open. A costa coffee had opened within Nuneaton but people mostly complained about how expensive it was; they advised that it was cheaper to go to the café in Asda. *Not quite the same,* thought Fred as he imagined a group of old biddies sitting drinking black sludge from cheap white mugs with their shopping trollies parked beside them.

He contemplated going in. He could get a coffee and begin writing his debut novel. The story that would awake the entire world; the story that would allow him to tell 8b to fuckoff; the story that would allow him to sit in those bars and drink as many £13 Gin and Tonics as he liked. But the thought drifted away as whimsically as it surfaced: the warm bulbs and sober faces disappeared. Fred continued along the street. *Something will come along,* he thought. At the end of the street, the bars and crowds began to thin. He turned around and returned the way he had walked, back past the coffee shop, and the bar where Michael had left him. He was getting desperate, and cold. *Oh Fuck,* he thought. *Fuck. Fuck. Fuck.* He stopped and leaned against a wall beside the entrance to Miss Saigon. He took his cigarette packet from his pocket, went to take one but couldn't stomach another. He pushed it back into the packet and put the packet away. He felt exposed. *What the fuck am I doing?*

Nuneaton provided for Fred. He knew it and he belonged in his own way. Despite its crappy pubs and the usual bemoaning of amenities, he never felt alone or lost as he did now. No matter where he walked, London was snootily ignoring him. He could drift around its streets all night, but the only thing the city would bring is pneumonia and pick pocketers. Fred's notion of excitement spilling onto every street corner was dissolving in proportion to the quantity of streets he actually walked. The depressing reality of Covent-Garden street-jugglers and motionless mimes replaced his romance. While they certainly added a buzz to the general atmosphere, standing alone, watching the damn things, Fred felt utterly flat. *That's it,* he thought, *I don't give a fuck if it costs me £100, I'm going back to that bar and I'm getting pissed.*

He returned generally the way he came, but like a giant spider web, London's small curvy streets fed into one another, and so, he didn't need to walk the exact-same streets twice. Back on old Compton Street, he decided against the humiliation of returning to the Michael-bar. Instead, he surveyed the options and decided on the place that survived his criteria best: busy, cheap, non-creepy, most people under 50. Fred was terrible at estimating age. His under 50s referred more realistically to under 30s. Consequently, he entered the liveliest bar on the street with the most explicit name: 'G-A-Y'. A bouncer eyeballed his red shirt and black chinos, in a disapproving manner, but he stood aside to allow Fred entry.

Inside, the place was more like a small nightclub. Madonna blared her lyrics through speakers while she danced on the many screens built into the walls. Men danced together in little clusters and Fred slipped between them like a small fish thrown back into water. He was far from comfortable, but his intense feeling of exposure was fading. There was so much noise and distraction, it would be easier for him to blend into the atmosphere; he could give himself a break from himself. He shouted his order to the barman, "a Pint of Estrella Damn please!" He anticipated that a pint would be significantly cheaper than a spirit and was pleasantly surprised when he received change from a £5 note. His spirit lifted. He didn't especially like larger, but it got him drunk quickly, and it was cheap. He could be here. Even if he was alone, he could get pissed and watch people dance. He relaxed.

"Alright Fred?" Nick shouted over the music.

Fred's mood went disproportionately south. London was his thing, his separate life. Even when it ignored him – made him feel lonely and exposed – it was his experience. It made him different from everybody else back in Nuneaton. Nick, by his mere presence, took it away. He made the night meaningless, a waste of money, a waste of heartache. Fred was furious. His teeth clamped hard on his own tongue biting it so intensely that he almost drew blood from himself. *How dare he?* He thought as he slammed his pint onto the high circular table he stood beside.

"Fred?" Nick repeated his name and turned to try and look at him. The loudness of the music prevented him from verbally ripping Nick apart. He couldn't waste his rage to an environment that would soak half of what he had to say. Fred puffed his chest, and pumped breath in and out. He cheeks steeled and his lips scrunched into a paralysed pout.

"Fred, are you alright?" Nick said again. He was alarmed at Fred's weird reaction. He reached his hand toward Fred's shoulder but before it made contact, Fred swiped at it. The blow caused his entire body to twist backward unexpectantly. His other arm swung instinctively to balance himself, but his pint glass slipped and smashed into a thousand ricocheting pieces. The larger splashed onto a cluster of men dancing close by. Fred didn't react. He was too angry. Nick looked like a loveable puppy that had been kicked by some beastly arsehole owner. The men flocked to see if he was ok. A few frowned in Fred's direction, and the most flamboyant among the group said rather firmly and with several expletives bolted onto the end, that he had better watch himself.

Nick assured them that everything was ok and reluctantly they returned to their dancing. Belinda Carlisle had replaced Madonna. Fred remained stiff. Nick was used to him being unpleasant but never physical. It didn't suit him.

"It doesn't suit you." Nick said.

Fred continued to stare directly ahead, his cheeks steeled, his mouth pouted. After a brief silence, he finally spoke, "Fuck. Off. Nick." His words were demarcated. Each its own sentence. His face did not move as he uttered them. Nick was confused. He now recognised Fred was angry, irrationally angry, but this made him think something serious had happened. He decided that it was best to appease Fred, or at least, pretend to appease him.

Nick left. He moved to stand near the bar where he could still see Fred, but where Fred would need to loosen and turn from his eerily ridged posture, to see him. He took his mobile and text Sasha the details of what had happened.

'His date must have gone badly :(hope you're ok x', she responded.

'Whose his date with? Yeah I'm ok, just bit freaked. Never seen him like this.'

'Some guy he met online. Don't leave him x'.

Nick sighed as he read the message. *Easier said than done,* he thought, looking across the room at the mummy dancing like a corpse. He continued typing into his phone: *'Of course... not sure how I'm going to do that though...'*

'You'll find a way. You're brilliant, Mr Head of Year ;) x'. Sasha typed.

Nick smiled and put his phone away. He ordered a fresh drink and stood drinking it at the bar. He kept his eye on Fred, who had moved to sit down on one of the benches built into the wall. He still looked crazy but less insane than before. *Progress,* thought Nick.

Christina Aguilera had replaced Belinda. A few guys had approached Nick at the bar. He refused their offers of a drink. Of course, Fred didn't see it, but Nick was attractive. He was a few years older than Fred, and although he had a youthful appearance, he somehow came across mature, somebody comfortable in his own skin. He was masculine but simultaneously unafraid of his campness. He ordered another drink. He sensed Fred's nuclear self-destruction hadn't been averted just yet.

Like a parent, Nick enjoyed himself but never forgot about his responsibility for Fred. He humoured guys coming onto him and danced a little. Periodically, he peeked over his shoulder to check Fred was still alive. Nick's friends had said their goodbyes to him over an hour ago. They did not understand his decision to stay and look after a weird colleague who had tried to assault him, but they acknowledged his old-fashioned honourable personality and knew it was futile to argue with him. They kissed him on the cheek and went onto bigger clubs, urging him to find them later.

Fred's temper had eased. He had moved from his spot of isolation to visit the bar several times and fortunately, the population of the pseudo-nightclub was more transient than an international airport, so hardly anybody knew of his freaky outburst. This reduced his leprous status: crowds, like jungles reclaiming abandoned settlements, moved back into the space around him and he danced between them. He was hammered – not enough to forget that *obnoxious* Nick was around and needed snubbing – but enough to overcome his self-conscious defence mechanisms that would have ordinarily prevented him dancing alone. A few older men approached him but his eagerness to make them dance scared them away. In the way drunk people misinterpret their strength, both underestimating and overestimating it, he grabbed their wrists with an inappropriate force and tried to spin them. Eventually the crowd learnt to leave him alone and the little darling danced his heart out, perfectly happy.

Nick pulled himself away from a little group he was dancing with, appeasing their protests by reassuring them that he'd be back. He re-took his drink from a ledge tacked onto the wall and stood watching Fred. He smiled, a non-creepy, fatherly smile. He took pleasure in the knowledge that Fred, a self-obsessed, neurotic pain-in-the-ass gobshite, was at peace with himself. Plastered, and though capable of transforming into a stinging nettle at any time should he be provoked, it demonstrated that there was more to him, something happier and free beyond his surface thorniness.

Around 11.00pm, the place thinned out. Fred didn't notice. It wasn't certain that he noticed when songs changed as his dancing moves remained pretty much the same irrespective of the music's tempo or rhythm: his arms flopped over his head and his hips twisted as if he were rolling a hula-hoop around it, over and over. Nick had moved beyond dutiful guardian. He had enjoyed watching Fred enjoy himself. *Oh Fuck,* Nick thought, "Shit", he laughed to himself, "No, I can't," he said, knocking back his last gulp of lager, hiccupping at his own ridiculousness. *There's no way I'm sleeping with Fanny-Fred,* Nick declared to himself. The dregs of the club filtered out leaving the proper filth. Nick was hammered now too, perhaps as much as Fred. *Now or never,* he thought, braving himself to make contact with Fred for the first time since his blow-out.

He stumbled across the now empty space, twisting his own hips to the music. Nick, unlike Fred, did have a natural ability to synchronise with whatever was playing. He slowed his approach once within arms reach of Fred and danced on the spot adjacent to him. They peeked at each other while twisting their hips, swaying their bodies, and crossing their arms behind their heads. They pressed forward toward one another with their chests peacocking into the air as if they had lives of their own. Their bodies brushed. Again, but each time a little harder, until the default position was that they pressed against one another and temporarily separated. The time away decreased and within minutes their bodies were permanently one. Their arms wrapped around each other's shoulders. They kissed, their foreheads touching. Nick moved his arms down Fred's back and rested them on his lower back. He pulled his head back a little to stare at exactly the same time the music stopped, and normal lights flicked on.

They smiled drunk ecstatic, uninhibited smiles at one another, an intensity that would never occur in sobriety. Nick took Fred's hand in his own and led the way out. They didn't speak but stumbled and embraced one another with intermittent kisses and laughter. Outside, neither of them felt the cold. They continued holding hands and walked along old Compton street to find a dodgy taxi that would take them to the station. They just managed to catch the final train back to Nuneaton and together, they stayed the night at Nick's.

CHAPTER 3: Horse Teeth

For the second time that weekend, Fred awoke to a throbbing headache. Memories of the night before trickled through his mind. He opened his eyes and the sight of Nick's flat, the one he shared with Sasha, horrified him. Nick's face pressed onto a white pillowcase facing away from his side of the bed. His bare shoulders lay above the duvet and his naked body beneath. Fred breathed as quietly as he could and lifted the corner of his side of the duvet so that he could sneak out undetected. Nick's eyelids flittered; he woke, and the memories flooded to him too. He swallowed silently, the lump rolling down his adam's apple invisibile to Fred on the other side of the room. He was intent to be equally quiet, his woken state undetected.

Fred fumbled around, collecting his clothes off the wooden floor and putting them on. With his teeth softly pinning his lower lip as if to stop the sound of his breath falling out of his mouth, he bent down to put-on his shoes; then, tiptoed across the room and left. He exited the hallway in the same manner of stealth as the bedroom. He was crossed between mortification and disgust; undecided which side of the bridge was most appropriate. He gently kept his palm on the front door and let it close at a painfully slow speed. He took a large breath on the doorstep and then descended the block's staircase. Outside, he let the glass door of the fancy apartment block (in comparison to his own) bang close. He ran and didn't stop until he was past the garages at the end of the street.

He leant over and his gut spewed sick onto the street pavement. He heaved four times, and the sick become waterier with each. An elderly woman walking her cockapoo stopped and glared across the street: she watched Fred, aghast, as if he were taking a shit in the middle of the street. "I hope you're going to get that up." She said knowing with certainty that he was not. Fred wiped his mouth with his hand and straightened his back. He ignored the woman and ran until he was off that street too.

Fred took the jitty wedged between a row of otherwise terraced houses. It led him onto the canal and then the fields behind. He began crossing them to get to his side of town. On the open grass, he felt into his pocket for a squashed packet of cigarettes. He removed one of the three remaining, placed it into his mouth and realised that he no longer possessed a lighter. "Fuck," he mumbled with the thing hanging on his lip. He removed it and kept hold of it as he walked. On the other side of the field, two women were pottering along the path. The one pushing the pram smoked. Fred ran over, smelling of sick, and asked them for a light. They scowled and told him to fuck off. Fred, now settled on the mortification side of the bridge; he scuttled away feeling like utter trash.

He walked past the closed chippy as his stomach continued eating itself. The only one open on a Sunday was on the other side of town. There was no way he was going. He conceded that he'd have to fork-out and buy the expensive bags of chips from the Chinese restaurant. *What's another fiver after last night?* He, self-piteously, bemoaned to himself. At home, he crawled into bed and only left again that day to walk to the Chinese to buy three bags of their expensive shitty chips. February needed to end.

Bea's crappy ford fiesta honked outside Fred's flat. Despite the miserable rain splashing onto the dashboard, she unwound her window slightly and lit herself a cigarette. She sat, knowing that her honk had only woken Fred, and that he'd be at least ten minutes getting ready, before coming-out. She finished her cigarette and lit another – not wrong about Fred.

He ran down the path in a scruffy jumper and his backpack over his head. The jumper at least, concealed the creases of his un-ironed shirt. He slammed the door shut once inside the car. Bea started the engine and the radio returned to life.

"Good weekend?" She said.

"Yeah, not bad," Fred said blanking-out Saturday night, "How's yours?" Bea shrugged whilst holding her open cigarette packet toward Fred. "Ta, lovely," he said in an exaggerated northern accent. He borrowed her lighter from the open compartment beneath the radio dials and lit-up. "So, how's Thomas?" He said remembering Bea's encounter Friday night.

"We're not going to mention that." Bea said declaratively. Usually, Fred would have poked at her vulnerability, and not let it go, but a thick knot of shame bubbled within his own stomach. He mustered all his strength to contain his own embarrassment and had no time to mock Bea. They rode the rest of the way to school in silence. Fred was plagued by hypothetical conversations with Nick.

The staff lounged on the comfy chairs of the staffroom, waiting for the leadership team to surge through the door and energise them for the week ahead. The Deputy head led the entourage. Her unfashionable yet professional black heels clipped the tiled floor between her squattish, shuffle-like steps. Despite her plump short stature, she was a formidable woman, a long-serving veteran of Eliot High. She strode to the front of the room without greeting any members of staff personally. The Assistant Headteachers followed next. The younger bloke had put on significant weight since taking the job a couple of years ago. He smiled and said hello to several teachers as he walked the aisle. The older, but not old woman, flicked her greasy hair and puffed her chest as she passed the teachers. She gripped her diary and plunged her eyes into its contents once at the front of the room, averting eye contact with anybody. The Head sauntered in at the end, smiling earnestly at anyone that would look in his direction; the upward creases of his lips curved so high that he appeared unnatural, as if his skin had been stappled or as if he had been seduced by some crazy cult that had indoctrinated him with the idea that God would smite those with even the slightest remnant of a frown. They were utterly dysfunctional as a team, but each, in their own way, contributed something that made the school work, just about; the bell rung on the hour and the children shuffled along in compliant response, as children generally do.

The Head spoke first. He pronounced his words very slowly as if he were speaking English to uncomprehending Spaniards or infants about to parrot his words, "Good morning everybody…" - *Good morning Mr. Bates,* said no-one aloud but a few members of staff had been conditioned over the years and so they couldn't help but think it.

He paused after his formal greeting and did a sweep of the room with his creepy smile. The staff collectively avoided his direct gaze, lifting their hands to scratch their foreheads, plopping pens into their mouths whilst faking gestures of deep contemplation. Several of the ladies looked down to adjust their skirts, and the men pulled at their jumper sleeves. The Head continued, unfazed by the response, in his painfully slow pace. "We have an exciting week ahead that Mrs. Addison will tell us more about in just a moment." He paused again to look over at Mrs. Addison, the Deputy Head, who expressed the irritation that many of the staff felt but dared not show. "Then, we will hear from Mrs. Barnaby about the upcoming Mock examinations for Year 11." He did his creepy pause again, staring the female Assistant Headteacher up and down, who smirked to herself, the only person in that room pleased with his attention. "And finally," he continued, "We'll hear from Mr. Huckett about our most vulnerable students." On the word vulnerable, his upward stapled smile sagged exaggeratedly downward giving a glimpse to the room of what plastic surgery gone wrong looks like. His pronunciation lingered too, more than it did for his other words; each syllable dripped from his cracked lips like sticky honey.

Mrs Addison, unable to tolerate him any longer, cut him off. She articulated herself confidently and although she stared into the room, she did not make eye contact with anybody. "Good morning," she said matter-of-factly, "firstly, we have our Head-of-Year interviews taking place at the end of this week. Thank you for those who have submitted applications. You will be informed this morning of the time of your interview. Secondly, the cover supervisor has an operation scheduled this week, so therefore, please check the cover announcement thoroughly. Obviously there will be a greater strain than usual. People will need to do their bit."

"Bet she won't be doing her bit," Tom said, under his breath, to Heeta with a smirk.

"Too busy shagging Mr White," Heeta replied, implying that Mrs. Addison was having it off with the severely overweight and under-socialised ICT technician who seemed unable to work his own computer let alone anybody else's and so baffled the staff as to how he had remained as an employee at the school for so long.

Mrs. Addison paused her announcements, "Do you have anything to share Ms. Rumbi?" She said to Heeta, who, quick-wittedly, replied without hesitation.

"Mr. Wilkinson just said that his Year 11s are prepping for the English Mocks this week, and so he'd be more than happy to do cover in the extra free periods he's picked-up."

"Wonderful, Mr. Wilkinson." Mrs. Addison said to Tom, looking at Heeta, and then him with genuine appreciation, even though she knew full well, Tom had no altruistic desire to take cover lessons.

"No problem, Mrs. Addison," Tom said imagining booting Heeta like one of his rugby balls.

"That's it from me." But before the Head sensed an opportunity for more ceremony, an opening to reintroduce his Assistant Headteacher, Mrs Addison saved the staff, "I'll hand over to Mrs. Barnaby."

She waffled-on about examination procedure and left more staff confused than they had been before the announcement, and then Mr. Huckett did his bit. Eventually the leadership team left the room in the single file they entered. The staff sighed relief. They could begin psychologically preparing for the semi-known battles that lay ahead.

Sasha placed her fingers on Nick's wrist, "let me know as soon as you hear." He smiled at her and nodded. Fred, from the opposite end of the staffroom stared at his every move. Heeta punched him on the upper arm.

"What are you staring at weirdo?" She said scanning the side of the room, on which Fred's eyes were locked.

"Nothing," he said, attempting to sound cool and nonchalant, but came across evasive and even aggressive. Like a dog hearing the squeak of a squeezy toy, Tom's head tilted instinctually toward Fred.

"Freddie's got a secret!" He teased, forgetting about the revenge he needed to plan for Heeta. "Come-on Freddie, tell us what's up? What've you done now?"

"Oh fuck-off. It's Monday morning. That's what's up. I've got 8b in ten minutes. I haven't marked their books, not that they've done any work anyway. Then, 10C and I promised them that I'd look at their coursework over the weekend. Today is going to be shit." Fred said.

"Fuck off!" Tom said, not falling for his bullshit. "You never mark books and 10C know you won't have looked at their coursework. Something's up with you." He said learning forward thrilled by the challenge, "And I'm going to find-out."

Fred knew they wouldn't leave him alone. It was the lesser evil to confess. He cleared his throat and looked at the floor, "I slept with Nick."

"Is that fucking it?" Tom said, shaking his head, severely disappointed and underwhelmed at the revelation. The others, unlike Tom, never raised their expectations in the first place. Heeta, Bea and Tom walked away, leaving Fred in his melodramatic discomfort.

By the end of the week, Fred had recharged, a by-product of the routine imposed by the school day. He couldn't get wasted, stay-up past midnight, or sleep-in throughout the afternoon. He worked throughout the day and so was physically tired at night. He slept better each night, ate less badly each day, and became less resentful of actual work, class by class. But his increased stability, ironically, also fuelled his neuroticism: without the hangover, the poor quality, intoxicated, weekend-sleep, and the onslaught of anxiety about the week of work ahead, he became more articulate, dramatic and imaginative. He became more himself. By Friday lunch, he was voicing elaborate self-narratives of capitalist exploitation annoying everybody around him. He, as a working-man who clocked at least 30 hours that week, was being forced into the role of proletariat-slave, a member of society exploited by the relentless bourgeois establishment, which conspired to kill the creative potential of the working-class.

"For fuck sake, Freddie," Tom snapped, "if you want to learn to play the Guitar, then buy a fucking guitar. If you want to be a ballet dancer and have Nick come to watch you pirouette. Do it. Stop going on about burgers."

"Erm one: how do you know what a pirouette is?" said Heeta, impressed. "Two: it's bourgeois not burger; have you not been listening to anything Fred has been going on," she slowed her voice, "and on," and slowed it even further before resuming her normal speed, "and on about?

And thirdly: I agree. Fred, stop bitching about things you can't change. If you want to be more creative, do it."

"We've introduced ballet into year 9," Tom said in response to Heeta's first point, impressed with himself, and before Fred could both protest and defend against the just do it argument. "Nick and Freddie made me realise that we need to be more inclusive; make sure there's something for the poofs to enjoy,"

"I don't think you can call them poofs, anymore, just like you wouldn't call me a Paki," Heeta said chewing on her bacon sandwich.

"And not all gays like ballet, you dick," Fred said getting drawn into the dumb conversation, shuffling Nuneaton canteen chips into his mouth.

"Don't they?" Tom said earnestly, "Don't you like ballet?"

"Well, yes," Fred said, "I've only been once for a school thing, and I thought I was going to hate it, but actually really loved it. I thought it'd be an upper-class pompous thing, full of pretentious; but you're missing the point." He said returning to his focus, "sexuality doesn't have anything to do with the type of sports or culture you enjoy."

"Doesn't it?" Tom said, again quite earnestly, "But being a boy was how I know I'd like Rugby…"

"Being a boy isn't the same as your sexuality. I'm not a girl," said Fred, "And even if I were that still wouldn't…"

"You are wasting your time," Heeta said, kissing the bacon grease away from her fingers, "Dumbness isn't racist; it comes in all shapes, colours and creeds. Tom here, definitely has it," she took a chip from his plate, "Don't you baby?" She wrapped her lips around the chip and sucked it into her mouth sensuously while winking at Tom.

"Yeah," Tom agreed, forgetting the conversation that, honestly, he really wasn't all that interested in anyway. He returned to the origin, "So do you think I should take it off the curriculum? Ballet?" Earnestly worrying that he'd not done the great thing he thought he'd done.

"No," Fred sighed, and Heeta laughed.

Bea walked into the canteen; she'd been out for a cigarette. She plonked herself beside Fred and Heeta, so all three of them faced Tom. "Got bloody year 11 next. Some tosser, timetabled me for a double with them Friday afternoon." Bea was most irate by Friday lunchtimes. Unlike Fred, lack of alcohol made her groggier as the week went on. Of course, she still had a bottle every night, but by Friday she needed seriously topping up.

"Nah, all of Year 11 have got extra English this afternoon." Tom said, both pleased that he could be the bearer of good news for Bea, and both sore at the misfortune it had brought to him: "but because some little twat," he gave an evil stare at Heeta, "volunteered me for cover, I miss out on the free period I would have picked-up – I have the other half the year group at the same time," he said enjoying the connection to Bea, despite its utter meaninglessness to her.

Heeta laughed, "serves you right for calling Fred a poof."

"One: Fuck off. Two: Stop stirring," Fred said.

"Which class you covering?" Bea asked.

"Nick's year 10s. He's in his Head of Year interview. Suppose, at least, his classes will be pretty good." Heeta and Bea both nodded. There was a general consensus that Nick was a good teacher but one who didn't fit into the twat category. He was one of those rare types that just got on with the job quietly. He didn't platform himself; didn't come across aggressive, shouty or overly sergeant major with staff or students; his classes liked and respected him, and they achieved good results without gaming the system. He didn't fall into that annoying category of ambitious moron, who lingered around till half 6 every night for brownie points; he didn't constantly volunteer to share best practice or tell everyone else how to teach. He was successful without being a douche and most of the staff preferred the idea of having him, over their own manager, despite his relatively young age.

"Fuck. I knew he'd get the interview. I bet they give him the job too." Fred said.

Bea smirked. Heeta rolled her eyes. Tom laughed.

"Don't be jealous. He'll make a better manager than most teachers I've met," Heeta said, "and besides," she said with devious glee, "he'll be your boss, so better start sucking up to him." She had made the pun deliberately, knowing that Tom could use it to make a joke.

"He's done that already!" Tom laughed, banging the canteen table as he stood.

"Fuck off," Fred sulked.

"Sir, have you marked my coursework yet?" A student asked Fred.

"Simon!" Heeta scorned the student with her glare more than her words, "Sir is on his lunchbreak. Go away!" He scuttled away with a 'sorry miss'. "You can buy me a drink later to say thanks," she said to Fred, also standing, "off to teach 7P, the little dicks."

Fred's favourite time of the week arrived: the bell struck three and freedom rang throughout the school. Students fled slightly faster than the staff. Fred waved goodbye to Pam the cleaner and made his way to the staffroom. An unusual orange, summery sun illuminated the winter dirt amassed on the large panes of glass. Fred sank into one of the comfy chairs, closed his eyelids and enjoyed the warmth on his skin. As he reopened them, Nick entered the staffroom. The spring in his step withered upon seeing Fred, who averted his gaze immediately, but it was too late; for the first time that week, they had looked each other directly in the eye and so now had to communicate. Nick walked stiffly over to Fred. He sat on the edge of the chair opposite indicating that he didn't intend on staying long. He looked over his shoulder to check that they were still alone.

"Look, Fred, about last weekend," Nick began. Fred's skin tightened as if he were a corset being strung-up by some zealous matron. "I'm sorry." He continued. "I didn't mean to," he took a breath and searched for the words, "didn't mean to, well you know, lead you on."

Fred felt as if the matron had overreached causing the corset to explode. *How fucking dare he,* he thought, and expressed it via his scrunched lips, and backward pull of his face. "Stop," he told Nick, "I absolutely am not interested. In-fact I'm beyond mortified," Fred turned to scan the room as if to make his argument more persuasive.

"So everything's ok then?" Nick said, relieved that the situation wasn't going to be as awkward as he anticipated. Fred was outraged.

"What did you expect?" He said, his words spat out, and he regretted his lack of control immediately. "Look," Fred said with less hostility leaking, "it was a drunken mistake. I'm not into you; I mean come-on your obnoxious Nick." Nick almost laughed at the way Fred identified him.

"Great," he said interrupting his burgeoning rant before he said anything too awkward, "so there's no hard feelings, and we don't need to avoid each other."

"I haven't been avoiding you. This is in your head, Nick. Not mine." Fred was trying to sound confident but was coming across shrill, and despite his protestation, very hurt.

"Ok. Well maybe it has been, and I'm sorry. I accept I have been worried about upsetting you. I get we're not the best of friends, but I don't want to see you hurt, and now I know that I've been reading way too much into it and that the awkwardness is all on me," he slowed his speech, "I'm sorry for avoiding you." He said this with complete honesty, complete responsibility and Fred couldn't say anything to it. He felt a surge of tears generate at the back of his eyes. He breathed in and trapped the breath in his stomach, stopping him from being able to take another. He felt paralysed as Nick lingered in his confessional stare at him. Nick, of course, thought it was helping, but Fred felt like a grenade. Each new second in this state could be the one that triggered his detonation. Fred needed Nick to get away from him. He was desperate for Nick to get away from him. Nick was unknowingly suffocating, drowning him, but as if he were chained underwater, Fred hungered for breath without opening his mouth, without showing tears; fought without being noticed. His organs, invisible to Nick, spasmed against the murderous self-control killing them.

Nick eventually broke the stare. He stood up, "I'm glad we spoke," he said smiling at Fred with honest affection, which jabbed at his skin like a dagger. His body couldn't take much more. It was now assaulted from within and without. "See you at the pub," he said. Fred scrambled the last of his resources, mustered the smallest nod and upward crescent on his lips. The moment Nick left the staffroom, he began heaving breaths like a soul washed up to shore after a terrible shipwreck.

He managed to pull himself together before any staff entered. Heeta, Tom and Bea arrived within a larger group. Fred told them he was just popping to the loo and then he was ready.

"Fancy trying somewhere new tonight?" one of the crowd said drawing looks of heresy and causing a most unusual Friday afternoon crowd-silence.

"Where?" a brave soul eventually joined the conspiracy and caused the silence to continue.

'The Anchor' was suggested and settled on. When Fred returned from the toilet, the staff set out on a new voyage. Tom, Heeta, Fred and Bea set sail, in Heeta's little, yet hardy, red micra, for the Anchor.

"You going to text Sasha to let her and Nick know where we're going?" Bea said to Fred, in her factual, not questioning tone. Fred, not feeling himself, did not act impulsively on his emotions. He wanted to say, *no. They can fuck off to the George*, but he knew that it would draw attention, and this time, not feeling himself, he really didn't want any.

"Yeah, good idea," he lied.

"What's up with you?" Heeta said. She could smell irregularity in Fred's psyche more effectively than a piranha smells blood.

"Hang on," Fred said pulling his phone out, gesturing that he was about to text Sasha. Heeta knew something serious had happened: Fred responded to her interrogation with calmness and successful evasion. He never did that; deep down he always wanted to spill information. He loved the idea of secrets, but never the reality; he was too dramatic, too eager to overshare and create a moment. *What's going on with him?* Thought Heeta.

Fred typed into his phone, *'Going Anchor instead'*. He acknowledged to himself that he would usually add an *'x'* and considered whether he should add it, make it normal. He couldn't. He didn't feel normal. He could not, even in a text message, imply his affection. *They don't deserve it,* he thought, unconcerned with the reality of whom *'They'* exactly referred. It was beyond Sasha and Nick, that was all that was certain.

The new pub didn't work. After a few pints, a good chunk of the staff decided to retire earlier than usual, and more still decided to head off for a curry way before they might ordinarily. The atmosphere was flat, out of alignment with the freakishly good weather for late February. It was only the little group, Sasha and Nick that remained.

"Fuck this," Tom said, "let's just sack this off and go back to the George." Bea shrugged and although Heeta sympathised, she said,

"I can't really drive: I've had three pints."

"And, it wouldn't be the same. Nobody'll be there," Bea added. A heavy, depressive silence layered itself onto an already heavy, depressive atmosphere.

"Fuck it", Nick said, "let's go into London." Tom perked-up immediately, and so did Bea. They were all pleasantly shocked at Nick's unusual lead.

"London?" Bea said, her horse-teeth making their first appearance in a week. "I don't think I've ever been on a proper night out in London," She said with an uncharacteristic bounce of excitement.

"Sounds good," said Heeta, "about time I saw some more brown faces."

Fred didn't know how to react. In theory, it was a brilliant idea. He'd much rather go for a night out in London; *that can always lead somewhere,* he thought. But it didn't feel right, and not only because he wasn't feeling his usual self. It was two worlds colliding, two worlds that were separate. School and friends were for Friday nights. Saturday. London. Being properly gay for another. Going to London wasn't the same as going to the sleezy Nuneaton gay club. In London, being gay was real; it was normal, a fantasy, but a realistic fantasy. In Nuneaton, it was a bit of fun and escapism, nothing serious; perhaps a hook-up but it would never lead anywhere. London had promise: the promise of a future life. It was his place, his future. They would infect it. They would remove its promise, its potential. They would colonise it; make it nothing more than an extension of Nuneaton. He didn't want them to go. It was his.

"They're not going to want to go to a gay club." Fred said to Nick directly, the first proper interaction since the staffroom. They all recognised that although this is something Fred would say, he would never say it in this way. Usually, it would have come out as a child-like attempt at reverse psychology, but this time, it whipped out and lashed them. It sounded accusatory, as if he were judging them all for being conservative, prudish, prejudicial.

"I will!" Tom exclaimed reclaiming the positive energy that was otherwise sparse that evening, "there must be some magic to that place if it finally caused you two queens to have it off." Nick was rarely embarrassed, but his cheeks reddened; he didn't know that everybody knew about him and Fred. They all laughed, except Fred. Seizing the momentum, Tom continued. "You never know, it might work for me. I could actually sleep with Bea and not just make it to her bed!" The table roared, again except for Fred. However, he did reveal the smallest resemblance of a sincere smirk.

"But Fred needs to make us a promise first," Heeta said, arousing intrigue and seriousness among the group. She left a dramatic pause, "He needs to promise to lighten the fuck up and leave this moody bullshit in this shitty pub."

He smiled at Heeta. His feelings of anguish evaporated. If he thought about them going to London, he still wouldn't like it, but Fred had entered a more comfortable and desired mode of being: reckless intuitive, anti-thinking. Like a lever he flipped attitudes. He gulped the remainder of his pint and switched-off his mind: "Come on then bitches, let's get wankered!"

Bea's horse-teeth made their second appearance of the night and even a neighing sound might have come out. Everyone lifted their drinks, banged them into one another, shouted cheers, and finished them in one glug - even Sasha, even Nick.

CHAPTER 4: Electricity

Tom was a hit in Old Compton street. The guys wrapped their hands around his biceps and admired his torso. They lifted his shirt and patted his muscular stomach. This helped Bea to appreciate Tom more than she had before: *Perhaps there is something to him,* she thought. Like shares, Tom was on the up and Bea was buying in. Tom recognised the correlation between Bea's increased interest in him and his humouring of the gay guys, his allowing them to squeeze his arms, pat his thighs and articulate vulgar performatives at him. So naturally, he encouraged them. Absolutely worth it if it even nudged Bea to properly consider him.

Heeta returned from the bar with six more shots of tequila on a little tray. Sasha took the salt pot, tossed a little on her thumb, then passed it on. Everybody repeated until they all stood with salty left thumbs. They each took a slice of lemon in the same hand, and held the tequila shot in the right. Sasha shouted, "to Nick! Congratulations, Mr Head of Year!" He protested that he didn't know whether he had the job yet, but on the train journey he had told them how well the interview had gone, and they all thought he'd got the job. Their glasses clunked together, even Fred's – he'd abandoned his Nick-hostility and general glumness; London was simply too exhilarating with friends. He was in a great mood; the evening was wide open and could lead anywhere. That outweighed anything. They drank the tequila with one twist of the glass, licked their salty thumbs and then bit down on the lemon.

"Oh God!" Bea's horse-teeth were out, "I hate tequila!" she exclaimed whilst laughing and stamping on the spot. Tom slapped her arse.

"Me too!" he said laughing at the same time. They giggled together.

"Oi!" She said, "that's my arse you're slapping," she bent forward and pressed it further out a little as if wanting him to do it again.

"Yeah - don't slap hers, slap mine!" one of the men said playfully. Everybody laughed. "I don't know what you're all laughing at. I mean it." He added deadpan. Fred, who was now fairly drunk, lent forward and smacked the guy on the arse. The group gasped in surprise, including the rather camp man whose bottom had just been planted with a fierce slap and who ordinarily seemed incapable of surprise: he did the provoking not the other way around.

He turned to stare at Fred, and his plan had been to mock outrage, but Fred went for his arse again. "Woah! Hey, hey, hey!" he said deflecting Fred's wrist and springing backwards to safety. The group laughed. The hunter had turned into the hunted, and little prey-like Fred had metamorphosed into a tiger.

"All talk!" Fred said scaring the men away for good.

"Well done white boy!" Heeta said, "you're learning!"

"Yeh – now if he could just learn how to get the drinks in!" Tom said.

"I'll get them. It's my round," Bea said.

Fred agreed to go with her and help carry them out. They were making the most of the weather by standing outside on the pedestrianised street, which was clogged with people who had the same idea. The moon rested above, but its light was outshone by the neon signs illuminating the street. The place was electric.

"He's come out of his shell." Nick said to Tom, Heeta and Sasha.

"He's got the home advantage, hasn't he?" Tom said.

"Only you could bring a football metaphor to Old Compton Street," said Heeta before changing the focus: "Bea seems genuinely interested; perhaps there's something for the away team too."

"I hope so," said Sasha referring to herself. "It's been way too long. Unlike Nick," she elbowed him, "I haven't brought a man back in forever." Nick gave an awkward nod. Sasha didn't know that it was Fred that he had brought back last weekend.

"Oh yeh – I'd forgot you too were here last weekend," Tom said taking a larger scan of the street, "so this is where the magic began." Sasha cricked her neck in that way dogs do when they try to show they're listening to you.

"You mean it was Fred?" Sasha said taking her cricked neck so that she could see Nick's face, "you slept with Fred last weekend?" It wasn't a question. Her words were an outlet for surprise. "I can't believe it". Again, she did believe it; her words were just outlets of expression. "Fred Baker... but you've always said you've never been interested."

"I was trashed Sasha," Nick looked over his shoulder, "look, let's not talk about this now," he looked over his shoulder again. Then at Heeta. He considered his words before speaking, "I'm not interested. He was really drunk, got into a bit of trouble, so I stayed to check he was alright. I got as drunk as he was. You get the idea. That's it though. We're," he considered his words again, "We're different. It really was a one-time thing."

Bea and Fred spilled out the doors with two large trays of drinks. The dance music from within the bar flowed onto the street and joined its medley, the mismatched beats escaping from the diverse venues. Bea had never been to New Orleans, but she imagined this is what it would be like. She placed the tray of sambuca shots into the centre of their little circle while Fred put his tray of pints onto the floor beneath. Everybody reached in for a glass. Tom counted down from three and they tipped the clear liquid into their mouths where it plunged like flame, down their throats.

"Woah!" they moaned and stepped on the spot. Tom slapped Bea's ass again. She neighed in pleasure. Fred impressed by Bea's reaction thought he'd try it out. He, impulsively, slapped Nick's.

Everybody stilled.

Nobody was sure how to react. It was beyond awkward, so Fred did it again.

"Don't do that!" Nick snapped.

Fred looked like he was the one that had been slapped, "Sorry, I was only," he said.

"Don't be so precious." Heeta said to Nick, "he's only cupping a little cheek. Not as if he hasn't had a bit of it before." It released the tension. Tom and Bea laughed. Sasha didn't. *Am I the only one that didn't know?* She thought. Fred used the diversion to bend down and pick his drink up from the tray on the floor. The others followed his lead.

Nick stood embarrassed. He bent down to pick the last drink from the tray.

"Well I fucking love your arse," Tom said to Bea, leaning in for a pinch this time.

"I thought it was tits that you loved," She said squeezing them toward him.

"I love them too. I love your tits and I love your arse," he lent forward and blew a raspberry into her cleavage. She cackled as if being tickled against her will, unable to get her breath or stop him, but loving every second.

"Stop it!" she said, only half wanting him to stop.

"Fred," Tom stopped blowing raspberries into Bea's cleavage, but with his head still in the general area, he twisted toward him, "don't do this to Nick. I don't think he'd like it." They all laughed, and Bea swatted Tom's head away from her cleavage.

As the bars along the street began to close around 11.00pm, young men in hotpants and skimpy t-shirts strutted along handing out fliers for free entry to the 'G', 'A', 'Y' nightclub – each letter is pronounced separately. The boys squeezed themselves between Sasha and Fred so that they could place a flier into Tom's hand whilst admiring him up close.

"This the place where you two hit it off?" Tom asked.

The boys handed fliers to all the others. "No, this is the club. We just went to the bar," Fred said before leaning forward with the intention of smacking the boys' asses: "This place looks way better!" He exclaimed as Heeta intercepted his hands. She gave the boys an apologetic look, but they'd moved on.

"We can go if," she paused for dramatic emphasis,

"You get the first round in!" Tom finished her sentence.

Heeta patted Tom's arse and whilst retaining her eye contact with Fred, said "if you get the first-round in." Fred laughed at her and his energy decreased from a nine to an eight.

"How're we going to get back though?" Sasha said, "that place doesn't even open until 11.30pm – the last train homes not long after that."

"Fuck it. We'll chip in for a taxi together," Tom said eager for the night to continue. Bea's cheeky horse-teeth popped out,

"Or we could get the first one back in the morning?"

Sasha was uncomfortable with both options. She thought the others were unreliable and was worried about the solo cost of a taxi should they get separated: "a taxi would surely cost us an absolute fortune."

"Not really. It's probably only like all of us getting another round," Nick said to her surprise. Sasha relied on Nick as an ally. "If we each put "£20 into our sock, between us, we'll have made sure that we have £120 to get home."

"I love this fucking Math's nerd. Where's he been hiding?" Tom said hooking his arm around Nick like an American jock. Nick enjoyed the struggle out of Tom's playful headlock. Bea felt a little jealous of their contact: he had seriously increased in value to her this evening.

They finished their drinks, placed the glasses on the ledge of the window and set out along Old Compton Street. Once they were walking, Sasha tried to pull Nick aside. She didn't want to go to the club. She wanted to go home.

"Nick, I don't think it's a good idea,"

He cut her off, "Sash, you don't have to come. If you want to go home, I get it. It's alright. But I quite fancy it if I'm honest," his tone was pleasant, supportive even. Sasha prided herself on her ability to remain calm and controlled; she rarely displayed anger and definitely not any form of personal upset; but Nick's response upset her. She struggled to hide her emotions, especially given the unusual amount she'd drunk that evening. Her relationship with Nick was sensible. They left socials together early. They never missed deadlines. They kept their flat tidy, took it in turns to cook. They were perfect companions. *Why doesn't he want to come home?* She thought, struggling to think of anything to say back to Nick, which conveyed her pain.

"Sash?" Nick said questioningly to see if she'd heard him. Nick failed to read her emotions completely. He thought she was just drunk. He laughed and called to the others, "Hang-on guys!" They stopped and turned to see what was up. Nick called to them: "Sash's had too much to drink and is going to head back…"

Bea's face tightened, her horse teeth scared into the pits of her mouth, *Oh shit, we're not all going home are we?* Bea panicked. She didn't want them to stop being together, enjoying the night together. Nick continued speaking,

"I'm going to grab a taxi so it can take her to the station."

Sasha crumpled internally like an autumnal leaf on its last reserves of sunlight. Words fled her. She was stumped. Silent. Nick waved at the guy smoking outside a taxi rank. He climbed into his car seat and drove over. Like a gentleman, Nick opened the passenger door and held it open for her, "I'll see you tomorrow, Sash. I know this isn't your thing, but thanks for coming. It's been great. I'm really glad you came," he waved his arm at the street, "… you know, to see this place, where I come; the stuff outside of work; you know, the real stuff." He was completely earnest with her, not knowing that his words were stabbing her repeatedly in the back as she climbed into the taxi.

The real stuff, she lingered on that phrase the entire journey back. It crushed her. Their routines, their life, work, was the real stuff.

After the taxi disappeared, the five of them cheered aloud in the middle of the street. They weren't being rude about Sasha, just expressing their delight at where they were going. In a horizontal line, their arms rested on one another's shoulders. Beneath the moon, and among the haze of neon light and drunken souls, they stumbled, and sung their way toward the club.

"Wait!" Nick announced in the queue before they shuffled forward together, "we need to add a tenner to our sock now Sasha's gone. For the taxi." They did. They hopped forward slowly and made it into the club just before midnight. The bouncers padded them down one at a time. The one wearing only black leather stared at Fred for what felt an eternity. *Don't slap his fucking ass; don't slap his fucking ass; don't slap his fucking ass,* is all Heeta could think as she watched Fred stare back at him. They made it through the security check without Fred creating any problems. Inside the club, the thud of human generated thunder and lightening struck them repeatedly. Their bodies joined the twisting, rubbing, bobbing, gyrating, euphoric hands-in-the-air, bouncing masses. Their arteries pumped electricity not blood.

Bea and Tom bought drinks over to the dance floor. The five of them huddled in a circle and danced together. Some of the drinks made it into their throats; a lot went directly to the floor. As the night progressed, their group naturally blended with those around them. Strangers danced with strangers; their bodies pressed against one another; legs rubbed against legs; chests against chests. And then the whole thing cycled; more strangers switched places to dance with more strangers like thousands of fish brushing closely past one another. This kaleidoscopic and fluid bodily intimacy consumed them all. It only stopped once magnetic attraction held a duo so tightly that they could withstand the onslaught of movement; their energy could repeatedly draw one another back. Fred and a guy in his early thirties emitted this to one another. They danced together, song after song, not that anybody could really tell when one began or ended.

After several hours of dancing, they slipped away from the dancefloor. They bought water from the bar and found a quieter area of the club to relax for a while. Nick, although thoroughly enjoying himself, had not found the same magnetic attraction on the dance floor. He noticed Fred had gone after a while, as did the others. Tom and Bea were pressed against the slimy wall, their tongues explored each other's faces in beat with the music. They momentarily paused their attention toward one another, and said to Nick, not to worry about it, that they'd find him at the end. They returned to jabbing one another with that most muscular instrument of the human body. Heeta lay her palm onto Nick's sweaty arm, "Fred will be fine", she said as loudly as possible so to be heard over the music. She suggested that they get a shot and go back to the dance floor. They did.

At the end of the evening, the thunder and lightning of the club seized. The God's were turfing the mortals from their home. The masses dripped into the exit and bulged outside of it. Hundreds of people spaced onto the streets. Bea, Tom, Heeta and Nick stood together, looking-out for Fred. Eventually he turned-up with the guy he'd met inside. In his lost voice, he tried to tell them his friend's name. They, also in their husky voices, tried to exchange hellos. They all felt two things: famished and parched. They didn't feel dizzy or drunk in the way they did at the end of a night at the pub. In many ways they'd sweated half the alcohol out. They were frazzled, rather than drunk; they felt like guitars that had been strummed for hours upon hours.

"Let's get some food," Tom said in his deepened smoky voice, and to which they nodded despite only just about hearing him with their tinnitus-ringing ears. Together they entered the kebab shop across the road and queued.

They sat on the kerb outside eating deep-fat-fried chips and cheap kebab meat in harmonious silence. Nick finished first. He stood to attract a taxi predicting accurately that it'd take a while for them to get one. Eventually a six-seater pulled-up. Bea and Tom climbed in the back-back; Tom slapped her arse as she bent up and in first. Heeta shoved the seat flat so that she could dive across the seats and settle by the window. Fred and his new friend climbed into the remaining two seats. Save the passenger seat at the front, the car was full. "Oi, what the fuck man," Nick said in an unusually aggressive, butch tone, his voice still husky from the club.

"Just sit in the front Nick," Heeta said leaning her head into the head-rest of the passenger seat in front. Tom and Bea, tucked away in the boot-area seats, jabbed away at one another with their tongues. Fred turned hostile. From the middle seat, he shouted at Nick.

"What's your problem?" He went from zero to hundred in a second.

"He is!" Nick matched Fred's anger, "what's he doing?"

The taxi driver, alarmed at the shouting, turned to see what was happening in his car. "No trouble," he said in his Bengali accent. Heeta lifted her head from the rest, straightened her arm into Fred's torso, which forced him to sit flat against the seat. She leant over him and said,

"Get in the front now. Or we're going. Your choice Nick." She turned away to leave the decision with him. After a moment's silence, Fred's new friend unclipped his seat belt and said,

"Look I don't want no trouble. Clearly I'm in the middle of something." He began to climb out of the taxi. Fred was furious at Nick. He climbed out after the guy, bashed Nick on the shoulder with his own as he moved past him.

Fred and the guy walked away from the taxi to talk in private. Nick climbed in and sat where Fred had been sitting. Heeta shook her head but said nothing. Nick clipped his seatbelt into the socket. The taxi driver said that he was starting the meter; his finger clicked the device, which flashed a sequence of red digits before he had even finished his sentence. After it had tallied up by at least £10, Fred returned to the taxi alone. He climbed in, fastened his seatbelt, and said nothing. He slammed the door closed and the taxi began taking them back to Bea's house.

CHAPTER 5: The kerb

They arrived an hour later. Obscene red digits flashed on the device above the dashboard. Heeta's head pressed against the window, her eyes were closed. Nick's head rested on Fred's shoulder and Fred's head rested on Nick's head in turn. Both their eyes were shut. Tom and Bea's heads both flopped forward; their eyes were also shut. The taxi man said they were here a couple of times in his normal voice before realising that he was going to have to shout at them.

They stumbled out. Each took the £30 from their socks, gave it to Bea. She shoved the cash into her purse and gave the driver her credit card. She paid the total bill, which came to much more than their combined £30s. They drifted into her house as the morning sun promised its arrival.

Tom and Bea collapsed onto her bed. Neither removed their clothes. Heeta whipped her top and trousers and climbed under the duvet of the double bed in the spare room. Nick was a newbie to Bea's sleepovers. He followed them upstairs to realise that there were only two bedrooms, and Heeta had made quite clear he wasn't getting in with her. Fred had folded himself onto the couch downstairs; Nick descended the stairs and entered the lounge. "Sorry for being a twat before," he said to Fred.

"Don't worry," Fred was too tired to speak let alone argue.

"I'm going to head home."

Fred opened his eyes on the couch, stunned at what he'd heard, "home?" He lacked the energy to form a full sentence let alone consider the idea of walking home.

"There're no beds left and I think I've pissed Heeta off, so…"

Fred squeezed his body into the back of the couch creating space, "Heeta's not pissed-off. She's knackered," he said re-closing his eyes. Nick stood motionless. *Is he offering to share the sofa?* Nick thought to himself with two reservations: *what he if isn't? and even if he is, there's hardly room for us both.*

"For fuck sake," Fred said with his eyes still closed, "just get on, and go to sleep. I'm supposed to be the neurotic one."

Nick closed the door to the hallway, grabbed the blanket from the shelf of the alcove beside the fire. He wafted it out and then laid himself and the blanket over them on the sofa. Fred wrapped his arm around his chest, more due to the lack of anywhere else to put it, than an expression of affection. Nick's back, bottom and legs pressed deep into Fred. Nick's neck tingled in response to the warm breath flowing softly from Fred's nostrils. They lay still in that position for a few minutes. Nick's breathing slowly synced with Fred's and just as Fred was almost asleep for good, Nick turned over so that his face brushed Fred's. Nick kissed him and Fred kissed him back.

Heeta took her paracetamol, tossed water in her face, and filled a glass for Fred and Nick. She sat on the blanket covering their legs. "Want a lift home?" she asked them. Nick pretended to still be asleep. He was still on the edge-side of the sofa, but his face was back in its original position, facing away from Fred, whose arm wrapped over his body, his now shirtless body.

Fred twisted his head upward to make eye contact with Heeta, who despite her petite frame was crushing their legs. Fred smirked at her while shaking his head, as if warning Her to not say a word.

"You've got five minutes," she said as she bounced herself off the sofa, "I'm going to freshen-up, then we're off."

The three of them left the house. Fred waited for Nick to move past so that he could pull the handle upward on the door.

"Oh shit," Heeta said halfway along the path, "my car is at the Anchor." The unusual warmth of yesterday had ended. A grey sleety sky rustled over them.

"My place is a twenty-minute walk. I can drop you guys home," Nick said, "call it an apology for last night."

"I might as well walk," Heeta said, "It'll only take ten minutes longer to go straight home… but thanks." She smiled at Nick, a smile that said, 'don't fuck him around'. They walked out of the cul-de-sac together. On the main road, Heeta turned left, and the boys right.

A heavy silence accompanied Fred and Nick for at least 15 minutes of their walk. The hangover and tiredness didn't help, but neither of them could find anything to say. As they passed the spot where Fred had thrown-up after fleeing Nick's apartment last week, he decided he needed to say something and so reverted to work: "good luck with the job. Obviously, I'm only saying this because I'm still pissed… you will be a good Head of Year though," Fred said.

Nick laughed, "Fuck off. You think I'll be shit. You're just saying that to make conversation."

Fred laughed, "well yeah, but I've decided that I need to make more of an effort."

"With what?"

"I dunno… with people," Fred kicked a pebble onto the lawn, "with life… I think I've been passing it by a bit too much… dismissing stuff… waiting for the weekend."

"Where's this coming from?" Nick asked.

"Don't you think about the stuff you want to change about yourself?"

"Not really," Nick considered the question only after he replied to it.

"So this is what you want your life to be - Nuneaton? A flat with Sasha?"

"No, of course not."

"So what do you want?" Fred asked.

"I dunno. I suppose what everyone wants?"

"What's that for us?"

"What do you mean?" Nick asked confused at the question.

"I mean. You said 'what everyone wants', and I mean, what does that look like to us?" Fred paused, he hated referring to himself with labels; with certain labels, "gay guys… gay guys from Nuneaton? I just don't see it. I don't see us having what everyone wants; I mean here; having what everyone wants here."

"What's our sexuality got to do with it?"

"Oh come on, Nick. It's not the same and you know it."

"I'm lost. What are we even talking about? Nick said.

"Family. A house, kids, normal life."

"Well, I wasn't sure that's what I meant." Nick said.

"What did you mean then? What does everybody want?"

"A partner. Love."

They had arrived. Fred sat on the kerb outside the apartment block. He wasn't ready for their conversation to finish. "What're you doing? We're here," Nick said.

"I just thought I'd sit for a couple of minutes." Fred said. Nick lingered on the pavement unsure what to do. He wanted to go inside, not sit on kerb outside his apartment block. He sighed to himself and sat down next to Fred, their backs toward the building.

"I get it," Nick said after a long silence. Fred's mood perked. He turned his head and he smiled at Nick earnestly. He never smiled at men sober. Nick continued, "I can't really see my proper life here. It doesn't make sense because if you meet someone that you want to be with, it doesn't really matter where you live. Rationally, Nuneaton makes just as much sense as anywhere else…"

Fred shrugged, "it just doesn't feel right."

"I know."

"So, let's go," Fred said to Nick.

"What?" Nick's teeth twinkled as a large smile opened on his face, "Where?"

"Anywhere! Barcelona? Paris? New York." Fred listed the cities he'd always imagined himself living.

Nick shook his head, his teeth were still visible, but his smile faded. "I'm serious, Nick." Fred turned to him and took his hand. "I don't mean as a boyfriend. Let's go as friends." Nick stared back at Fred, properly considering him for the first time.

"You're serious."

Fred nodded and clutched his hands tighter, "I'll die if I stay here." He said it, with oceans building behind his eyes. The intensity of feeling was overwhelming, but his eyes like solid glass, would not allow a single drop to pass by. Nick swallowed and, for the first time in his life, he did not evade the emotion. He locked onto Fred's stare and nodded. He didn't pretend to not understand. He didn't pretend that he hadn't felt the same way. He nodded and shared a terrible truth, a buried feeling that let him know an unhappy destiny awaited, should he not take courage and stray from the path of wilful ignorance. He nodded at Fred.

Sasha moved the curtains aside in the apartment behind Nick and Fred. She was watching them; she watched as Nick clutched Fred's hand back in response; as he said to Fred, "Let's do it."

CHAPTER 6: London, six months later

Their apartment smelt of cumin, nutmeg, and turmeric: Fred wanted to be close to zone 1 and Nick wanted a place that didn't absorb their entire salaries. This is how Shadwell became their new home. The move caused upset: the school hated that their rising star had not only snubbed a prestigious promotion, but resigned mid-term, forcing them to employ supply teachers; Bea was distraught at endings, period; and Tom was pissed that the boys' departure had encouraged Bea to emigrate into a new group, which did not include him. Heeta was happy that Fred was taking control of his life, making decisions rather than subjecting himself to fate. But she felt sad too. Sad that she had lost her friend and sad that Nick had been the one she had lost him to. Whereas Sasha was devastated. Unlike Heeta, she hadn't lost a friend: she'd lost a husband. Sasha had unintentionally learnt to see Nick not as her colleague, flatmate and friend. Nick had become the person she relied on. The person she trusted. The person she wanted to see first thing in the morning and last thing at night. She had fallen in love with him. She knew he was gay, but it didn't matter. Sex didn't matter. Their life did. When he left, her life, as she knew it, ended. She took some time off work, leaving the school with yet more supply teachers. But Fred and Nick had made the best decision of their life. They absorbed the stench of curries brewing in the block of shabby ex-council flats and bathed in their progressive self-narrative of liberation.

They hadn't slept together since moving from Nuneaton. Fred felt the desire occasionally, but the acquisition of a friendship that he truly valued, outweighed bodily desire. He worshipped Nick like a benign God: he wanted to share things with him, speak with him, think things through with him. Sex with him, over time, became an increasingly odd sentiment. To Fred, Nick figured as an extension of self rather than an object of desire. A virtual body part, a nobler, more refined inner voice that had been within the entire time but that had just required fleshing out. They returned from their new schools in the evening, spent time exchanging stories, relaying their respective experiences; they prepared lessons and meals for the days ahead. They planned activities to make the most of every weekend. They were being the people that they wanted to be: proactive, energetic, alive.

They were no longer drifting through their lives, waiting, waiting for destiny to make them happy, to make them accepted, to make them feel and have what everybody else presumably wanted. They were orchestrating and executing their lives and not attempting to be normal. They were done with trying, pretending. They weren't normal. They were gay. They didn't want to save-up, buy a house, and pop out kids. Or if they did, they forced themselves to stop; to create a space in which they could begin to entertain notions beyond these options; to think of living a life other than the life they experienced in their own childhoods, which on the whole, had been happy.

London was a blank slate. It could be cold and snotty, refusing to help, but it never oppressed or dictated. For better, for worse, it left them to decide what to do with their lives. Fred and Nick felt free, properly free, for the first time in their lives.

Fred shut the door as he returned home from work. He held a cheap old guitar that was new to him. He had decided to learn how to play an instrument, and the guitar seemed most fitting; he imagined himself performing for a group of friends, unplanned, spontaneous, the sort of thing that happens at the end of a night-out, at a small afterparty perhaps.

He crept along the hall with it in his hands and outside the living room, he strummed his index finger across the strings. An awful, untuned whinging noise leaked into the room. Nick withheld his reaction. He wasn't going to roll his eyes to a half-opened door. The terrible noise plunged into the room as Fred strutted in like Freddie Mercury. Nick laughed and shook his head at the same time.

"Play us a tune." He said.

Fred dropped onto the sofa beside Nick and laid the guitar on his lap. "I've always wanted to learn," he said stroking the wood.

"You should. Guitar playing will definitely help your image."

"When did you become a such a shady queen?"

"It was buried deep, deep, deep," Nick paused to exaggerate his point, "deep down. Some of us had parents that actually tried to instil manners and etiquette."

"Yeh - look where that got you. Almost married to Sasha."

"Ouch," Nick said embarrassed and feeling guilty for the way things had ended, "I still feel bad when I think about her."

"Oh, come on. You can't blame yourself forever. It needed to end. Think how bad it would have gotten had you stayed. She'd have continued moulding you into the perfect provincial husband that you could never be, and…"

"Hang on. Who says I could never be the per…"

"I do," Fred said definitely, "you're a free spirit," he lifted his guitar so that it sat vertically on his lap, "which is why you need to learn the guitar with me." Fred smiled, a hopeful plea-like smile. "Oh, come on. It'll be fun. We can learn together, and then when we're utterly amazing, we can bum around Europe, playing to lost old souls, drinking themselves into oblivion in European bars and taverns."

"There are about fifty things wrong with what you've just said."

"Come on, Nick. I mean it." Fred whinged.

Nick sighed. His habitual response was to reject any sort of groupie request. He didn't start commitments at somebody else's whim. He determined his own interests, which of course had led him to Sasha. She placed no demands on his identity, offered no challenge to his innate conservatism, and it ended in a sham, hollow life. All of this shot through Nick's mind as he sat there on the sofa of his Shadwell nutmeg-cumin-and-turmeric smelling ex-council-house flat-home. He reacted in opposition to his instinct. "Let's learn the fucking guitar." Before Fred could celebrate and make him reconsider his decision, Nick added, "But we're not learning on that piece of shit." He gestured at the busted guitar Fred had brought home from the school's derelict music department. "If we're going to do this, we need to buy a decent guitar."

Fred's teeth showed. He was delighted at Nick's response; if he was honest, also a little apprehensive. He hadn't fully committed to learning the guitar. Rather he'd experienced a bit of a whim while covering a music lesson in the day and brought one home with him – unlike Nick, Fred hadn't secured a permanent position yet, and so was working as a temporary supply teacher; today he had spent the day in the music department of an East London Academy. But as Nick resisted his innate conservatism, Fred evaded his instinct to be non-committal. He put the busted old thing onto the floor and looked at Nick, "You're serious?"

"Why not?" Nick replied.

"So, we're going to buy guitars and seriously learn to play?"

"For fuck sake, Fred. It was your idea and now it sounds like I'm the one asking you!" Nick said shaking his head, "if you don't want to…"

"No!" Fred interrupted, "Definitely! I think it's a great idea. Let's do it."

"Good." The decision was made. "Let's meet in central after work tomorrow and we'll go to one of those music shops opposite the Astoria." Nick said.

"A proper music-shop?" Fred said surprised.

"Where else do you think we'd get guitars from?" Nick said genuinely interested in Fred's thinking.

"I hadn't really thought about it… but definitely. I mean makes sense: a music-shop will sell musical instruments."

Nick rolled his head so that his chin pushed into his chest. He then shook his head in disbelief, "let's stop talking about his before I change my stupid mind."

"Deal," Fred said not wanting to spook him away from the plan. In his own head, he hadn't really thought seriously about learning; that isn't to say that he didn't want to, he'd love to follow through with a plan; to put the effort in to learn something as amazing as playing an instrument. It was just that Fred knew himself despite an abundance of evidence that supported the opposite conclusion: Fred knew he would drift into fantasy if it were a mere matter of disciplined, solitary work… but the proposition of learning with somebody – with Nick – changed the fundamental nature of what he was doing. He wouldn't be grinding away laboriously. He'd be having the time of his life.

Fred enjoyed supply teaching much more than he anticipated. He knew he'd appreciate the lack of guilt derived from never having to worry about marking, but he assumed that he'd find the lack of routine and relationships difficult. His anticipations made no sense – Fred was terrible at routine and his relationships were never as strong as he thought they were. Supply worked and to his surprise, behaviour was better than his actual classes back at Eliot High. The bell rang at 3.00pm and he walked along the corridor, past teachers stumbling with piles of books and trotting off to pointless meetings. He was smug. He said bye with confidence to the Headteacher who stood by the school gates waving his kids home. He didn't need to worry about the impression his leaving at 3.00pm gave; he was supply. It was expected.

He walked along the main road among the hundreds of students. It cut through the estate toward the tube station. The kids didn't know or bother Fred and so they walked together without awkwardness. He also got away with wearing chinos and a jumper rather than a proper suit so that helped him not stand out so much, which he liked. Happy dance-pop music poured into his ears through his cheap white headphones and the sun of late April warmed his smug face. He minced along completely in love with life. That narrative of liberation played his mind.

At the tube station, he flashed his oyster card over the yellow-orange pad beside the turnstile. A feeling of connection shot through his entire body: the little bleep and the release of the barrier made him feel like a local. This stupid little sound and mechanical lever made him feel a religious sense of belonging; it metaphorically told him that this was his city. It confirmed that he was doing his life right. He strode through the barrier with his teeth visible to the world. On the escalators, he joined the masses in walking down on the left. Each step downward gave expression to his contentment. The tube shot him through miles of underground-London, and he felt as happy as a little kid on a baby rollercoaster for the first time. He exited the train, his adrenaline pumped.

On the escalator ascent, his imagination lifted to fantastical heights. He envisaged the red carpet at the premier of the Hollywood movie based on his novel. The black limousine doors closed outside the Odeon in

Leicester Square. Velvet ropes shimmered under a crystal blue London summer sky. Beautiful dresses glimmered and swooshed. Meryl Streep blew a kiss. A-list celebrities smiled for photographs. Everyone linked arms and walked in at least duos. His friends from Nuneaton trotted along the red carpet too. They had looks that reflected his euphoric feelings. Heeta, Bea, and Tom smiled along as a threesome.

He stumbled at the top of the escalators, back into the equally fantastic reality of Tottenham court road tube station. He was on his way to meet Nick and buy a fabulous guitar. He took his phone and flicked the track on the playlist backward again. He had listened to the same song on repeat for the entire journey. He never configured the settings so that it repeated automatically. Each time he felt the desire fresh to relive the last 3 minutes and 28 seconds of life. Soundtracks were Fred's crack.

He wasn't meeting Nick at the music shop until 4.30pm so he had an hour to spare. Old Compton street was close by and so Fred headed for a drink. Two Spanish men with styled beards finished their pints of Estrella-Damn and stood up to move away from their little table on the street. Fred plopped himself onto the warm seat and ordered himself a pint when the waitress came to take his order. He felt so cosmopolitan. He removed his phone and flicked the track back again as it finished for who knows what time it had played. He sipped his beer, which the waitress had brought over in one of those classy European glasses that wasn't a wifey half-pint glass, nor a blockish full-on pint, but rather somewhere between. He indulged in his fantasy of the premier for a little longer. Nothing happened it in. The images, like that track in his headphones, just kept recycling themselves over and over: red velvet, Meryl Streep, black limousines, Bea, Heeta and Tom in lined arms; they walked like a boomerang, up, down, and back up, that red carpet.

Half of his beer had gone, and his song was coming to an end again. He went to take his phone to reset the track before taking another sip, but a man approached and stood immediately in front of him. His deep red lips moved. They mesmerised Fred who heard only the lyrics of this song. He pressed the pause button and took his headphone out his ear.

"Sorry, I couldn't hear." He said to the man with the deep red lips.

"Do you mind if I take the seat?" He stared at Fred with a charming smile.

"Of course not. Go ahead."

"Thanks." He said in his northern accent, sitting down in the chair resting against the window of the bar beside the little table with Fred's drink on. They both faced the street in their chairs, as did the other customers. Fred wasn't sure on the etiquette: could, should, he put his headphones back in, or was he expected to say something to the man? He compromised. He put one earpiece in, on the opposite side to where the man had sat down.

"So, you're a Londoner then?" the man said.

Fred's heart leaped as if it were a child jumping out of bed on Christmas morning. "I suppose I am, yeh," he said to himself as much as to the man.

"Suppose?" the man repeated Fred's own word.

Fred turned to make and collect a brief glance at the man's face, "I live here now, but we've – I've – only just moved, so I'm not sure on the official requirement; how long it takes before I can say I'm a Londoner."

"We've?" The man repeated his word again; his face strained a little too.

"Yeh – me and my friend,"

The strain in the man's face relaxed and he smiled, a large, friendly northern smile. "So, do you, or your friend, have a boyfriend?"

Fred had never been asked that before in his life. He blushed. He didn't understand why it caused him to feel embarrassed, but it did. It wasn't as if he was in the closet in Nuneaton, but he wasn't treated as a proper gay man either. He was barely treated as an adult, a man, and adults, men, were asked if they had boyfriends. Deep down, Fred viewed himself as a boy still. This realisation surfaced within him sitting there next to this beautiful man. He ignored the red pigmentation of his cheeks and pushed his feelings into his stomach. With the most mature, and unafflicted voice he could muster, he said, "No boyfriend. You?"

"Yeah," The man responded deadpan. Fred felt betrayed and a little stunned at his own potent emotional response. "I've got three," the man added before laughing. The intensity exited through a controlled push of air Fred forced through his nostrils as he expressed jovial surprise at the man's comment.

"Three?" Fred said now intrigued rather than embarrassed, betrayed or stunned.

"Yeah. I love them all. We love each other – we couldn't decide who got the cut – so we decided not to," he laughed, and Fred smiled at this strange man.

"But you don't seem", Fred began.

The man raised his eyebrow in anticipation of how Fred was going to finish that statement. Fred heard himself, heard his own judgment and stopped.

"It's ok. I promise to not be offended at whatever offensive thing you're about to say."

Fred thought he shouldn't say what he was going to, but he'd never been good at self-censure: "You don't seem overly gay though?"

The man laughed a guttural laugh, his northern-ness illuminated itself. He took a cigarette from his packet and then hovered the packet, open, with a strong accentuated flick of his wrist. across the table, toward Fred. Fred hadn't smoked many daytime cigarettes since leaving Nuneaton, but he was drinking in the afternoon mid-week, so thought why not. He took a Lambert and Butler cigarette. The northern man leaned across the table and ignited his lighter so that Fred could lean into it with the cigarette in his lips. "So what's overly gay about having three boyfriends?" The man asked.

Fred inhaled and replied with the smoke in his system, "I don't know; perhaps the promiscuity, the open relationship," and then exhaled.

"Who said anything about an open relationship?"

Fred scrunched his eyebrows, "Wasn't it implicit to the fact of having three boyfriends?"

The man exhaled and put an end to the nonsense, "Look I was just trying to see if you were interested. I don't have three boyfriends," he laughed, "and despite my appearance, I am 'overly gay,'" he said mocking Fred's phrase. "But I'm not into open relationships and I prefer to know if the guy I'm chatting-up is, before I carry on."

The red pigmentation in Fred's cheeks returned. He lifted his drink and finished most of it in one gulp. This was the first time a man had ever come onto him, in daylight and in public. He usually met men under strobe lights and after drinking at least eight pints.

"I take my comment back."

Fred glanced through the side of his eyes at the man. *What did he mean by that?* He thought to himself paranoid.

"After speaking to you for five minutes, I'd never think you were a Londoner."

Fred was relieved that he hadn't changed his mind about coming onto him, although he wasn't too thrilled about the loss of his Londoner identity.

"You're too sweet." The man exhaled smoke and unashamedly looked over at Fred.

The waitress reappeared and asked Fred whether he'd like another drink. The man held his card-out for the waitress to take, "we'll have two more of whatever he had before." She took the card and left before Fred could respond.

"Thanks." Fred said.

Fred's phone vibrated within his chino pocket: Nick was calling him from the music shop around the corner. Fred had checked the time at least twice and knew he was late, but he didn't want to leave this charming new man that seemed genuinely interested in him. He took the phone and silenced the call.

The guy paused, anticipating that Fred would take the call.

"I've got to go," he said.

"That's a shame. Can I see you again?" The man asked. There was no reserve or expectation. Hope perhaps, Fred thought. He grinned like a sultry teenager attempting to conceal an overwhelming joy; he was going for cool – casual.

"Sure." Fred replied as he stood. He lingered on the spot and the first awkward silence emerged.

"For God's sake," the guy said laughing. Piteously, he looked at Fred standing in front of him holding his phone in both hands. "Are you ever going to ask for my number?" He saved Fred from stumbling to a clumsy response, "It's 07822255007". Fred typed the number into his Nokia mobile afraid the numbers would evaporate into the warm air if he didn't clutch them quickly. Yet the guy had to repeat them at least three times before Fred finally got them saved.

"Ok." Fred said unsure how to say goodbye, "I guess". His phone began ringing.

"Take the call, and then text me. Nice to meet you Fred." The guy scrunched his fist, drew it toward his deep red lips, kissed it. He then flattened his palm and blew the kiss along his skin toward Fred. He left his lips open so that his teeth shimmered beneath his dazzling eyes. Fred's grin expanded. He squirmed though, not knowing how else to react to the guy's open affection toward him. He shook his head in mock judgment. He turned, walked a few steps, and then answered Nick's call.

"Hey, sorry I'm on my way," he turned around while talking. The guy sat relaxed in the chair staring directly at him without reservation. He placed his palm onto his chest where the heart is and breathed in exaggeratedly. Fred had to stop himself from laughing. He twisted back around and kept walking. He told Nick that he was only around the corner and that he'd be there in two minutes. He didn't look back, but his heart told him that the guy never stopped looking.

Once Fred had left the street, he took his mobile into both hands. He text a line of words, deleted them, re-wrote them, deleted them, wrote new ones, deleted them. This continued until Nick called again. "Sorry, I'm here. I'm here," Fred said before Nick could complain down the phone. He put his phone away and returned to walk at a pace that meant he moved past more than one shop per minute.

He kept his eye out for an opening on the road, and when one emerged, he darted across. Nick stood outside the music shop in his suit. His jacket was tucked into the strap between his nicely ironed shirt and brown satchel bag. He clapped his hands as Fred arrived.

"Sorry," Fred said.

"You're pissed."

"No. I've just had a couple of pints."

"I wasn't judging – just jealous!" Nick said affectionately, "perhaps we can go for a couple afterward," he paused for a couple of seconds slightly disappointed in Fred's lack of enthusiasm. It was usually his job to curb Fred's excitement, "if you want to have a few more." He added lowering his expectations.

"I'd love to," Fred said.

Nick smiled at him, his enthusiasm returning. "Great. Well come on then. I think I'm more excited than you about this bloody guitar!"

They left the shop with guitars strapped to their backs.

"God, I felt like a complete idiot!" Nick said laughing.

"I know. The guy looked at us like we were heathens."

"How dare you dare to learn."

"I knew there was a reason I'd always been afraid of those places," Fred said.

"It feels a bit fraudulent – don't you think?"

"Yeh – but it's amazing so I don't care," Fred scanned the stream of pedestrians around him, "they think we're musicians, able to play these things."

"I don't think they think anything," Nick said piercing Fred's bubble of stardom, "still fancy a drink - Old Compton street?" He suggested nodding toward the other side of the road.

"Yeh – we need to take these babies for a walk."

They sped across, between a double decker red bus and black cab. They turned the corner and Fred searched into the distance to see whether his man was there. He hoped he wasn't. He'd love to see him again, but it felt weird with Nick and the guitar. Fred felt a deep need to impress this guy he'd met for less than hour: the guitar would reveal his whimsiness. It would highlight something that he couldn't do. He didn't want that. He wanted to showcase strength. He tensed as they progressed into the street.

"What's wrong with you?" Nick asked.

"I'm just a bit anxious that someone's going to ask us to play."

"We'll just tell them we're beginners… like brand new beginners… besides nobody'll ask us to play. We're only going for a couple of drinks. Also, what's it matter?"

Fred smiled at the table where he and the guy had met earlier. They settled on a grungier place further down the street. Nick removed his guitar, satchel bag and suit jacket. He sat on a short stool around one of the small circular tables. He took a £10 note from his wallet and handed it to Fred, "get me a pint of Amstel please." Fred rested his guitar against the bench, took the £10 and headed to the bar.

Long blond hair, tied into a ponytail, bobbed on the barman's left shoulder as he pulled Fred and Nick's pints, "Where you playing tonight?" He asked moving his gaze toward their guitars.

"Ah. No. We're not…" Fred stopped himself. People didn't want the truth. They want stories. He considered a venue but wasn't the fastest of thinkers, "we're erm just practising tonight, got a gig in a place around the corner tomorrow."

"Ah yeh – where abouts, Madam JoJo's?" he asked.

Fred exemplified the problem with telling a lie: it leads very quickly to more lies, "Erm no. I can't remember the name now. We're pretty new to London – still getting used to everywhere."

The guy raised his brown eyebrows, the colour of his hair beneath the peroxide blond. He sighed placing one of the pints on the bar, "well we always need a few performers, nothing serious, just a bit of ambiance before it gets busy." He took a card from the shelf and handed it to Fred. "Give us a call if you're any good; pay's terrible, but you know, good for your visibility." Fred took the card and went to give him the £10 note.

The man smiled – it looked odd on his plastic face. "On the house; supporting our gay musicians and all that," he said. Fred felt like he was stealing; though, he put the £10 into his back pocket quick enough. He thanked the barman and went back to their table.

Before he could tell Nick what he'd said, the guy came over to their table. Fred leaned his top teeth onto his lower ones as if bracing for a car crash. He bent toward the small table and placed the card he'd attempted to give Fred, onto it. "You forgot the card." He smiled at Nick and returned to the bar without stopping to chat.

"What's that about?" Nick asked.

"Nothing, but if anybody asks, we're playing at a gig tomorrow night someplace around the corner that neither of us can remember the name of."

Nick laughed. "Why'd you tell him that?"

"Oh, I don't know. He asked where we were playing and I started telling the truth, but it sounded so lame, so I made something up."

"Yesterday you convinced me," he pointed to the guitar, "and you're bailing already?"

"No. I want to learn," Fred reassured Nick.

"You just don't want anybody to know you're learning…" Nick said confused.

"No. Yes. I mean… I don't know… sort of…"

"Fred, you are a wierdo." Nick said taking a sip of his pint. "There's no shame in learning. Everyone had to at some point."

"I'm not a kid," Fred said a little snappy.

"Fine," Nick withdrew not wanting a fight.

"I know it's silly. The truth is I met somebody earlier."

"Oh yeah…" Nick took another sip from his pint and eagerly smiled, "you mean a real-life man with legs and everything?"

Fred scrunched his eyebrows. "I've just been freaked-out a bit since."

"Why?"

"Well, you know".

"I have absolutely no idea." Nick said.

Fred took a sip of his pint and looked away. "I'm being stupid. Ignore me." Fred stopped himself from plunging into a broody cycle of internal soul-searching. He shook his head vigorously and rolled his shoulders as if he were warming himself up for a PE lesson out on a frozen field. He energised himself. "I really liked the guy. It's why I was late meeting you. He just came over to sit next to me while I was having one drink while I waited for you."

Nick chuckled, "why didn't you say you plonker. That's great." He was sincere.

"I don't know. I suppose I felt guilty."

Nick dropped his jaw wide open in perhaps the campest gesture Fred had seen of him. His eyeballs rolled upward exaggeratedly, "don't you feel bloody sorry for me!" He pieced together Fred's internal dilemma.

"You sure you're ok?"

"That's why we're here. I think it's great. And I don't want to be a party pooper, but you met the guy an hour ago; it's not as if you're moving in with him." Nick took another sip. Then looked across alarmed, "Oh God Fred, you're not moving in with him - are you?" He was afraid for Fred, not himself: "only a psychopath would invite you to live with him after an hour."

Fred's anxiety melted like hard butter in an artery. He breathed loosely, freely. "No – come to think about it, I don't even know his name." Nick laughed.

"But seriously," Fred said, returning to the more serious tone, "What happens if we do meet people. I like being with you." He looked away as he said this, slightly ashamed of the open display of emotion.

Nick laughed and squeezed his shoulder, "Fred, we can still be friends and have boyfriends." He now had to tilt his pint higher to get the drink into his mouth. "I like being with you too." He said much more comfortable than Fred in showing his emotion, but not completely at ease either. "Let's promise to stay friends no matter what."

Fred lifted his gaze away from the floor slowly and met Nick's. He looked at him and said, "promise."

PART II
Flying
2009

CHAPTER 7: A single chair

The hearse stopped at the crematorium. Fred watched his mum and aunts step out of the car leaning on one another's arms. They patted tears from their cheeks. Nick rubbed the back of Fred's arm, but Fred lacked strong emotions. He knew the situation was theoretically sad, but he found it difficult to feel it. As the coffin came out, the crowd funnelled into the building after it. A short ceremony flickered by. The family weren't religious so pop songs performed the role of hymns.

People trickled out of the building a different way that they entered it, a symbolic gesture of life's journey, its ever-onward acceleration. Fred thought about his move to London, the decisions he'd made over the last year. He told himself that, unlike all these people, he was doing life right; that he wouldn't get into that box at the end of his life and have people standing around looking at him indifferently. Nick asked if he were ok when they got outside where people naturally spaced out more than they could inside. He nodded. He wanted to spill to Nick that he felt very little, guilt mostly, guilt of not feeling the appropriate sadness. But he nodded instead and performed the expected role.

They dawdled around and Fred chit-chatted with aunts and cousins he hadn't seen in a long time. He asked about their lives; occasionally they asked him a question about work. After enough time elapsed that it wouldn't be considered rude, Fred and Nick jumped into their hire car and drove away from the crematorium.

"Do you miss it?" Nick asked.

"No way!" Fred said immediately. He then asked in anticipation, "do you?"

"Sometimes," Semi-detached houses flickered past like head shots from a photographer's camera, "but not enough." He added and Fred's tension loosened. "I mean I never disliked the place like you did."

Fred disliked Nick's perspective. "That's a bit misleading. It wasn't that I..." But Nick cut him off,

"Because I don't fall in love with places the way you do." Nick took his eyes away from the road to glance at Fred with an affectionate smile. It appeased and silenced him. They drove to the wake in a comfortable silence. Fred paid attention to every detail of the town appearing and disappearing outside the car window. He knew every house intuitively; he'd absorbed every detail growing up: the colours and styles of front doors; the shapes and conditions of driveways, the bends and gradients of the streets they sat upon. It took Fred leaving to appreciate how well he knew the place; how deeply Nuneaton imprinted itself on him, how ingrained it existed within. He looked at Nick and wondered if it was the same. He knew it wasn't – Nick had moved around as a child – but Fred looked and wondered anyway.

"So, you don't fancy moving back?" Nick brought some energy back to the car. "We could beg for jobs back at Eliot High, go to *Chicos* every Friday, and you know, perhaps look forward to when we're old enough to go to the meat Bingo."

Fred smirked grateful for Nick's silly humour. The engine stopped and Nick went to open the car door as Fred pulled at his shoulder. "Thank you." Fred said unusually open in feeling let alone displaying a graciously affectionate manner.

"For what?" Nick replied with tenderness and curiosity.

"For agreeing to leave. I wouldn't have done it without you."

"Of course, you would Freddie." Nick's chin dipped into his chest. "I should thank you. It was me that wouldn't have left." He kept his head low feeling some shame. "I used to judge you, Fred. I mean, not aloud, to people. But to myself, I did think you were a melodramatic mess."

"I am a melodramatic mess." Nick laughed at Fred's self-deprecating sweetness.

"No, you're not." He paused and reconsidered, "Well, yes you are; but, in the best possible way." He rolled his chin and face upward to lean it onto his shoulder and the headrest. He stared at Fred and Fred stared at him. Nick lent forward and kissed him. Fred's lips didn't resist; they reacted slowly, softly, to the warmness of Nick's. Nick's palms rested on Fred's cheeks. Fred though, gently, after a few moments, lifted them away from his face and pulled back from the kiss.

"I'm sorry." Nick said. "I didn't mean…"

"It's ok. It's a weird day." Fred said. He remained in the closely intimate position, staring at Nick. "I don't feel overly sad about my gran. It's sad of course, but you know, it happens. Death. We weren't that close. But the town. It doesn't make any sense… I feel, I feel like, the town; I do feel sad about it. I don't know why. It's like the mourning everybody else feels for people, I feel for the town." Nick listened without judgment. "And it doesn't quite make sense because obviously it's still here, unlike Granny Em. But it isn't, at the same time. It's feels like a ghost; it's the only way I can think to describe it."

"I get it." Nick said.

"No, you don't," Fred said laughing.

"Well, no I don't, but you do, and that's what's important."

"You're sweet, Nicholas."

"Erm. I think you're the sweet one. I'm obnoxious remember," he said mockingly.

"Oh, shut up." Fred said pulling his body upward. He opened the car door, "Come on. Let's go in; let's say goodbye properly."

Alcohol turned the mood at the wake from austere awkwardness to sentimental warmth. People shared stories and spoke more honestly to one another. Their fear and self-consciousness lessoned; they became family. Uncle Joe fiddled with the sound system and eventually, eighties music blasted through the speakers attached to the walls. He quickly reduced the volume so that it was loud enough for people to dance and still hear each other if they raised their voices to a soft shout. The overall noise and energy increased within the little clubhouse which was tucked away from the houses blooming off the main road. Fred's older brother poured rows of sambuca shots at the bar. Fred's mum took the first glass, lifted it into the air, and announced a toast to her granny Em. Seven or eight extended family members took a glass, lifted to clink it to hers, and before tossing it down their throats, echoed her words,

"To granny Em,"

"Granny Em,"

"Em," they said over and with one another.

As everybody sucked their lips in and popped them back outward, shaking their heads and shimmying their shoulders, Jack re-filled all the glasses. A few aunts withdrew, but cousins took their place. Somebody else proposed another toast, "To life!"

"Life!"

"Life!"

"Life!" everyone shouted together.

Jack re-filled the glasses. People switched places. Some stayed for another toss; others bowed out; others joined. The toasts continued for half an hour. Jack re-poured and re-poured. Liquor bottle after liquor bottle emptied. Fred and Nick joined several rounds: Fred more than Nick. Some aspects of him had changed in London. Other's hadn't.

The atmosphere had metamorphosised from funeral to pseudo-nightclub. Uncle Joe had turned the main lights off and people moved the seats to the edges of the room. The wall lamps emitted a gentle glow; it wasn't quite strobe lights, but people danced together and unlike an expensive nightclub, the alcohol flowed freely.

Fred walked onto the terrace, where the half of the room not dancing, congregated in plumes of smoke. His mum opened her cigarette packet and offered him a Spanish knock-off, Trevor had brought her back 50 duty-free packets from Malgret-de-Mar a few weeks back. Fred took one and leant into the flame she'd created with her lighter. "How's London?" She asked.

"Yeh – good," he responded.

"When was the last time you came back?"

"Probably Christmas," Fred changed the topic. He didn't want to recount trivial bits of immediate History for the purpose of evoking guilt about his decision to leave. "How's things with Dad?"

"Same." She said before changing the topic. She didn't want to recount trivial bits of immediate History for the purpose of evoking guilt about her decision to not leave. "How's Nick?"

"He's good." Fred said. They sucked on their cigarettes and blew smoke into the now darkened evening air. "We've been learning the guitar together". She glanced at him with disbelief.

"You haven't." She loved the idea of him playing an instrument but couldn't envisage it. "You could play something now?" She said accusatory, not meaning to be offensive, but seeking certainty for her conviction that Fred hadn't followed through.

"Yep." He said enjoying the surprise he generated in her. "Obviously, we're not amazing, but after a year of practising every day, we can hold our own."

She smiled heartily. Fred rarely saw his mum smile properly, as if she really meant it. When sober, an insecurity often sat beneath it, and when drunk, an insanity. He enjoyed the moment. She didn't insist that he should play. Fred was sure that she believed doing so would risk exposing the truth: she'd take illusion; the thought of him performing was enough. Why jeopardise that with a failed reality? She blew smoke and smiled at him. "You've always been brainy," she said.

"How's Nana?" Fred diverted the conversation away from them.

"She's alright…" Fred's mum took another drag on her cigarette, she continued speaking as the smoke circulated, "Granny Em was a tough old lady," she exhaled. Her words were affectionate and kind. "She was so different to Nana", she paused thinking for a word to emphasise her point, "hard." It was a compliment.

Fred nodded. Truthfully, he didn't know his granny Em as a person, but only great-granny Em, an old lady that had always been an old lady. Her youth, her love, her heartache, her joys, were unknown to him. Great grannies didn't share their stories, their lives. Nobody did. Fred thought of his life in London and felt bitter. Like his granny Em, he had a life that these people knew nothing about. Why didn't they want to know? He flicked his cigarette onto the floor and stamped it out. "See ya inside." He said to his mum.

Nick danced with Fred's cousins. Fred left him to it. He walked to the bar, passed beneath the hatch, and helped himself to a good glug of whisky. His brother shouted over to him, "pour out some shots, bro." He did. People came up, took shots of whisky, tossed them back, made hedonistic toasts and then sauntered back to the dance floor. Fred lingered behind the bar, pouring out shots, doing something, keeping busy. He didn't want to dance, and he didn't want to talk. He didn't want to go either. He was content behind the bar, at the edge of things going on.

His dad came over. "Alright Freddie? How's London?"

"Yeh – good, Dad."

"How're the bars down there? I bet they're great." Fred didn't want to talk about London with his dad.

"Yeh – they're good."

"Bet you go to so many different places. Not like round here. Bet there's a new place for every weekend if you wanted," admiration flowed freely, "God, I wish I'd moved to London. Mind you, was pretty rough when I was younger; bet nothing like nowadays." He pointed at the whisky bottle. Fred poured it until golden brown liquid surfaced at the top of the glass. His dad bent over the bar and slurped the liquid reducing it down a little so that he could lift it without spilling. "Made many friends down there? Bet they're fun, the people."

"Yeh – a few. They're nice." Fred said almost on automation. His dad knocked back most of the whisky in one. He made a husky 'brrr' sound, the sort of noise people make as they feel the warmth of a fire that makes them realise how cold they were in the first place. "I'd love to come down. We could see loads of pubs. Have a good knees-up," he said.

Fred poured fresh whisky into his glass and responded non-committal and disinterestedly, "yeh – sounds good, dad." He placed the bottle back onto the bar and ducked under the hatchet, "see ya in a bit dad."

"See ya son," he said.

Fred's phone vibrated. He looked at his screen, a text from his man: *'hope today has been alright baby. Thinking of you x'*. Fred snook through the changing rooms beside the bar and headed outside, to the back of the clubhouse. He called his thick red lipped London-man and was soothed by the northern accent as soon as it channelled through the phone.

"It's a weird day. I can't wait to get back though. I don't fit here anymore." Fred spoke into the phone pressed to his ear. His foot rested against the brick wall of the clubhouse.

"Baby they're your family. Of course, you fit there. Enjoy them. You'll be back before you know it. Trust me, these moments are special. They'll be fewer and fewer of them, so make the most of it while you can. London is your future – I'm your future – and there's a lot of it ahead of us. So, savour your past while it's there."

Fred softened. Like the breach of a dam, currents flooded his body. The pain and joy of his family throbbed but he felt better immediately for not resisting the emotions, "I hate the person that I become when I'm here. It's not even their fault. It's me. I can't relax and be normal," Fred said as if he were at confession.

"I'm listening," the northerner said after a short silence.

"It's like I'm enguard unable to stop looking for threats."

"I get it."

"I know." A warm long silence rested between them. "Thank you." Fred said.

"I can't wait to see you."

"Can't wait to see you either."

"I wish I could be there right now."

Like water to the face, this lifted Fred out of his sentimentality. He meant what he'd said, but the thought of his northerner being there right now terrified him.

"I'll be back soon. You'd hate it here."

"No, I wouldn't, but I didn't mean it literally. It's your family – the relationships we have as gay men, well, it changes the dynamics. I know that. It might never feel comfortable with me there, and that's fine. I just meant that I want to be there with you, standing out back or wherever you're hiding, just for 5 minutes. Then I'd disappear and you'd go back and enjoy yourself."

Fred's lips lifted and his incisors twinkled beneath the moonlight. The 2-minute conversation had fully recharged him.

"Put your teeth away," the voice in the phone told Fred. "Look I'm going now. You're clearly feeling much better and I've got lots of my own fabulous things to be getting on with."

"Are you working tonight?" Fred asked.

"Yeah, got a few stories to finish for Monday, but I want Sunday completely free so I can spend the entire day kissing and pampering you."

"Oh yeh – well I was thinking of coming back tomorrow."

"No, you won't. You're going to go back into that party-wake, get hammered, have an amazing night with your family. Then tomorrow you're going to wake up, see your friends and have a great night out with them too… you're going to feel like you're back in love with the place but then you'll miss me even more than ever and call me drunken, horny and affectionate."

Fred laughed at his prescience. In his heart, he knew it was correct. "Now bugger off and start missing me," he said. "I'm hanging-up. See you soon."

"See you soon," Fred said. The line ended. Fred put his phone into his pocket. He removed a cigarette from his packet of Marlborough lights and lit-up. His back rested on the brick wall. The moonlight softened the darkness of the woods, cricket-field and rugby pitches surrounding the clubhouse. He inhaled and exhaled smoke and felt at peace. Full. He felt like a man. Strong, stable, at ease with the moment. He didn't require action, internal or external. He wasn't afraid of the darkness or his family. He was ready to be with them.

He flicked his fag butt into the ground and squashed it out. Back in the bar, he walked past his dad still sitting at the bar. He joined Nick and his female cousins who were dancing to Whitney Houston. "Hey!" Nick said loud enough to be heard over the music, "on the phone to your northerner?" Fred grabbed Nick's hands and twisted him around. His cousins matched the energy he'd brought over. They twirled each other and hopped to a faster internal rhythm. As soon as Fred let go of Nick, his cousin grabbed Fred and twirled him thrice and thrice again. They sang aloud to the lyrics at the top of their voices, as did everybody else dancing. They stopped only to go to the bar to pour themselves more shots, the terrace to regain their breath while smoking a cigarette, or the toilet where they gossiped about nothing important with all the importance and passion of a grand council. Fred's mum and aunts joined the dancing. They too twirled, their shoulders shimmied, their waists circled like hula hoops. The men then joined too. Fred's brothers, his uncles and cousins twirled, knocked back shots and pints as they pumped their bottoms back and forth, thrusting themselves across the room like superstars performing at Wembley stadium. Eventually, even his dad saucily joined the dancing. He shook his hips and like a Rockstar rotated his wife while singing the lyrics to 'Sex on Fire' at the top of his husky whisky voice. The room was electricity. The airwaves throbbed. The clubhouse wombed them joyfully together. For that night, everybody danced and submitted themselves to a superior lifeforce. They worshipped spontaneity, the free-flowing movements of the body, the euphoria of syncing to a rhythm beyond self. They were alive and celebrated life. They said goodbye to Granny Em.

Fred woke beside Nick in his childhood bed. They wore boxer-shorts beneath the single duvet they shared. Nick's arm wrapped over Fred and their bodies pressed together tightly. They'd paid for rooms at the Holiday Inn, but an afterparty had spilled to Fred's mum and dad's home.

Fred untucked himself from Nick's arm and rolled gently onto the floor, attempting to sneak out without waking Nick. He grabbed his black trousers and T-shirt from the floor, tossed them on and crept out of the bedroom. He closed the door very slowly, turning the handle to soften the sound of the click. Downstairs, an aunt slumbered on the sofa, an uncle lay with his head pressed into an armchair; both of his legs flopped over one side of the arm. Two of his cousins lay spooning one another in the conservatory with an old blanket sprawled over them. Fred drifted into the kitchen, looked out of the window onto the front lawn. A crisp clear blue sky awaited them outside. Empty bottles and beer cans filled the worksurfaces inside. Plates with slivers of grease from the piles of pizzas and oven chips cooked when they got home, piled on top of one another beside the sink. Fred cleared some space so that he could fill the kettle with tap water. He clicked the power button and waited for the steam to shoot out. His fingers rubbed the skin above the edges of his eyes. He thought about Nick in his bed upstairs, and then to the times he'd sat in that room as a teenager telling himself that he had two choices he could make: leave this place: be gay but leave family behind. Or stay: get married to a nice woman, have children; deny himself but keep his family. The two options were mutually exclusive. It was inconceivable for them to co-exist, and now he sat waiting for the kettle to boil with his openly gay best friend asleep in his bed in the room next to his parents. The steam escaped. He blew it away from his cup, toward the window, as he poured boiling water into his Nuneaton Football mug. He smiled and slurped tea. Uncharacteristically, he pulled an additional mug from the cupboard and made an extra cup of tea. He retraced his steps through the lounge and up the stairs to his old bedroom. This time he didn't attempt to control the noise of the door opening.

Nick's eyelids struggled to open but they mustered tiny reserves of energy from somewhere to force themselves to open for just long enough for him to make-out Fred's figure, but importantly an outstretched arm and cup of tea in hand. Like a guillotine they dropped back shut but he was comforted that when he did finally rise from his feeling of deadness, there'd be a cup of tea waiting. Fred wedged his bum over Nick's body so that he could rest his back on the wall. His legs drooped over his torso like a car over a speedhump. Nick moaned as he regained more awareness of his hangover. He twisted himself over so that he faced inward toward Fred and the wall. Slowly, but with more promise of long-term success, his eyelids opened. He smiled at Fred and Fred from high, smiled back.

"So, this is your bedroom then - where all that secret internet dating first began?" Nick jibed. Fred jabbed his side with his fingers poised like steel. "Ow!" Nick grunted. "But I don't get it Fred: your mum and dad are so cool."

Fred wanted to say that they hadn't always been like this, but it would have been a lie. They had really. It was more complicated. "It's more complicated," he said.

"Fuck, my parents would never let loose like that. Ever. No matter who I came back with. Your parents are really fun Fred. I expected..." Nick thought of the moment that Fred had pleaded with him to leave – *I'll die if I stay here* – the stories he'd listened to Fred tell, the stories he'd heard about Fred's family, "I dunno. I expected them to be hard, you know, intolerant. Dangerous."

Fred knew that he'd fed this characterisation, not intentionally. He lacked the poetic ability, the language and verse, to express what his family are. He'd never meant to depict them as intolerant in its Middle-class sensibility. They aren't. Fred still lacked the language. He couldn't explain them to Nick, but he didn't feel as angry and suffocated for not being able to do so. Fred took a sip of tea, "I didn't ever mean to paint them in that way. They're not homophobes, or racist, or anything like that, but just because they can have a good party doesn't mean they're properly accepting of difference either."

"What do you mean? They seemed pretty hospitable to me."

"Look it's different. Parties are different to everyday life," Fred said.

Nick let it go. He didn't have the energy for the intellectual jousting, and it was doubly hard having to do it in a whispering voice. He looked around the room and noticed the rows of CD cases blue-tacked adjacent to one another on the wall. There were three rows, one on top of another. Savage Garden, Tracey Chapman, Blink-182, Britney Spears, Now that's what I call Music, 38! Texas, Aqua, Cyndi Lauper, Titanic, No Doubt,

Meatloaf, The Cranberries, The Verve, David Grey. "That's a bit of a very gay eclectic mix – how'd they not know?"

"Oh, shut up. There's a tea on the window-sill." Nick bent his arm to reach for the mug.

"So, what's the plan for today? We need to confirm and pay the Holiday Inn if we're stopping tonight," Nick said.

"I thought I'd want to go back, but I think it would be fun to stay another night if you still fancy it?"

"I'm up for it," Nick said, "Shall I ring the Holiday Inn and confirm the room," he gestured to the single duvet by tugging at it, "I mean as much as I've loved this, I think I will probably need a proper bed tonight."

"Yes. I don't think anything good will come of our sharing a bed again," Fred said.

"What do you mean by that?" Nick said seriously.

"Nothing," Fred hadn't meant anything serious but as he listened back, he realised it was awkward. He attempted to brush it off, "I mean you'll end up trying to sleep with me obviously." He'd made it worse.

"You forget we've already done that." Nick said restoring some joviality.

"Not properly."

"Well let's leave this conversation, hey. Mr, 'I've got a boyfriend'." Nick referred to Fred's northerner and it made Fred tense-up. He didn't want to discuss him with Nick. Sharing a bed with Nick, even a kiss, cuddle and intimate talk about their past sexual activity, didn't cause Fred any inner turmoil, but poking fun of his northerner, felt wrong. That wasn't Nick's place. Fred discovered he had boundaries and it made him uncomfortable, ashamed. He sprung himself from the bed, pretending to ignore the comment and hide the reality that he had a problem talking about this with Nick.

"Come on," he said to Nick, "I'll make you an egg toastie." Fred left Nick in his bed as he walked out of the room, pretending things were normal between them. Nick's leg bent out of the duvet and his foot pressed into the carpet. His other foot followed. He pulled the duvet away from his body and stood out of the bed in his boxer-shorts. He rearranged his parts and searched for his clothes. He couldn't find his jumper, so put on one of Fred's.

The mess and difficulty of finding enough space to butter a piece of toast let alone boil eggs, caused Fred to abandon the plan of egg-toasties. They walked into town instead. They decided against a McDonald's breakfast in favour of something greasier and more wholesome. They headed to the no-frills, Nuneaton café, Mrs Parkers. Fred sank his lips into a crusty baguette filled with bacon, mushrooms, and tomatoes; Nick chewed his way through a thickly sliced sausage sandwich smeared with so much ketchup that it had become a sauce. They ate while walking the rest of the way into town.

Nuneaton town centre was an urban watering hole. Its population gravitated there under the guise of need, the need for a new CD, the need for a new top, the need for a new computer game, the need for lunch, the need for an 11 o'clock cheap pint, the need for new knickers, the need for hair gel, the need for a birthday card, the need for a wedding hat, the need for dog food. But like animals who stay even though their thirst is quenched, the people stayed even though their shopping was purchased. They lingered, lingered in town as the animals lingered at the watering hole. Like a beautiful multi-coloured kaleidoscope, swathes of people criss-crossed through each other, around and around the pedestrianised streets. They stopped to chit-chat, laugh and gossip.

With full stomachs, Fred and Nick didn't need anything. They strolled through the shops and pointed out the things that had changed, or more numerously, the things that hadn't changed since their leaving a year ago. After three loops around the town, they hadn't bumped into anybody. They had expected to see ex-colleagues, school friends, extended family, random people that they knew but didn't really remember why or how they knew them. Nobody. This isn't how it worked. Like a stubborn dog and child unwilling to return home from the park, they perched on the benches looping the fountain at the heart of the town. Nobody.

"Bloody hell. We haven't been gone that long. Where is everybody? I haven't seen a single person that I recognise," Nick said, and he was by far the less social of them.

And as he finished speaking, a blond bob, on a black leather jacket, bobbed toward them. She carried two shopping bags: an orange Sainsbury's in the left and white top-shop in the right. Bea's horse teeth spread across her face and the boys smiled back at her. She lumbered toward them; her shopping bags increased their swing as her legs trotted that bit faster than before.

"Oh, I've missed you!" She said leaning in to kiss each of them on the cheek with her shopping bags still glued to her hands. "How long are you here for?" She said. It was always how long, never why. Purpose was irrelevant, only time mattered.

"Just till tomorrow," Fred said.

"Well, I needed a new top, so I popped to New Look but couldn't find anything, and then I found this in Top-Shop," she placed her food bag on the floor so that she could take her top out to show the uninterested boys." With people shuffling around her, she held the low-cut top to her chest and smiled.

"Very nice," Nick replied. He didn't have an opinion but gave the response that made her smile.

"I'm so glad because I didn't have anywhere to where it, but now I do," she said. "Shall we go for a little drink now?"

"It's 11.30," Fred said deadpan. Bea's smile faded a little. "Where's best to go?" He added, and her face looked like three 7s aligned on the slot machine.

"The George," she responded instantly in case they changed their mind.

Nick sighed, "I'm not sure I can drink yet... last night's shots aren't even out of my system." Bea looked hurt.

"You were here last night?"

"Funeral." Her hurt dissolved.

"Ah," She picked-up her bag and gestured in the direction of the pub, "Come on tell me about it on the way". They meandered through the Saturday crowds, through the market men advertising the price of their apples and pears; past the flower stalls wrapping dozens and half-dozens; past kids begging their mums for ice-creams; past old ladies gossiping about last night's episode of coronation street; past teenagers gossiping about who fancied who. Bea handed her bags to Fred and Nick inside the pub. It wasn't full but it was more full than empty. "I'll get the drinks. You find us a seat." As Fred and Nick went to saunter through the deeps of the pub, Bea called back to them, "Outside! It's a nice day, let's sit outside."

She brought out a tray of sambuca shots, and three double gin and tonics. Fred felt the same as Nick, but he didn't let it impact his actions. He clinked the shot of sambuca with Bea and tossed it back. Bea then lifted the shot for Nick and tossed that back too.

"Brrr," she said shimming her shoulders in the warm sunlight. She then took a large gulp of the gin and tonic to wash down the unpleasurable taste of the neat spirit. Fred did too.

"I don't know how you can after last night," Nick said shaking his head. Fred licked his upper lip and shook his head vigorously.

"Carpe Diem!" He said pushing through the protests of his stomach. He'd decided that today was going to be goodbye. A proper goodbye. He looked around the pub, seeing through the walls into the town beyond, through the streets, through the shops, through to the rows of houses, through to the schools, the hospital, the clubhouses, the country lanes, the fields, parks, and forests. He was saying goodbye properly to all of it. He recalled his thick-lipped boyfriend's words, *London's your future. I'm your future. Enjoy your past while it's there.* He thought to himself that he'd been playing at London with Nick. When they went back this time, he was going properly, this time, he was taking his heart with him. The least he could do was give Bea a good time. He didn't even get into a mood with Nick for not intuitively reading his mind and adopting the same mentality. He didn't give him a hard time for refusing to drink. He, uncharacteristically, leaned into Bea, rested his palm on her forearm, and conveyed his happiness openly. Her smile stretched even further.

"Let me call, Heeta, and Tom. They have to be here," she said taking her cigarette packet from her handbag before her phone. She handed the Marlborough lights to Fred and a lighter, then, phoned Heeta.

Three pubs later, Fred vomited for the second time. He cupped water, threw it onto his face, washed the bits out of his mouth and went back to the party. They'd moved to Wetherspoons where half of Fred's family from the wake also congregated. The spring sunlight had retired; the market stalls had packed-up, and Nuneaton's nocturnal inhabitants had begun emerging. Women in short skirts, low-cut tops, heels and jewellery replaced daytime shoppers. Daytime drinkers, shabby clothed, either hid into the backgrounds or left. Bea had changed into her new top in the toilets and dumped her food bag in Heeta's car. There was no way she was going home, not even to change.

Fred re-entered the bar. The lights had dimmed, and the music had increased while he'd been in the toilets. He swaggered through the pub, assuming that people were looking at him even though they weren't. He spun 360 degrees back at the table and then jabbed his outstretched hands into Bea's fleshy sides. Her body jerked and she screeched while instinctively slapping Fred's now tickle-intent arms away from her. The others laughed. He leant inward evading her slaps. He licked her cheeks with his post-sick tongue. She screeched louder but the music and boisterous level of noise in the pub prevented attention from other tables.

She struggled to speak in her involuntary, suffocating fit of laughter, "Get-off!" She said. Fred withdrew, laughing, she winced and wiped her cheek, "Yuck. You smell of sick!"

"Rotten!" Tom said, "I've got to kiss that later."

"You haven't kissed that in a long time," Bea replied, referring to her cheek.

"It's been so long since we were all together," Heeta said. She had caught up with the amount Bea and Fred had drunk. "Seriously guys," she reached out her arms in both directions, placing one palm to her left on Fred's knee, and the other to her right on Tom's, "we need to do this more often." She hiccupped.

"Yeh, you bastards," Tom said, "since you fuckers left, these bitches hardly ever let me come out with them." Heeta lifted her palm from his leg and brought it down with a stinging slap. Tom sucked on his lip.

"Don't you call us bitches," she said caught between a laugh and another hiccup. Her attention turned to Fred, "We have to come down to London." She focused her eyes onto his. It would have been far too intense were she sober, but a large part of the stare was merely for the sake of letting her focus catch-up. She took some time to remember what she was going to say. Everybody waited in anticipation. She searched internally despite fixating on Fred.

"Right, I'll get another round", Bea said.

"I'm coming to London," Heeta said, remembering what she wanted to say. "To live!" She hiccupped again. She placed both of her hands onto Fred's knees. His face tilted back slightly apprehensive that she might hit him, not aggressively. He mustered the strength to not laugh directly at her face. Red wine stained his otherwise twinkling teeth. He emitted S.O.S sonar glances to the others.

Tom leant toward her and placed his hand on her shoulder. She swiped at him. This time it was slightly aggressive. Bea, Nick and Fred sucked air and pulled their faces a few millimetres backward. They'd seen Heeta drunk plenty, but no matter how much, she had always retained a trace of self-control. Pure irrationality wasn't her. "Get-off!" She said. She placed her hands back onto Fred's knees and re-focused her stare onto him. But this time she was not searching internally. Her consciousness was on Fred. She was looking into his soul. "It should have been me. Not him," she meant Nick. "I would have gone with you." The others were silent. They had never seen Heeta vulnerable. Exposed.

Fred saw oceans behind her eyes. He saw the oceans that had consumed his own being. The oceans that he'd shown to Nick sitting on that kerb. He turned away and broke the connection between them. He resented the way she was making him feel. She could have come, "You could have come," he said.

An unstable silence lingered. The oceans in Heeta boiled: the still waters of sadness and love swirled into tempestuous showers of fire and rage. How had he responded to her so cruelly? The trace of self-control returned to her. She stood like lightening bouncing from the earth to strike back at the heavens from which it came. She swallowed, considered saying something, but left without doing so. The others experienced delay. Eventually, Tom went after her. Bea went to the bar, and Nick said that he was going back to the hotel. Fred sat alone, furious at everyone including himself.

Laughter continued in the rest of the pub. More dolled-up women entered together, one group glanced at Fred and his empty table hoping he'd move so they could grab it. He didn't. He sat and sulked. The women came over anyway and asked if they could take the chairs.

"Help your fucking selves." They took the chairs, and largely ignored him.

He sat on the only chair left at the table. He pulled his phone checked for messages. Nothing. His chair legs scrapped backward. It didn't screech because of the carpet. He stormed out. Bouncers had arrived. Their eyes suggested to Fred that his leaving was one directional. He didn't care. He was done. He stomped along the centre of the street, undecided on where to go.

Inside, Bea returned to the table with a tray of drinks. She sat on the single chair and dipped her head.

Fred plunged into the booth at the posh chip shop where you could sit down. There weren't waitresses as such. He ordered chips, a battered sausage, and mushy peas as he entered and then one of the staff brought it over. He wolfed the food, shovelling the funky crinkly chips into his mouth before he'd finished the ones already there. He hadn't eaten apart from the sausage baguette on the way into town. The man returned with a can of coke. He plonked it onto the table without communicating.

After his stomach began to relax its demands, he slowed down. He fingered the remaining chips into the mushy peas repeatedly before eating them. The fizzy bubbles sank through his throat and bleached his insides. He started to feel some remnants of humanity again. He wiped as much grease from his hands with the serviette and then pressed his fingertips into his forehead, massaging the skin softly and only smearing a little unwiped grease onto himself. Regret worked its way through his system. He visualised Heeta's eyes, recalled her towering figure stood in front of him; disgust poured onto him. He took his phone and opened a message to her. Again, most of the grease had been removed, but a few slithers made their way onto the number-pad. *'Sorry. I was a dick'*, he typed. He deleted it and rewrote leaving the apology and changing the tense, *'I am a dick'*. He sent the message. The little swooshing noise confirmed it had sent. He stared at the screen for a few minutes thinking about what she said. He never considered that she would want to move with him. He then gave himself a hard time about his selfishness. *How'd I never think about what she wanted? Why didn't I just ask her?*

'Can I see you?' He typed into his phone. His finger hovered over the button that would fire his message through the atmosphere and into her phone. The future was that he wasn't sure if he wanted to see her. What if she replied and came – what would he say to her? Fred was sure the northerner was about to suggest moving in together. His proper life was about to begin. It just wasn't the right time for Heeta to move. He'd moved on. He ignored this voice and pushed the button. She wouldn't come anyway.

'Where are you?' her reply came through immediately. *Fuck,* he thought.

'Wales,' he replied.

'???'

'The chip shop," he clarified.

'Be there in ten minutes,'

Fuck, he thought again. *'Great, see you soon x'*.

He thought the time would drag but the anxiety and uncertainty of how he was going to handle the situation consumed the minutes quicker than he had consumed his chips. He saw her sturdy little palm, flat on the glass door, push. She walked past the counter without ordering anything. She saw Fred in the booth and came over. She sat opposite him.

"I didn't mean it in a Sasha way," was the first thing she said. Fred hadn't even considered that. The idea of Heeta being obsessed with anybody, let alone him, was absurd, incomprehensible, to Fred. She hadn't meant it to be funny, but he laughed aloud. It cleared the greasy air between them, at least a little.

"I hadn't even considered that."

"Good."

Fred wondered whether he should fill the silence and decided against it. He acknowledged that he'd likely say something wrong – better let her speak. She looked down into her chest, ashamed. It was unlike Heeta. She was strength itself.

"I need to leave," she said.

Fred prevented the questions spilling out. And with great effort pursued his plan of silence. He was going to listen. Listen. Not speak.

"Things have become a bit difficult..." she said. Fred, now intrigued, found it a little easier to stay quiet. He wanted to know what had happened.

"You've never met my family," she said in Bea's factual tone. Fred nodded. He'd never really thought about it. It wasn't unusual to not meet a friend's family, sort of.

"Well, my dad. He's sort of..." she searched for the words. She'd never spoke about her family to anybody before. She ignored them, defied them without making an issue of it. "I don't want to be around him anymore," she said regaining some firmness. She lifted her head away from her chest and looked more like the Heeta he knew.

"Come to London," he said and meant it. "We'll figure something out. Make it work." Fred found his compassion and asserted it confidently. He felt unbelievably better for it. Heeta smiled at him. She stretched out her hand and he took it.

"I don't fancy you, or even necessarily want to live with you. In fact, I definitely don't want to live with you," she meant it. "But I want to be friends. I'm going to move to London, and it would be nice to know you're there."

Fred nodded.

"I'm not telling anybody where I'm going though." Her voice became serious. She expected confidence from Fred. "You cannot tell anybody. Can you do that?"

Fred nodded instinctively, "of course." He wanted to ask her what was wrong but exerted the miraculous self-discipline to stick to his listener role.

She smiled at him and tightened her hand on his. They sat in a warm, comfortable silence. She ate the few remaining chips off his plate.

Outside the glass window of the chip-shop front, Heeta leaned into Fred and gave him a hug. Her small arms viced him. He bent his head and rested it on her shoulder; his hands were stapled to his sides beneath her arms.

"Thanks Fred. You're a dick, but a dick I want in my life," she said. Her chin perched on his shoulder; a cheeky smile stretched across her face. "I've got stuff to sort out, but I'll give notice to work first thing Monday and start applying for jobs tonight." She released her locked arms and allowed Fred to breathe normally. "I mean it. I've already seen a couple of schools that I like the look of. There's a few Head of Department positions that I'm going to apply for too."

"You're really coming then?"

She locked eye contact with him, "I will tell you everything once I've sorted things here, but there is no doubt, none." She paused and stared with her most serious face, "Fred, I love you."

"Not in a Sasha way," Fred, rather emboldened, softened the emotional intensity without disregarding what she'd said. He smiled and told her back, "I know. I miss you too." He was sincere. Although if he was honest with himself, he was surprised. He hadn't actively thought about Heeta, about their relationship over his last year in London. He hadn't consciously missed or felt an absence, but standing outside Nuneaton's finest chippy, he rediscovered a depth that he'd forgotten about. He loved London and couldn't wait to return. He loved its lightness, its voyeurism, its endless capacity to live on the surface: new pubs, new clubs, new restaurants, new shops, new galleries, new schools, newness, diversity, constantly. But he craved heaviness too. He wanted things in his life that endured the newness and difference. Constants, with whom he could co-sail, in an otherwise world of oceanic fluidity. He wanted Heeta. Heetas. But this realisation made him doubt his relationship with Nick. He began to think: 'Nick and I are only doing lightness. Our London life involves soaring, higher and higher. Endlessly upwards. We're migratory birds, nesting only to rest. We're afraid'. He sank into his re-wired self-narrative: 'We've been afraid the entire time, running away, when we should have been building, rooting.'

"Fred?" Heeta said sensing he'd drifted away from her. "I've got to go, but I'll give you a call in a few days," she reached in and gave him another hug. But Fred had created an internal black hole. He nodded and hugged her back, but his soul was absent. "same old Fred!" She said with an affectionate pat on his back, "you never change." She gave him a peck on the cheek and left.

'You never change', the words slid into the maelstrom beginning to swirl in his mind. All his thoughts spun into that black hole of depth opening within: 'Shit, am I throwing everything away? Is this heaviness just a load of crap to undermine what Nick and I have done? What's wrong with flying endlessly? Is it naïve to think we can have it all? 'O heavy lightness'… wasn't Shakespeare taking the piss? Romeo was lost, indecisive, impulsive – his thirst for heaviness killed him… he could have just lived perfectly happy if he just manned-up and made the most of his fucking privilege… it was his stupid, naïve craving for heaviness – for Juliet – that sent everything tits up. For Christ's sake Fred. You sound like Lady Macbeth… 'man-up?' You're telling yourself to reject the heaviness of truth and justice, conscience… what's right; that's going to end badly if you don't sort yourself out… and now look: you're full on talking to yourself. Get a grip. Stop."

Fred blinked repeatedly. He pulled his consciousness away from himself, his dark fruitless inner rabbit-hole. He'd lost himself down there many a time. Not tonight. The sights, sounds and smells of Nuneaton refocused: the smell of back alley piss, muffled music from bars and nightclubs, and the railings stopping drunks from falling into the river. These simple things made him happy. He shimmied his shoulders and shook his head to energise himself and shake away his introspection. He felt the cold and his lips rolled instinctively like a car engine warming itself against the weather. He started walking back toward the centre. He was done, but it'd be easier to get a taxi.

He watched the metre the entire journey and re-calculated over and over how much the short trip would cost him. He hated taxis, or he hated paying for them. He told the driver to pull-up on the main road rather than looping around to the hotel entrance. He'd walk round. Even though he hated paying, he could never not tip - even if the drivers were rude. He gave a £10 note and told the driver to keep the change.

The corporate glass doors slid open and Fred entered the hotel. He pressed the button for the lift but walked to the staircase when the light indicated they were both on the 3rd floor. He looped up the staircase. Fred's fingertips brushed against the beige walls as he drifted along the windowless corridors. He swiped his key card and entered the depressing cell. The wall mounted T.V. filled the room with the voice of some smug politician promising waffle; Nick lay on his single bed tapping away on his phone, the news bleated on in the background. He didn't look up or say hello. Fred sat on the edge of his bed, bent over to remove his shoes, and then scooted himself up so that the headboard supported his aching skull. His hangover was kicking-in. His bottom right-angled on the bed – his torso upright, his legs flat. His eyelids dropped shut and were it not for the juxtaposed droning and hyperbolic headlines being intermittently announced on the news channel, he would have probably fallen asleep. He craved the energy to open his eyes, move his body toward Nick's bed so that he could snatch the remote and throw it at the screen.

"Please turn that fucking thing over," he finally said.

Nick picked-up the remote and changed the channel without looking at the T.V or acknowledging Fred.

"What's up with you?" Fred said with his eyes still closed and his head still resting on the board.

"I've just been thinking."

Fred opened his eyes, twisted his head slightly to glance over at Nick, but he couldn't commit to keeping it there. He'd acknowledged him though - that would be enough. "Go on then," he said. He didn't intend to sound dismissive: he just lacked the energy to sound enthusiastic, or even civil.

Nick placed his phone onto the bed; it rested beneath the triangular arch of his legs, of which his arms wrapped around. "I think we should move out."

"Oh yeah?" Fred sounded unenthusiastic now, not only because of his lack of energy but because he was expecting his northerner to ask him to move-in, so he didn't really want to commit to a new place.

"Move-on," Nick added.

Fred puzzled with the information. He couldn't have this conversation seriously right now. Telling Nick that he was going to move-out would be hard enough at the best of times, let alone with a delayed hangover from the day before, and one from that day breaking through. He opted to play along – he could break the serious news to Nick later. "Where shall we go - East or West?" He said referring to London, with his eyes still closed.

"I was thinking separately."

Gravity pulled on each of Fred's organs harder than it had before Nick said that. "What?" He pulled his body away from the headboard. He crossed his legs on the bed and lengthened his spine. He faced Nick's bed. "Are you serious?"

"It makes sense." Nick rested his chin onto his peaked knees. He spoke down toward his sloping legs. "You're going to move out soon. It's only a matter of time," he paused. He had more to say but wanted Fred's silence to confirm his anticipations. It did. "I just think that it makes sense. We've done it, Fred," Nick turned to face him, his head still resting on his knees, but his face tilted. He smiled, "We've moved to London. We've helped each other settle in. And you've even found a boyfriend!" His voice amplified happiness, but Fred could only smell the sadness hidden beneath it. The problem was that he couldn't refute what Nick was saying. He was stuck. He couldn't think of a single word to reply.

"It's ok. I know he hasn't asked you yet and so you can't respond". Nick articulated everything that went through Fred's head: "You can't say, 'no let's carry on living together', because when he does ask – and you obviously say yes – you'll feel wretched for breaking a fresh commitment to me. But you can't say, 'yes, good idea', because there's no guarantee that he will ask you, and so you need me as an insurance option." Fred felt terrible at the phrase 'insurance option'. Tears swelled at the back of his eyes on behalf of Nick. It was true and he hated the way it sounded. Exploitative.

"Don't feel like that. You're not a bad person," Nick said. Warmth poured from him, "This is life, Fred. It happens. You're not a bad person. And neither am I. But I need to protect myself." His voice strengthened. *If this were a poem*, Fred thought, *we've definitely hit the volta.* "I can't come home waiting anymore. Waiting for you to tell me you're moving-on. It's not fair on me. I get on the tube everyday and think he's going to tell me today; today's the day he's telling me that he's going." He paused momentarily. "I can't live like this. I hate it. We need to accept the reality that our time is over. I don't want to be the person that secretly hopes, everyday, that his best friend isn't moving on with his life. I don't want to be that person, Fred. I want to be happy for you, and I can't do that sharing this much with you. We need to give each other space."

They sat in silence for a while. He had spoken the destructive truth and pierced the veil of ignorance that enabled their continued relationship. They both knew it. They were both helpless. Voiceless. Neither could pretend any longer. Truth brought them to London. Without it, what were they doing there? Nick had done what needed to be done. Fred knew it. But he felt afraid. Not abstract, existential fear, emerging from the swirling nonsense of his internal maze-like wonderings. Cold, blood-fear. Fear beating simply, inescapability, rhythmically; pure feeling, independent of thought. Fred uncrossed his legs and lay back; his head melted into the pillow. He lay and experienced his fear. He stopped thinking. Just lay there. Feeling. He was alone. Properly alone.

Nick also laid back into his pillow. He switched off the T.V. They lay on their single beds in the soft lamp light and among faint sounds of electricity. They eventually drifted into sleep. Although it wouldn't be the last night they would sleep in the same apartment, it was the last night they would sleep together.

CHAPTER 8: Tower blocks, new friends, & old enemies

Grey tower blocks blotted the horizon. Fred looked at them through the train window. He wondered what it would be like to live in one but couldn't get much past the image of gangs loitering at grubby communal entrances. He needed to find somewhere to live though, and so he tried to scrub the image of his having to go into a Russian-looking concrete tenement from his mind. It didn't work. He was scared senseless and the imagery of horror only multiplied the harder he tried to control it: grimy lifts with crack addicts shooting up in them; psychopathic murderers eying him up, from the other side of their peep holes; bleak graffitied corridors echoing screams. His awful imagination wouldn't stop. The harder he tried, the thicker the images became. But Saturday was approaching, and he needed somewhere to live. As a supply teacher in London, it needed to be cheap. Very cheap.

Heeta was moving-in with Nick. They'd found a flat to share in south London. They weren't the best of friends, but that made the arrangement ideal. They both wanted the comfort of living with somebody that they knew, but they both also wanted independence. Nick didn't want another Fred. He wanted to get out into London and start making proper friends, a life of his own. And Heeta just needed space and a place where nobody could find her.

But Fred, holding-out for a proposal from his northerner, hadn't faced the reality of finding a new home. He hadn't seriously thought that he'd have to live alone. He knew Nick and Heeta would let him stay on their couch – they'd never let him be homeless. But he'd lied so lavishly about his northerner asking him to move-in, that he was too embarrassed to tell them the truth; that he hadn't told him about moving out. Fred had failed to discuss the situation with his northerner: he had no idea about the breakdown of Fred and Nick's friendship, their wilful moving-on from one another. Each time Fred thought he was about to tell him, an internal clamp locked onto his voice box. Words thickened in his throat like soreness, an awful sore throat soreness, that razorblade feeling. He couldn't have the conversation. It was too intimate, too pushy. Fred thought it might scare him off and then he'd have to live alone, which is exactly what not talking to him was resulting in. Awareness of the irony made no difference. He couldn't talk about Nick with his northerner, just as he couldn't talk about his northerner with Nick.

The grey tower blocks faded into the grey London skyline and the train shot forward through several tunnels before it finally committed to the darkness. The rest of the journey happened underground. Fred exited the train and the station in his work chinos, jumper and water-proof jacket. It was too hot for the jacket; the air was sweaty inside the station, and muggy outside, but Fred put it on anyway because too much rain had begun to fire down from what he considered to be rather angry, vengeful clouds. The school Fred headed toward liked him. The principle wanted him to sign a contract and take a permanent contract, but Fred liked the lack of commitment. The freedom.

The rain increased in its severity. Droplets came down faster and harder, and so Fred ran the remainder of the way to school. He darted past teenagers clumped together under shared umbrellas in their school uniforms. A few of the more boisterous students shouted out, "Go on, Sir!" as he sped past them.

Inside, the headmaster and deputy greeted him. "Morning, Fred – you need an umbrella."

"Yeh – I always leave them on the train though, so don't bother anymore." Fred had never carried an umbrella, ever, but he thought this sounded better and his default mode was to tell his employers what he thought they wanted to hear, despite his rants and self-idealised anti-authoritarianism, his disdain of perceived 'yes-men'.

"Have you thought anymore about joining us properly?" Fred prepared his instinctual response, but the image of the grey tower blocks flashed before him and caused him to catch the reply before it came out. He took in a larger than usual breath and decided to speak before thinking too much about what he was doing.

"Actually, things have changed, and I am looking for a permanent position, so yes."

"Fantastic," the headmaster said initially surprised, but as headmaster's do, moved straight onto business: "I'll get Janet to message you so that we can have a chat; I knew we'd win you over."

Fred left before he could reconsider. He did not want to sign a contract and commit to working at the same school, but the pay would be significantly better, and he needed the money. He headed to the English department, logged onto one of the shared computers and checked the cover e-mail to see what lessons lay before him. He already knew a couple of classes he'd teach – 9W and 10A – English classes he'd been covering since he'd started; they belonged to a lady who had been working part-time but was now signed-off for stress. The rest of his timetable filled with whatever was needed that day: drama, chemistry, and business studies appeared next to his name. *Fuck – not Drama,* he thought. He had to work in the drama studio; had to keep an eye on what the kids were up to as things could unravel quickly with the wrong class.

They did. 8b entered the studio first period, hyperactive from walking to school in the rain. Upon seeing that their normal teacher wasn't taking them, their energy levels boomed. "Yeh- Ms. Ain't here. We got sir!" One wretched kid said before three others swarmed straight into the costume cupboard and began pulling out outfits.

"Hey! I need to do the register first. Out!" Fred attempted to assert himself. He walked over to the cupboard and stood with his hand on the door handle. "Come-on. Out!"

"Oi! I want the green one," one of the wolfish urchins snatched a wig off the head of another wolfish urchin.

"Fuck-off!" the other one replied. Like cats, they clawed at one another in pursuit of possession. In the end clumps of hair came loose and neither wanted it any longer. It ended-up tossed on the floor by Fred's feet.

"Get-out!" Fred now shouted at them. He summoned his most masculine, deep throated voice.

"Calm-down, Sir! We're not ready yet."

"Out." He repeated, meaning business.

They put the stuff down and left but it was never a guarantee. They walked with wandering eyes. It was only a matter of time before their attention locked onto something else. Nothing took their fancy until they reached the main room. Fred pulled the door shut, ensuring the click noise was audible as if it reinforced his authority. It didn't.

The boys ran around the laminate floor chasing each other with maracas. They dived between clustered groups – the rest of the class had splintered into mini-clicks for their own protection. Fred would usually have not given a toss. He was a supply teacher, he'd tell himself; if the school hadn't developed a good enough culture where kids acted at least moderately civil when routines were slightly disrupted, then that was their goddamn problem. He wasn't feeling guilty about controlling them because the school and parents had failed to properly socialise and raise them into functional human beings. He'd go on a little internal rant about the school and parents' desire to control, ironically, contributing to the utter lack of control and buy-in from the kids. But the permanent position – the one he didn't want – dominated his thoughts. He couldn't stop thinking that if the Head walked in, the offer would disappear, and those grey tenements would become his new home. The maracas clanging evoked in him the image of keys dropping into his hands; keys to that horrid tower-block and a rage floated to his surface. Those thick little shitbags were not going to make him move into some murderous, gang-ridden shithole. His temper thickened: he huffed and gritted his teeth. He stomped his left foot repeatedly on the laminate floor so that it shuddered. He slammed his right hand repeatedly onto the blue matt, atop of the pile. "Enough!" he said three times, louder each shout. The entire class stopped chatting; the boys stopped running; and silence emerged into the studio as everybody stared at him. He stopped stomping his foot, slamming the mat, and screeching, but he tested their patience for just a few seconds too long. One of the wolves burst into laughter as another shook the maracas into the air above his head while shimmying his body and elongating vowers for what seemed perpetuity:

"Eeeeeuuuuuuuwwww" it said. Others joined in, either with the sound or just laughter. Fred didn't have anywhere to go. He couldn't stomp any harder. Slam any louder. He couldn't deepen his voice or increase his pitch.

"Sit down, you little twat!" He could swear though.

"You can't say that!" the little twat said, and he was correct. Fred couldn't and he knew it as soon as it came out. *Fuck,* he thought immediately: *shit, shit, shit.* He didn't even bother trying to downplay or bribe the class. Schools can't keep secrets. Everything gets out. He knew he was in trouble. The little twat's little group joined the outrage party, "Sir, you can't say that!"

"Sir, you're goin' to get fired now."

"Sir, what did you call him?"

"Sir, did you just call him a twat?"

"Sir… Sir… Sir…" Fred was done. He couldn't be arsed with the endless meetings that the incident would trigger. They'd all lead to one outcome. If he had a permanent contract, it'd be fine. He'd get a slap on the wrist, and a note on some yellow form stored in a cabinet file that the real world didn't give a shit about; the head would defuse the situation and things would be forgotten. But Fred didn't have a contract. He was supply. He wouldn't be asked back. Fred ignored the hordes of children calling his name and walked out of the drama studio. He collected his jacket from the English department. A young teacher sat marking books in the office; she looked at Fred and said that she thought he was covering drama. Fred ignored her. He couldn't be arsed to explain himself. He left the office and headed toward the exit. He'd pass by human resources to tell them he was leaving; that the discipline was too poor, and he wouldn't be returning.

As he reached the main reception, he dreaded bumping into the headmaster; he knew it would unnerve him; that he'd end up babbling, and probably sitting in some meeting room where he'd begin undergoing the series of meetings he dreaded. The headmaster wasn't there. He said his short, rehearsed piece to the stout admin-women that dealt with the supply agency. He left before she could really say anything back. He strutted out of the building after having to buzz the main doors and wait for the receptionists to release the lock.

The rain hadn't stopped but it had softened. Droplets poured down his cheeks. Fred felt alive. Reckless and unpredictable, but fearless.

He envisaged those grey tower blocks and told himself 'to bring it on'. He didn't care anymore. He didn't have anything for a gang to take anyway, or at least, this is what he rationalised to himself. He placed his white headphones into his wet earlobes and turned the volume high so that Avicii poured restless rhythms into his soul. He walked back to the station with a euphoric smile tattooed across his face and ignored the vibrations of his phone ringing in his pocket. He was done with teaching.

That afternoon Fred applied himself. He popped to Tesco to buy himself a notepad and stationery, then plonked himself into a booth of some greasy café near Elephant and Castle tube station. He ordered a cup of tea and a full English Breakfast, and while waiting, he searched Gum Tree for apartments. With his new pen, he noted the address, cost and phone-number of potentials into his new pad. The ones that didn't completely petrify him received an asterisked star next to it. Stratford and Lewisham emerged as favourites, largely since his Northerner lived in Stratford while Nick and Heeta's new flat was in Lewisham. Thick lines scratched out the places in Stratford – *it'd look too stalkerish,* he thought. Then he scratched out the places in Lewisham, *too pathetic.* He re-scrolled, lists of properties floated up the page. He hadn't even heard of half of the areas: *where the hell is Gravesend?*

A Polish lady placed his food and tea onto the table, and smiled at him, "you look for home?" She said. Fred assumed she was Russian. He looked up and smiled at her, *she seems normal,* he thought before responding.

"Yeh – my flat mate is moving out, so I need to find a new place, and now I've been in London for a year, I realise that I need something way cheaper. London is expensive and I need more money to be able to actually live."

"You work?" She said declaratively but meant it as a question.

"Yeh – I teach," Fred always phrased his job as a verb, something he did; never a noun, it wasn't who he was. He hated those little words: *I am…*

"Good," she smiled, earnest yet functional. Fred sensed that if he had said 'no', then she would have walked away mid-conversation, "teaching, good." This time it was a statement. She wasn't suggesting moral or social approval of Fred's occupation: "teaching pay regular and good. We have room in apartment if want. £360 month. Me, Chinese man, and German boy have room. Last girl she leave to home in Romania." She tilted her palm toward his phone, "I show?" A question.

Fred gave her his phone instinctively. She wiped the grease from her hands onto the apron tied around her waist, and then tapped a link into his phone. "Signal, not very good, but it load slowly," she said moving the phone so that it rested between them, allowing them to see the screen together. A picture of a grey tower block loaded floor by floor on the screen. *For fuck sake,* he thought. Her finger slid the picture upward to reveal three pictures of the inside of the apartment.

"Looks nice," Fred said surprised. He'd expected the inside to look like the outside. It wasn't Buckingham palace, of course, but a clean spacious kitchen with modernish units encircled a good-sized table and a large glass window, which looked like it had decent views. The other picture showed a good sized bedroom, and again it suggested excellent views. "When's it available?"

"When is?"

"Yeh," Fred nodded, assuming she understood him.

"Interview is Saturday. You want?"

"Viewing?" Fred assumed she had used the incorrect word.

"No. Interview is at flat if you want. We have 12.30 left."

"Interview?" Fred said again. *It's not a fucking job,* he thought. "You mean like asking questions sort of interview."

The Polish lady laughed. "You know interview other?" She placed his phone onto the booth table, took his pen and scribbled the flat's phone number onto his pad. "12.30, Saturday. You call if no want interview. But you like flat. It good." She left him with his breakfast and tea.

Fred unravelled the serviette from the knife and fork. The sausage sliced into bits and once dipped in egg, journeyed into Fred's mouth. His focus fluttered between appreciation of the food, visualisations of being at school teaching 9W – where he would have been had it not been for that drama lesson – and walking around a new apartment. The interview surprised him though. He'd never considered he'd have to interview. The truth was he hadn't thought properly about the situation. He had been envisioning living alone, rattling around a large, terrifying haunted house come tower block. Empty space began to appear on his plate, and the realisation that he wasn't going to literally live alone sank in. His self-inflicted abandonment would result in him being around more people, not less. *Solitude is for the rich,* he thought, rather impressed with himself. The Polish woman took an order at the counter and Fred watched her from his booth. *She seems nice,* he thought. He reloaded the details of the apartment on his phone and examined them as if they were the objects of a new infatuation. He'd gone from dreading the thought of living in a tower block, to feeling anxious that he might not be successful at the interview.

His toast absorbed the bean juice and tore into pieces. Fred popped a bit into his mouth, chewed and swallowed it, his eyes glued to his phone. He repeated until the plate was clear and his tea depleted to dregs. He looked back at the counter, but the lady had gone. He left.

He returned to Tesco to buy some food for dinner. The reduced items looked too grim, so he resorted to cheap ingredients for a basic spaghetti bolognaise. As he headed to the checkout his phone rang. He placed his basket onto the floor so that he could get his phone from his pocket without pulling his keys out too accidently.

"Hello," he said to his northerner,

"Hey – just a quick one as I know you're probably busy,"

"Yeh,"

"Fancy dinner tonight? I don't think I'll be able to get out until 6, but we can meet for a quick drink and head straight out."

"I'm a bit broke," before Fred could finish, his northerner laughed,

"Oh shut-up. It's on me. I'd never expect a struggling teacher…" he paused for dramatic emphasis, "or a southerner, to pay!"

"Fuck-off," Fred said with the largest smile on his face, "I'm not a southerner anyway."

"Well, you're a tight arse wherever you're from."

Fred continued smiling. He moved his basket to the side of the aisle with his foot, looked-up and down to see if anybody was looking and then walked away, toward the exit. "I was just buying some lovely ingredients for a nice spaghetti bolognaise, but I guess your offer sounds a bit better."

"How come you've finished work so early?" His northerner asked unpresumptuous.

Fred panicked, *Shit*. "Oh sorry, I've got to go – mum's calling. I'll tell you later."

"Cool. I'll text you when I'm leaving. Meet at Old Compton Street?"

"Yeh - sounds good. See ya later." He put the phone down, pretending to take a call from his mum.

Fred wandered around the dump of a shopping centre that is the Elephant and Castle. He liked it. Yellow tiles with flecks of dirt twinkled ahead; he thought of the Wizard of Oz, *follow the Yellow Brick Road,* repeated in his head. Elephant and Castle was going to be his new home, he could feel it. A small queue of waffs and strays formed along the glass window of Tesco. Fred joined the back of it and shuffled toward the cash machine, one unwealthy person at a time. His pin bleeped as his fingers pushed 1 – 3 – 5 – 8, he'd chosen the numbers because it created a 'Y' shape on the number-pad. His front teeth pinned his lower lip as a little circle span continuously on the small, smeared screen. His balance appeared, all three digits of it. He squinted to assist his eyesight – he could see the numbers clearly, but he wanted to ensure that he only withdrew £20, not £40, and he struggled to align the numbers with the correct buttons. He went for the one he considered closest and as the machine gurgled like some con man rubbing its hands together in anticipation of successfully mugging off some loser, he hoped the lower amount would pop out. It did. His card slid out the tight hole too. He put them both into his wallet and headed for the exit.

He calculated that by Saturday, he'd be able to afford two months' rent on top of the deposit, on the assumption that the deposit was equal to a month's rent. The yellow tiles transitioned to grey slabs as he exited the centre. He factored in two weeks' wages that were due to hit his account tomorrow, and unscientifically concluded that even if he didn't work for the next couple of weeks, he'd be able to make it through two months. It was enough to ease his mind so that he could focus on the interview. He placed his headphones into his ears, and as Alicia Keys bellowed out the lyrics to *Empire State of Mind* – "*Concrete jungles where dreams are made of... there's nothing you can't do... in New York...*" he looked upward to the pseudo-sky scrappers of Lambeth. A small grin of happiness defeated Fred's impulse to frown at a shrill wind freshly piping itself along the main A-road from Bermondsey. His pace quickened.

Funky murals of dolphins swimming through boulevards, Robert Browning's head on a green-tiled wall resembling a men's public bathroom, and a man pulling a fire hose through a busy restaurant accompanied Fred through the warren of underground passages joining the bits of Elephant and Castle together. He explored the place, imagined himself living here. It was fine. *The problem would be night-time,* he thought. The tunnels shipping people beneath motorway-width roads weren't issues during busy daytimes; but there was no way Fred would consider walking through them at night. The vision he'd had of those gangs loitering around the grey tower block had moved to the tunnels: he thought about them trapping already impoverished people, wavering knifes at their bellies, cowering, exposed, against the backdrop of the murals, until they parted with what little they had. *Nope,* he thought, *I'll take my chances against the buses ahead.* Fred's pragmatism won out. The thought of that nice kitchen, a clean bedroom, non-murderous, non-psychopathic flatmates – and one of the lowest rents – incentivised him to find solutions. He knew there was never going to be a perfect answer.

He pressed onward toward the Thames where the wind had become artic. The morning began continentally muggy, but unextraordinary for London, Nordic weather eventually turned-up to chase the heat away; at least, it pushed the clouds away too. Fred strolled along the greyish brown river, dry; his cheeks were freezing, but the sun pumped some needed vitamin D into his hungry skin. As he approached the Tate Modern, he checked the time on his phone. There were still hours between now and dinner with his northerner. The post-World-War 2 brown-bricked power-station (turned modern art gallery) sat along the bank of the river. Fred looked at it. He imagined bombers flying overhead during the blitz; *it must have been such a target,* he thought, *a mammoth energy creating machine – must have powered half of South London.* Fred didn't have a clue, but he enjoyed wondering. He loved London for its power to on the one hand, feed his egoism and journey of self-discovery, whilst on the other, take him so far away from himself: into history and a world beyond his immediate own. The brown bricks made him think of olden days. Low-quality British Education defined the olden days by two distinct periods: Tudor England and World War 2; the time between was merely a giant boundary. *Modern students graduate from schools with bigger budgets, but lower standards of real education, than ever...* Fred bemoaned to himself whilst staring up at the magnificently austere chimney. "Fuck it – this is what London is about," he said, slightly aloud, but not so loud that the people around him distanced themselves from some street lunatic. *I should know more about the world...* he thought, *I should make more of an effort.* He wanted to know more. He wanted to chop his timeline of History into more segments than Egyptians – Greeks – Romans – Battle of Hastings – Tudors – WW2 – Internet. So, he looked at the ex-power station as if it were an ancient God daring him to know more, in its deep deistic voice. Fred saw the building like an Arabian genie, some mystic entity only pretending to be bricks and mortar. It mocked him. It laughed at his pathetic knowledge, his ridiculously empty grasp of his own world, his own history. The Chimney, which once emitted thick black clouds into London's skyline now pumped out the genie's laughter. Fred saw what nobody else saw: plumes of scorning laughter filling the sky. Like little Sampson, he stamped his foot on the ground, and defied the goliath. People did stare at him this time; those walking past spread a little wider, leaving a larger gap between them and this odd man stamping his foot on the floor whilst staring at the Tate-Modern as if it were some bully, which he was no longer standing for. He stood motionless staring at the building, but internally, Fred was piously burning incense in devotion to a higher being.

On that spot outside the Tate, on the morning that he'd sworn at kids in the drama studio; on the morning, he walked-out of a job and the promise of permanent employment; on the morning, he'd scouted Elephant and Castle as a new home where he'd begin living a properly independent, adult life, he made a commitment to something bigger than himself – he didn't know exactly what this was – he was strictly speaking, not religious. His parents had never baptised him or discussed God, although the lady in the street, had taken a group of the kids (including him) from the small council estate to a happy-go-lucky Baptist church as children. So, Fred didn't vow, necessarily, to the Christian or Islamic God, the Jewish Yah-Wey, or the Brahmin almighty. He didn't visualise a golden Buddha or speak directly to Jesus, but he acknowledged some cosmic force that was bigger than himself; it could have been any of these, or some power or force that was here before, and would exist long after any of them. It didn't matter. Fred spoke to that thing, decreed to it; he told it that he'd make more of an effort. He didn't know if it listened, or whether it even cared if it did, but he told it, and it felt important. Like his mum looking at him with disbelieving eyes when he told her about being able to play the guitar, he felt more expectation in this thing – he imagined its eyes, unlike his mother's, to have expectation in them. He had vowed to something powerful. Breaking it would not only be letting himself down. And with that thought, with purposeful strides, he marched into the Tate Modern.

Fred left two hours later confused. The sky flecked with pinkness. He looked up and thought it was more beautiful than most of what he'd seen. He popped into a Starbucks and parted with his fresh £20 note for posh coffee. As the lady returned his change, his grandma's voice echoed within: '£2.50 for a coffee!' He grabbed an expensive bar of chocolate from the counter that he didn't even want, "Sorry this too," he said to the Spanish girl serving him. She took the bar, scanned it, and told him that it would be another £2.50. His attempt to defy his grandmother's voice backfired. She was louder than the first time: "£2.50 for a bar of chocolate that's half the size of a 39p Mars bar!" He knew his grandma would never refer to a Mars Bar but it didn't matter. What mattered was the reality that he was paying excessively too much for something he didn't want and couldn't afford to prove a pointless point. "Sorry, it's ok," he said to the Spanish girl. She looked confused.

"You don't want?"

"Erm, no. It's ok. I forgot, I already bought some chocolate," Fred lied.

She smiled, "Es really expensive – I would not buy also."

Fred's redness eased. "Yeah, £2.50 for that, no thank you." With the help of the Spanish girl, he embraced his grandma's voice, "I can just about afford the £2.50 for the coffee."

"Es expensive too. In my town, a coffee is no cost more than 1 euro. Everybody in London is stupid rich."

"More like just stupid."

"Es true," she said getting a funny look from her supervisor, "have good day."

"You too," Fred smiled and trotted along the conveyor-belt-human-queue of the modern coffee shop. He was processed and received his hot cup of sugary milk with a dash of espresso at the end by some machine-servant that nonetheless offered a human touch by writing his name on the cup, *Fret :)*. Fred slipped a sleave onto the cup and with it cupped into his hand, he returned to the Thames. He crossed the bridge and headed for the West End.

Fred used the change from his £20 for a couple of pints in old Compton street. A text alert bleeped: *'just out the tube station – be there in 2 mins x'*. Fred chugged the remainder of his beer. He felt nervous, which made little sense; they'd been dating months. Old Compton street cared nothing for what day of the week or month of the year it was – its neon lights flashed, its music bleared, and its pilgrims flocked come what may. Fred loved it. As he turned to leave the bar, an older guy bumped into him:

"Alex?" the man said.

"Fred."

"Fred, of course," the guy's tongue loosely clamped between his semi-open teeth. He tried to recall how he knew Fred. Before he could speak, Fred attempted to scuttle away. The guy pulled his arm, "Hey, wait – we know each other?" the guy attempted to charm Fred, who was having none of it.

"Yes," Fred said, "you left me to pay for your very expensive gin and tonic." The voice of Fred's grandma energised him. The guy scrunched his face; at first thinking Fred was being playful. Then realisation struck, and a squirming wrinkles emerged across Michael's face like lines of sand on a beach with a receding tide.

"I"

"Don't bother," Fred patted his arm, "I should thank you really." The squirming morphed into apprehensive eye lifts. "I slept with my best friend that night and it gave us the courage to move to London together. We've been here a year now.

"So where is this boyfriend?" Michael had rediscovered his smarmy confidence. He leaned toward Fred like a predator that had regained its advantage. His lips puckered outward, but before he could make his next move, Fred tilted his body to leverage himself around Michael's body without rubbing against him as much as possible in the crowded bar.

"There," Fred said, moving further away. Michael twisted around to see the specimen standing in a leather jacket outside.

"Tasty. I know…" Michael said.

Fred ignored the sleazebag and moved away causing him to not finish his sentence. He hopped outside the bar and called to his northerner who'd taken his phone out to text him. "Hey babe," the northerner said in his deep, husky, un-creepy voice. Michael hung his upper body outside the doorframe:

"Hey, sweet-cheeks," he said to Fred's northerner.

"Hey, Michael."

Fred looked back at him in disbelief. *He was telling the truth,* he thought. "You know this guy?" Fred said the words as if he had liquorish stuck beneath his tongue.

His northerner found the reaction amusing, "Sure – everybody on Old Compton Street knows Michael. He lingers around waiting to catch anything with a pulse." Fred swallowed instinctively. Shame flushed into his cheeks and his impulse was to censure any reaction to buy a little time so that he could manage his response. Before he could consider how to tell his man that this infamous creep 'waiting to catch anything with a pulse' had not only rejected him, but abandoned him mid-date, Michael stepped out of the bar and he and Fred's northerner embraced one another with a hearty hug. Michael kissed him on each cheek.

"How are you darling?" He asked.

"Good – so you've met Freddie?"

"I'm afraid so. We had a date, and I bailed on him," Michael's teeth slid over themselves as his face twisted sidewards toward Fred, and his eyes motioned an upside-down silliness that signalled an uncommitted sorry.

"Michael's one of the first guys that I ever met in London. He's a veteran queen; ugly as sin, but he's got a good heart."

Fred hissed. He didn't like Michael and although he was unusually comfortable in expressing this dislike, he wanted to withhold open disdain until he knew more about the nature of their relationship. Michael was far from ugly too, and so Fred interpreted his northerner's comment as a deeply irritating flirtation.

"I was positively naughty for abandoning you little Freddie, but you see I bumped into an old friend, and we got chatting; one thing led to another, and before I knew it an hour had passed. I felt terrible, but then realised that a young gorgeous piece like yourself, wouldn't be alone for long... so I didn't beat myself up... and I was quite right because as you said, you ended up sleeping with your best friend that night, which led you moving to London together, and which in turn led you to our dear Ryan here."

Fred's temper flickered and crackled like a fire chewing logs. He wanted to punch Michael in the teeth and push him back into the bar. He'd not told his northerner that he'd slept with Nick and now it was obvious. He spat out a bit of heat instead, "So you and Ryan have fucked?"

"He wishes!" laughed Ryan. "Michael tries it on – God love him, but I," he turned to Fred, "have way better taste." He leaned and gave Fred a kiss, his deep red lips briefly touching Fred's. But like an already too hot fire, the last thing Fred needed was further heat. He tensed at the kiss. He didn't want to be touched, let alone kissed by a man (even if it was his boyfriend) in a public street. Or more particularly, in front of that dickhead, Michael.

Ryan ignored Fred's awkwardness which he attributed to nothing serious. "Fred was probably more pissed off at the bill you left him with," Ryan said to Michael, "he's a tight-ass, and you're a flamboyant queen that probably ordered the most expensive cocktail on the menu." Fred had never told Ryan the story, but he had read the situation almost perfectly.

"It was a Gin and Tonic! They didn't do fancy cocktails in that dump," Michael said.

Fred's fiery mood went to the south pole. He usually loved his northerner making jokes at his expense, but this was raw and felt cruel.

"You know what. I'm not in the mood for dinner. Go with Michael. I'm going home." Fred detonated. He stormed away. Ryan said bye to Michael, who blew a kiss as a way of saying goodbye, his lips puckered exaggeratingly over his open palm. Ryan jogged to catch-up with Fred.

"Hey- hey," he said whilst reaching out his hand to pull Fred's arm. Fred stilled outside the corner of SoHo House. Ryan tried to encourage him to turn and face him, but Fred's body froze forward, his eyes locked onto some unidentified object in his horizon. "Fred," he repeated a few times, "What's wrong?" Appreciating that he wasn't turning, Ryan walked ahead and turned to face him. Fred continued staring at the same spot even though Ryan's face was now in his way. "What's wrong?" he repeated. Fred's silence continued. People walked around them, a few peeked over their shoulder, hoping to catch some of the drama.

Ryan poured his sweet, masculine affection into Fred: he rubbed both his arms with his hands, "you can tell me." His deep red lips hung open and his blue eyes waited patiently. Fred didn't see them though. He continued staring through Ryan.

"It's not going to work," Fred said as if his voice had been replaced by a soulless robot.

"What's not going to work?" Ryan replied. He was so measured. So calm.

Fred huffed, which was progress from his stiffness. Hot air shot through his nostrils. His mouth attempted to say something, but it repeatedly closed before any words escaped. He was in a fight with himself. Ryan had to control himself. Fred expected him to flee, to match with a counter rage, to suffer, to hurt; but all Ryan really wanted to do was laugh. He didn't elaborate on his question, but left Fred to stew and recalibrate his response.

"Us," Fred said. He continued to stare through Ryan, but something had melted within and Ryan sensed it.

"Oh shut up, you drama queen." Ryan pressed his thick, deep red lips onto Fred's and this time left them there until Fred loosened. Eventually, Ryan felt Fred's lips return to life. They squirmed and pulled away.

"Get off," Fred said, his stare fizzled downward. He now acknowledged Ryan but didn't look at him out of embarrassment, not wilful destruction as before.

Ryan took his hand and twisted to stand beside him. Facing forward, he said, "can we now go for dinner?"

Fred nodded and they began to re-walk along Old Compton Street hand-in-hand. Fred had thawed. Although he felt vulnerable, he also felt more alive and loved than he had felt in a long time. He was remembering happiness.

CHAPTER 9: Straw to the floor

The last box squeezed into the bit of space that wasn't really big enough for it. Heeta gave it a final shove and then slammed the boot before it had the opportunity to topple out. Bea squeezed her arms around Heeta's little body and attempted to suck the energy out of her so that she wouldn't go. Heeta had been slowly moving her things across to Bea's house so that she could disappear when the time came with her family finding out only after she'd long gone. That morning she'd left a letter in the top draw of her otherwise empty desk telling her family that she couldn't agree to the marriage and that she'd send letters every few months to let them know she was alive and well, but that it would be the last time they'd see her.

Bea's arms still crushed her, but Heeta didn't protest. She allowed Bea to grip as tightly and for as long as she wanted. "Don't go, Heets – live with me." A tender smile stretched across Heeta's face, buried deep into Bea's breasts. She wrapped her own arms around Bea and hugged her back.

"Come with us," her words muffled up Bea's cleavage.

"I'm too old," she leaned her cheek onto the top of Heeta's head. She smelt her shiny black hair, "you're leaving me with all these dirty boys. Their hair smells horrid; your hair smells lovely."

Heeta blew a raspberry into Bea's breasts, causing her to shake as if being tickled, "you love the dirty boys." She said, loosening from Bea's grip.

"I do," Bea said rearranging her breasts and the straps of her top. Her teeth shined in the early morning sunshine. A good blast of hot air on her chest always induced a smile.

"I don't. That's the problem." Heeta said.

"I know, darling," Bea took her hand, "I'll come visit, I promise." They absorbed the intimate sight of one another, "one more hug." Bea took her into her arms for one last time. She left room for Heeta to breathe this time, and it made the moment much more emotional. Bea pulled her body back, but clutched Heeta's hands. "You give those boys hell," she winked, "and enjoy as much fanny as you want. Fuck these jealous tossers," her voice attempted to remain sassy and jovial, but it couldn't help rubbing the vocal cord of affection, "you deserve to be happy and love whoever you want." Their hands unlocked. They held back tears that neither of them wanted. "Right come on. I never thought I'd say this, but time for you to sod off."

Heeta nodded. She was so grateful of Bea's love, "thanks for everything." She turned and climbed into her little red micra. Bea followed – she leaned to close the door after Heeta was fully inside, the motherly figure that everybody deserves. The window was already wound down. The ignition propelled the engines into motion. The radio turned on automatically: a modern rendition of Tracey Chapman's *Fast Car* played. Bea lifted flat fingertips to her lips, kissed them and flattened her palm back toward Heeta. She turned away from the car and walked back toward her house. Heeta pushed the clutch, found the bite point and launched the car into first gear. The car had barely accelerated before her foot pressed hard back onto the clutch and she motioned the gearstick into second gear. She was off.

The street faded into the background; the town faded into the background; her family faded into the background; her sexuality faded into the background. As she blasted along the motorway, overtaking car after car, she breathed deeply and felt free. The wind whipped her black hair and freshened her face. She screamed as loud as she could. A happy, liberating scream, a scream that carried away shame; a scream that carried away expectation; a scream that carried away worry; her shoulders shimmied, and her breasts shook liberally as her hands gripped the steering wheel tightly. Motorway signs with 'London' flickered past overhead. The number of miles on them reduced with each new song on the radio. Heeta thought that this is how they must have felt, this paradoxical feeling of being both in control and absolutely at one with the wind, like a bird gliding a breeze, a surfer riding a wave, a dreamer weaving a world. Predestined and self-willed.

The motorway lanes transitioned into dual carriageways which funnelled Heeta ever closer to London proper. Service stations and motorway landscape disappeared. Tenements, High rises, rows of Victorian houses, sprawling roads replaced them. The thrill of speed and feeling of escape eased and blank space began to emerge in Heeta's consciousness. She had defined herself by opposition for such a long time – she knew exactly what she didn't want to be. What did she want? The question wasn't daunting to her; it was serious, but in a good way. Between intensely focusing on trickier junctions, she contemplated futures for herself: she listed the things she wanted – the things she *could* do. She'd put it all out of mind before. Pragmatically, she didn't like to dwell on things out of reach. Now though, things were in reach. Item one on her list was a one-night stand. She'd watched so many of her friend's hook-up, casually engage and enjoy a sexual experience. She'd never. It wasn't something that she planned on making a habit of, but something that she wanted to experience. She wanted to have a girlfriend. She wanted to experience a break-up. It sounded bizarre, but she wanted to feel what it was like to ache for somebody she'd had but couldn't have any longer. To experience the ordinary drama of relationships that had past her by. She wanted to go to dinner parties. She wanted a career, a proper one. Once she'd broken through the first couple of ideas, they kept flowing. There was so much that she was going to do.

Her phone vibrated in the dip of the dashboard. She reached out her hand to accept the call without looking away from the roads. She double clicked the accept button so that the phone went straight to loudspeaker.

"Hey," Fred said.

"Hey, I think I'm nearly there,"

"Woop! How far away do you think you are?"

"Erm… I've just passed this big ugly Elephant thing on what looks like a shopping centre and not that it'll mean anything, going around massive roundabouts close to each other."

"You're in Elephant and Castle – that's where I'm moving to," Fred said without thinking,

"Really - so how far away is this?" Heeta didn't consider the implication of Fred moving to this random area – it didn't mean anything to her. Fred moved-on quickly.

"Oh, only about ten minutes I think," he didn't know. He'd never driven in London but he calculated that it was only a couple of train stops between London Bridge and Lewisham, and Elephant and Castle was close to London Bridge so it couldn't take that long to drive.

Heeta made an excited noise, "I can't believe I'm here!"

"Cool – well I'll let you go if you're driving. Give me a call when you're in Lewisham and I'll direct you to the flat."

"Brilliant! See you in ten minutes," she said leaning forward to run her finger over the buttons to feel her way to the hand-up one, so that she could keep focused on the roads.

Forty-five minutes later she eventually reached Lewisham. She pulled into a Tesco supermarket so that she could park-up and tell Fred to come and meet her. It was too complicated to navigate over the phone, so Fred agreed to meet her there. She was nervous. *When he arrives*, she thought, *it's real*. Fred's finger tapped her window, the biggest smirk stretched across his face. She had never been happier to see him.

Heeta opened her door and they embraced.

"I can't believe you're here," Fred said.

"It's all a bit surreal but I'm here; at last, I'm here," she referred to her life not Lewisham.

"I'll jump in and direct you to the flat; it's only a couple of minutes from here," he said while walking around the bonnet and climbing into the passenger seat. Heeta raised each of her thighs to stretch out her legs before she got back in.

"A couple of minutes, or a couple of Fred's minutes?"

"A couple of minutes. Come on."

She climbed back into the driver's seat, "Ok, let's go." The car reignited and headed for the exit.

"Turn right and then right again at the traffic lights,"

"How're you and Nick?"

"Good,"

"Good?"

"We're good, honestly. It was never meant to be between us," Fred glanced at Heeta as the car pulled up at the traffic lights, "Friends. We were meant to be friends and that's what we are."

"I hope you stay friends."

"Liar – you never liked Nick," he said laughing at her.

"True, but you obviously did, and I like him now."

"Only because you've got to live with him."

"I'm choosing to live with him because you've become all grown up and moved in with your boyfriend," Heeta shifted the car in first gear and turned right.

"Stay on this road until it bends around to the mini-roundabout then take the third exit." He waited for her to settle into the road and then continued, "I actually need to tell you something. I haven't said anything to Nick yet. In fact, I don't want him to know so you can't say anything."

"You're not getting married. Fuck off." she said.

Fred laughed, "No." He switched back to his serious voice, "actually, quite the opposite."

She twisted her neck to scan his face for a quick second before returning her focus to the road, "you've split up?" Her initial response was slight panic – would it mean she needed to find another flat?

"No." She relaxed. "But we're not moving in together."

"But you said you were moving to Elephant and Castle."

"He doesn't live in Elephant and Castle. He lives in Stratford," that information meant nothing to Heeta.

"You're cheating on him with another boyfriend?" she said playfully.

He smiled, "third exit, then I'll tell you when to turn off." He delayed his explanation until they were off the roundabout. "I haven't told him that I'm moving out. I kind of just kept waiting for him to ask me to move in, rather than me pushing the situation. I didn't want him to ask me just because I'm moving-out."

"That's stupid."

"Not really. It needs to be right. I can't push it."

"Push what?"

"Moving-in."

"I'm lost Fred."

"Straight on."

"No, you idiot, I don't understand what you're on about. Why haven't you told him that you're moving out?"

"I didn't want him to think I was hinting."

"No, I get that. It's stupid but I understand the argument. I mean, why haven't you told Nick you're moving out?"

"Oh," Fred hadn't expected that question. He knew the answer, but it felt awkward saying it aloud. He stared at the houses; he wanted to word his response properly, "oh shit, left now."

"This one?" Heeta said pressing the breaks so that she could turn if he responded, "Yes," she slammed the indicator and wrenched the steering wheel, leaving a slight burn mark on the road. "Sorry," Fred said, as he gripped that coat-handle thing above the door.

"No worries – a little bit of warning next time though."

"The flat's at the end of this road; there's a small carpark for residents. Nick's got a badge for you when we get there."

"Brilliant. Anyway – come on, hurry-up. Why haven't you told Nick, and what am I supposed to say to him if he asks?"

"I just didn't. He thinks Ryan and I are already at happy ever after, and…"

"Aren't you?"

"Well, I thought we were, but he hasn't asked me…"

"He doesn't know you're moving out!"

"I know, but surely if it was right, he'd ask anyway."

"He might not want to sound pushy. There is no way you can read anything into this. But it still doesn't answer why you haven't told Nick, and also, if you're not moving in with him, where are you going?" Each question triggered the need for more information: "and, where's your stuff?"

"The flat's on the left. There's a turning after that last car."

"Fred…" she pressed for some quick answers.

"My stuff's still at the old flat. I've got until five to hand the keys back.

"It's already twelve."

"I know. I was going to ask you to help me move after we've unloaded all your stuff…"

If she was honest, Heeta was a little annoyed, "You're telling me this now?" She turned left onto the drive. Nick waved at them from the entrance of the building. He started walking over to the parking bay. "What am I supposed to say to him?"

"If he tries to come, we'll just say that there won't be enough space in the car for all of us, and my stuff – he probably won't want to come anyway."

"Of course, he will. What did you tell him?"

"That Ryan was coming around to the flat with his car at 2.00."

"For fuck sake, Fred."

"Sorry… I wouldn't ask unless I was desperate."

"Well, I haven't really got much choice."

She passed the bay that Nick signalled to her to pull into, on purpose, and motioned to him that she'd turn the car around first.

"There's one more thing."

Heeta's didn't say 'what' straight away. Instead, she braced herself. "I've got an interview for the flat I'm moving into at 3.00." She gave him a murderous look. "So, if I give you the keys and directions to our old flat, can you load my stuff into your car while I go to the interview; then I can get the tube over to meet you or you can drive over if you're done…" He knew he was asking a lot, so he said it all as last minute as possible so that she didn't have time to refuse.

She pulled into the bay, and Nick smiled at them from the verge in front of the bonnet. Heeta smiled at Nick and concealed her fury at Fred. She said, without looking at him, "You better ace the fucking interview." She opened the car door, and Nick came to greet her with a big hug.

They unloaded everything from the car. Boxes lined the hallway of the new flat, ready to move into Heeta's new bedroom, but as she went to lift one, Fred looked at his watch again. He attempted telepathy with her, but she deliberately avoided his gaze. If he wanted to leave, he needed to take the lead.

Nick bent down and wrapped his new bulky arms around one of her boxes – he'd joined a gym and developed a bit of a healthy addiction to the weight machines. Meanwhile, Fred took his phone and pretended to read a message. "Ryan's just messaged, he's had to rush into work for some sort of emergency."

Nick placed the box back on the floor and turned around to face Fred and Heeta, "I thought he was a writer?"

"He is," Fred looked back at his empty screen and pretended to read as he thought of ways to elaborate. "Something to do with a printing Jam for the Sunday Papers going out tomorrow…"

"Surely that would require the engineers, not the writers?" Heeta said, her eyes telepathically telling him that he deserved to squirm.

"Look, I don't know exactly – but the reality is that he's not going to be able to get over with the car for a couple of hours," he looked at Heeta, "I know it's an absolute bugger but could you…"

"I'm done with unpacking for a while and it's probably a bit too early to start unwinding with a couple of glasses of wine, so why not?" she said. "Nick, are you coming?"

Before he could answer, Fred interjected, "There won't really be enough room for three of us with all my stuff,"

"Don't worry – I'll pop to the gym," Nick said, relieved that he didn't have to offer out of duty. "We can meet up in town later if you want, celebrate the evening? Ask Ryan – if he's finished with his toolbox."

"Yeh – cool. Sounds like a plan," Fred ignored Nick's jibe. He just wanted to get out of the flat. His stomach bubbled as if he had the beginnings of food poisoning – nerves for the interview and more potently, the possibility of homelessness should it not go well.

"How long will it take to get to…"

"Shadwell," Fred finished her sentence, "about twenty minutes if the traffic's ok."

"And then how long to get to…" Heeta didn't intend to finish this sentence but Fred cut her off.

"Stratford," he said, lying. "… about twenty minutes too, so we better get going if we're ever going to get into town for drinks tonight."

Heeta took her car keys from the kitchen work surface, and hugged Nick, "Thank you so much for finding this place, and agreeing to this. I'm so grateful. Drinks on me tonight."

Nick smiled, "Don't be stupid. You need your money now you're a Londoner." He gave her a peck on the cheek and watched her and Fred walk toward the front door of the flat, "I'll give you a text later to see how you're getting on. Good luck."

They said bye and headed down the communal staircase to the car. It seemed so spacious with all the boxes cleared. "I am such a good friend," Heeta said.

"Right, let's head back via Elephant and Castle – it's not far from here and pretty much on the way, so I can jump out."

"Is there anywhere to park at your old place? Can I have the address? Keys? How many boxes?"

"There's a few resident spaces to the left of the building, but you'll be fine," Fred said uncertain as to whether it would be fine. In fact, he assumed that there probably wouldn't be any spaces left, and it would be a problem, but he couldn't think about that. *One problem at a time,* he thought. *Get that fucking flat.*

"You haven't got a clue whether there's parking?" She said shaking her head and putting down the indicator as the car rolled out of the driveway. "Good job, I'm a very resourceful friend, who won't give you a hard time about this supreme selfishness until after you secure that flat." She meant her words to ease some of Fred's tension. She wasn't used to seeing him this worried – his skin was whitening. "Come on Fred, you'll be fine. Don't worry," her anger toward him completely gave way to compassion. "Fred, honestly, stop worrying," her tone hardened. "It's making you look pale," she took her eyes of the road to glance at him quickly and tugged at his arm, "I mean it. They won't want to live with you if you go in there looking like a ghost."

"I know, sorry. I'm just getting so into my head. I always leave things until the last minute and make a complete mess. I need to grow-up and sort my life out," his passion was at least inducing a little colour into his face.

"Fred, you're a dick," she said flatly, "but you're a good person. You don't need to 'grow-up', or 'sort' your life out. You just need to think a bit more about other people and be a bit more organised." She left a comfortable silence between them.

"I do need to grow-up a bit then?" He said eventually.

"What does that even mean?" She was serious and Fred hadn't expected the question or the intellectual response. It brought him out of himself, which is exactly what he needed. She allowed his mind to fill the silence.

"It means…" he repeated the phrase several times but struggled to screen an adequate answer. "It means I need to change; to become serious; together."

"The last thing you need is to become more serious," she laughed. "You're too serious; you need to get out of your head; tune into your real self and the world. It's already together if you just leave it alone."

"When did you become the Dalai Lama?" Fred joked.

"See!" she patted her hand on the steering wheel, "That's better already." She brushed her fingertips across his shoulder blade without taking her eyes of the road.

"Thanks," he said. "I'm so glad you're here. How did it go with your family?"

Now she pretended to focus on the road even though it didn't require any extra effort. She thought she needed to calibrate a response; it was her default reaction to any sort of question about her family. She patted the steering wheel to break her own pattern. She told Fred the truth, "no idea." For the remainder of the journey, Heeta told Fred everything: the arranged marriage; her father's unwavering hostility – cruelty to her and her siblings; her mother's meekness; the threats to return them to Pakistan for rehabilitation of what he perceived as minor defects. "God only knows what he'd think or do in response to his daughter being a lesbian," she said. Fred listened to her story without judgment; he didn't appropriate her injustice or rally a crusade on her behalf. He just let her speak and accepted her story.

"You see – never grow-up, Fred. Never become so formed in your opinions that you know every answer. Don't be like him. Treasure that loving child within. Honour that impulse to play and learn from others," she clicked her neck and took a quick glance at him: "The Dalai fucking lama," she flicked her fingers causing them to click like a rapper. They laughed together.

Fred jumped out of the car as a double decker bus hooted at the little micra in its space. "Be yourself," Heeta said preparing the clutch. The bus hooted again.

"Thanks – I'll call you." The door slammed shut and Fred ran behind the car before the bus moved forward. He had the tiniest spot beneath the left-hand side of his lower lip, and with his nerves he didn't leave it alone. He walked past the tube station, scratching at it. He walked through the shopping centre scratching it. He walked into the grey tower block scratching it. By the time he arrived at the flat, it had doubled in size.

The Polish lady, Chinese man, and German boy tried not to look at it in his interview, but their eyes kept wandering beneath Fred's clammy hands which were trying to cover it. They asked him questions each in turn, and Fred muffled responses. The Polish lady focussed on Fred's work and income. The Chinese man wanted to know how much time he'd spend in the flat, particularly the kitchen. The German was concerned with Hygiene and bathing rituals. Fred left feeling quietly confident. On the way in, the previous applicant walked out smelling of B.O. and looking like he hadn't been to a hairdresser since his stunted adolescence. But on the way out, a young attractive girl, not-smelling of B.O. and looking like she'd come directly from the hairdressers, passed him in the lift. *Fuck,* he thought, *those guys are definitely going to pick her.* He smiled, hating this girl he knew nothing about.

They'd told him that they only had one more person to see and so they should be able to let him know by 4.00pm. He drifted to the tube station unable to think about anything. His chest pumped oxygen so that his tissues could tie themselves into knots of stress. He knew he should call Heeta and begin his journey back to his old flat, but he couldn't leave the area until he knew the answer. He turned out of the tube station and headed to an uninviting pub that looked like it was for locals only. He'd just have one pint and wait for the call, for all Heeta knew he was still in the interview. *It's only half an hour,* he thought.

Dark wooden furniture filled the space. Despite the smoking ban, the place stank of cigarette smoke. It had either infused into the wood over the years, or the manager was afraid of challenging his nicotine loving patrons after hours. Fred didn't care. In fact, it made him want a cigarette. He scuttled around in his wallet for a five-pound note tucked away in one of the compartments and paid for his pint of beer. He stood at the bar and drank it much quicker than usual. He checked his phone repeatedly. Once the time hit four-fifteen, a message glowed-up on his screen. It was from Heeta, asking him how he was getting on. He tapped the screen to return it to its dormant blank blackness. He ordered another pint, digging into another compartment of his wallet where he kept the twenty-pound note for emergencies. He drank another two pints as the time now showed, five, zero-five. His phone vibrated several times as Heeta called. He couldn't answer. He declined each call, eagerly returning the phone to that blank state. Then finally, a message came through from an unknown number that wasn't Heeta. *'Sorry, you have not successful with flat – good luck in your search though!'*

"Is that fucking it?" Fred said aloud to his phone, still standing at the bar. He stood restless but didn't move. He pulled the change from his twenty-pound note and counted it – he could afford two and half more pints with it. He ordered them in one. The barmaid's eyes communicated to Fred that she had zero interest in hearing about his problem. Her bottom lip was pierced, her tongue rolled over it as she told him the price and held out her hand for the money. He paid and stood at the bar drinking his two and half pints. His mind cycled a half-thought in which he visualised himself as a drunk homeless man lying in one of those tunnels beneath the Elephant and Castle roundabouts, mixed with a fictional scene of Ryan dumping him, Heeta screaming at him for abandoning her, and Nick closing the door of his new flat as he stood outside it. The time showed Six, fifteen. His phone had so many missed calls from Heeta, but now Nick was trying to call too. "There's no fucking way I'm speaking to him," Fred said aloud. He now looked like the desperate drunk that the barmaid had an hour earlier, unfairly projected onto him. He asked her for another pint, but she told him the amount and held her palm on the bar first. He looked into his wallet knowing there was nothing in there. She moved her hand and pointed her finger at the sign behind the bar that said, 'No cards'. She walked away deeming their interaction finished. Fred sighed and internally murmured, *fucking bitch.*

He declined another call from Nick. "I'll go to the cash machine then!" he said to the barmaid who had moved far away from him and didn't acknowledge his comment. Fred lingered awaiting a response. The five and a half pints affected him. He swayed on the spot and lost interest. She wasn't going to respond. He went for a piss in the ugly lavatory that wouldn't look amiss in a movie scene of Jack the Ripper, and then left.

The fresh air slapped his cheeks and allowed his consciousness to catch-up with the knowledge of his being drunk. People strolled past about their business as usual, but Fred resented them. He wanted to push them over. He wanted to push everyone over. Everyone needed pushing over. Instead, he stumbled into walking among them, knocking into them accidently as he headed toward the tube station. People tutted and delivered evil stares at him, but wisely, nobody challenged his instability or lack of respect for personal space. They moved on and away quickly. His phone vibrated repeatedly: Nick, Heeta; Heeta, Nick. *They could fuck off,* he thought.

The tube ride into Soho was a longer and intensified version of the short walk from the pub. People exerted greater patience as he bumped and stumbled on the underground celled carriages that trapped them together. By the time, he returned to the earth's surface, he had a load more miscalls and texts, but now Ryan's name appeared in the list too. *'Fred, where are you? Your friends called to say you're missing and that you're moving?! Call me.'*

Fred ignored the message. *It was over. It was all over,* he thought. He exited the station and joined the queue for the cash machine. Tuts and grunts showered him from the other queuers. Once he reached the screen, he poked his pin numbers into the dial pad, shouting them aloud as he did so, "1-3-5-8! It makes a 'Y' shape, so it's easy to remember." He turned to face the person behind him as he spoke, but she avoided his eye contact. He opted to pull the maximum suggested amount on the options: £200. He didn't care about tomorrow. He was going to have a good time, "I'm going to have a good time," he said to the woman behind. She nodded at him still avoiding direct eye contact. He stuffed his bank card and the notes into his wallet. The constant vibration of his phone irritated him and so he turned it off. *They can all fuck off - wankers.*

Old Compton Street was alive, and Fred unconcerned about money decided to go into one of the swankier looking bars. "Mind yourself darling!" Another customer said as he swayed into them whilst walking inside. His pocket full of cash sweetened his mood.

"Sorry, sweetheart," Fred said back to the bloke with the biggest arms he'd ever seen. He'd never use the word sweetheart, especially not to a guy, especially not to a butch stud way out of his league.

"Whatever you're on, I want some," the guy returned. But unaware, as drunks tend to be of their own delayed speed, Fred went to say something back; too much time had elapsed. The guy patted him on the back: "you have a good night', he said encouraging Fred's moving on. He did. His drunkenness prevented embarrassment. He looked ahead to the bar for somebody else to talk to. His inhibitions had flown away. He was in the mood to mix.

"What can I get you, Mr?" the barman in the tank top asked Fred.

"I'll have a double gin and tonic,"

"No problem gorgeous," the man winked at Fred and then sprang into preparing his drink. Fred looked up and down the crowded bar. He read the room; who looked interesting?

"Hey – Fred, right?" A guy said to Fred.

"Moron Michael, right?"

Michael laughed, "I see you've acclimatised quickly to the scene. I knew you would. How's Ryan?"

"Why would I know?" Fred intended *nonchalance* but achieved bitterness and tantrum.

Michael didn't bite. The barman placed Fred's gin and tonic on the counter, "Let me get this. I owe you one." Fred didn't argue.

"You owe me more than one," again Michael didn't challenge Fred. He laughed at Fred's exaggeration, "Ok, sweetie, you can have another after you've finished that."

Fred grabbed the glass and sucked onto the fancy straw with its tiny circumference. He struggled to drink at the speed he wanted, but he wasn't in the mood to be defeated, especially by a straw. He tossed the straw onto the floor and pressed his lips directly to the glass. He knocked it back, not in one gulp as such; it was more a series of glugs, but it was one episode – spectacle. Michael watched the ice bobbing back and forth between the glass and his lips. He chuckled at Fred once the glass was finally empty and signalled to the barman for another.

"You're determined,"

"Am I?" Fred replied, "Carpe Diem!"

"I hate to admit this, but to an older gentleman that phrase doesn't quite hold the allure it does to youngsters."

Fred was too drunk to interpret or entertain Michael's abstraction, "What? Get to the point."

Michael laughed again, "Hangovers are a killer as you get older darling. Carpe Diem sounds good in the moment, but it's the devil's language," Michael handed his card to the barman and lifted the freshly poured gin and tonic into Fred's hands, "But you're a little imp, so drink up."

Like a child suckered by a bit of reverse psychology, Fred moodily slammed the drink back onto the bar. He wasn't going to be told to drink or condescended by some old queen, "I'm not going to be condescended," the pronunciation of the word was a hurdle, but Fred not only cleared it, he repeated the word to prove he could handle it, "condescended, by some out of touch queen,"

"Quite right," Michael said, his face and tone serious, no delay in the speed of his response. Fred was unprepared. In his drunken logic, emotion begets emotion. Michael's reaction didn't adhere to Fred's heuristics: he was meant to say something offense back and the interaction increased in nastiness until a dramatic explosion of verbal fireworks wrapped things up.

"What's your problem; bitter and afraid of being a haggard old queen that's going to die alone?" Fred pushed forward with the fight on behalf of both of them.

"Sounds about right. I am afraid, a little, I guess, but hopefully, I'm not bitter about it. I don't think I'm bitter. Do you?" Michael defied Fred's expectations again. He didn't get it. He was being a dick, why wasn't Michael ripping into him.

"Why are you being nice?" Fred said with the innocence of a child mesmerised by an enchanting spell, of which he wanted to know the magician's secret.

A flicker of a smile flashed on Michael's face, but as a professional, he rationed the emotion: a truce may have settled, but the war wasn't over. He considered his next response appreciating it would be a high-stake moment, the fulcrum of a treaty or nuclear detonation: "because the guy speaking to me when I was in your place many, many years ago wasn't nice, and I don't want to be that person."

Fred lifted the drink from the bar and drank through the straw. His consciousness thickened – and pieces restored. Objects in his view – the bar, the chairs, coats, glasses, bottles, the barman, Michael – they all took on a more substantial texture; they became recognisable as the differentiated entities that they were, albeit still a little wobbly. The smooth, coldness of the glass tingled; the sugar of the tonic registered in his mouth; the kindness and substance in Michael's eyes thawed Fred's screen, his separation from it ended. He sat in the barstool and reengaged with everything, allowed everything to re-focus. Michael stood next to him like a benevolent parent. The music, cloud of conversation and hustle of shuffling crowds all awakened within Fred. He was present.

"Sorry," he said; Fred's world continued to sway in his intoxication, but at the core of his being, he had stilled. Michael and Fred faced the bar so neither looked at one another any longer. Michael didn't reply, but Fred knew he accepted the apology and was listening. "Do you want a drink?" Fred asked, and Michael laughed.

"Yes. But put your wallet away. It's not clever to be advertising to everyone that you're walking around with that much cash," Michael said in response to the wads of notes sticking out of Fred's wallet, "I might die alone, but I'll at least do it in a bit of luxury." He handed his American Express card to the barman as he indicated two more with his fingers.

"I've messed things up," Fred began his confession.

"Oh yeh?"

"I abandoned my friend. She was packing up my stuff while I tried to find somewhere to live. I just left her; my stuff. I just left. Didn't tell them."

"I'm sure she'll understand."

"Not really. She didn't want to help in the first place. I pushed her into it, and then fucked her over."

"She wouldn't have helped if she didn't want to."

"Yeh, but I made her lie. Nobody else knew I didn't have anywhere to go."

"They know now?"

"Yeh – well, I think so."

"What are you going to do?"

"I have no idea," Fred said the words, but he no longer felt helpless or lost about his situation. It wasn't that he was happy, but to his surprise, he recognised that he was calm. It was still a problem, but he had perspective, and this dissipated the drama. His despair had gone. He felt for the first time, that he could resolve his problems if he really wanted. "I have been such an idiot," he said.

Michael smiled, "wasn't it that attitude that got you here?"

Fred's face scrunched, "huh?"

"Don't be hard on yourself. It doesn't achieve anything."

Fred listened like an earnest schoolchild. This narrative didn't structure his world, but equally it wasn't the wishy-washy sentimentality of an out of touch establishment either.

"Look. You want to stand on your own feet eventually," Fred's expectant eyes encouraged Michael to elaborate, "but let people help you up, and don't get sanctimonious when you're there." He sipped his drink. "People think about responsibility as a chore. A burden. That's very unhelpful. It's wonderful to be in a position where you can help other people. It takes a lot of work, but it's such a rewarding place to be. People punish themselves when they fall short and it's stupid – generosity is a destination, a place we're constantly journeying to. When you're there – properly there – it's ecstasy, heaven – love, not sacrifice, a blending – not denial – of self. Transcendence. So…" he paused and changed the gear of his speech, "you messed up. You've been selfish. So what? Get over it. Get over yourself. Move forward. People don't want your perfection; they just need to know you're trying; that you're heading in the same direction as them."

Fred thought of his family, his mum, his dad. He thought of Bea, of Nick and Heeta. He judged them. He wasn't a hypocrite: he judged himself too. But Michael helped him to realise the futility of measuring people. He had gotten things upside down. Whenever things went wrong – as people and life, of course, did – his default reaction was to admonish. He expected perfection and couldn't handle the disappointment of not reaching it. And thus, he lived in an endless state of falling short. Life played out as one perpetual failure, a long epoch of self-hatred. A feeling of never making the mark, both within himself, and through time, the relationships he formed.

A tear trickled down his drunken cheek and Michael placed an arm onto his shoulder. His fingertips pressed enough to transmit affection. Fred took that hand on his shoulder and squeezed it with his own affection. He embraced the intimacy and it felt as if years of blocked arteries flowed in the way they were meant to. His self-imposed dam unblocked, and life entered sealed-off spaces. His impulse was to respond to the moment with action – to use the energy as an opportunity to sort stuff out, but he judiciously, restrained his inner voices and obeyed this depth of feeling (and his drunken helplessness). Anybody else would have labelled it despair, but

Fred had finally tuned into his hope, a much harder, and more disciplined place for him to reach. Following inner voices came easily; tuning into a deeper more peaceful place, and staying there, took courage and perseverance. But he screwed himself to that un-sticky place; for the first true time in his life, he stuck it out.

Michael rubbed his back and took him home.

PART III
Redemption
Spring 2009

CHAPTER 10: Camp

A grand piano rested in the centre of the room. Heavy tied-back silk curtains bordered three large bay windows and a pristine parquet floor stretched across the largest apartment Fred had ever been in. He pulled the daffodil yellow duvet off his couch-rested body. Patches of lime green velvet illuminated in the glimpses of light that caught the couch between Fred's legs. He moved himself into an upright position and let the duvet fall to the floor. He leaned his head forward and it pressed onto his knees. Wretchedness filled the hole that vomit had created in his stomach.

"It's hunger, not sin," a voice said from behind. Michael, wearing a fury dressing gown, stood behind an open plan kitchen work surface. A box of eggs paraded in one hand, and a saucepan in the other. "I'll make us some breakfast. I shouldn't really have toast – keto diet darling – but I guess we're celebrating."

"Celebrating what?" Fred said with his head still between his knees. Memories from the night before began to unfold, but a drunken mind does not relive experiences during sleep in the effective manner of a soberly dreaming one. Like the light struggling to reach the couch between Fred's legs, the reasons for his being in Michael's apartment fought their way into Fred's cerebral cortex, past the inner streams of pleas: *O God, please I never; not Michael; please no.*

"Obviously not our first sexual encounter," Michael said.

The straw with the tiny hole, a man with big arms, and then the image of himself crying into Michael's arms in the middle of a crowded Soho bar coalesced into a single mental picture, not amiss in a Picasso gallery. Thirst struck his stomach like a chimpanzee attacking guitar strings, but mortification glued his head to his knees. He couldn't lift himself up.

"because that didn't happen," Michael ignited the hob built into the modern open planed kitchen surface. Slabs of hard salty butter dropped into the pan and melted into a golden lake, "… because despite being a haggard old queen that is afraid of dying alone," a blunt knife knocked open an egg's mid-air shell, causing gravity to pull a yolk and translucent goo into the now bubbling pan of liquid butter, "I have standards and tearful apprentice queens with delightful boyfriends, contrary to popular belief, aren't my cup of tea. Speaking of which, do you take sugar?"

Thankful devotions trickled into Fred's cesspool of consciousness: *thank God, thank God, thank God.* And then streams of panic crashed and drowned the short-lived gratitude, *fuck: Ryan… Heeta… Nick…*

"You'll have plenty of time – literally, weeks, months – to make up to them. The damage is done, so right now you might as well focus on whether you want sugar in that cup of tea."

A folded pair of chinos with splashes of vomit on them, lay on the marble coffee table. Fred reached for them intending to check the pocket for his mobile phone.

"It's charging – on the table by the door; but for Christ's sake do you want sugar or not?" Michael stood with a teaspoon lingering mid-air.

"Yeh," Fred said, his leg slipping through the trouser leg, "two please." He walked across the beautiful apartment with stately high ceilings, aristocratic expensiveness, and modern elegance. A full green bar displayed on Fred's otherwise black mobile phone screen. Michael handed a cup of tea to Fred as he waited for his mobile to reawaken. A keypad eventually appeared and requested his pin. He tapped in his 'Y' code and slurped his tea while it re-loaded. "This place is phenomenal," he said.

"See didn't take you long to let go of that shame did it?" Michael said putting a white plate with a piece of seeded toast on it.

"Why have you got bread if you don't eat it?"

Michael beamed delight, "Look at you, so out of your own head, you're picking up subtle little details like my storage of bread."

Fred smirked, quite pleased at himself, "well come on, why do you?"

"I keep a loaf frozen for special occasions, like when I wake-up with an attractive young man in my apartment." Fred pulled the toast away from his mouth and examined it. The idea of frozen bread unnerved him.

"Really, this was frozen?" the half-eaten slab tilted up and down and then returned to Fred's lips.

"Oh child, how simple are you?"

"You don't want to know,"

"Darling, I was being rhetorical. I know perfectly well." Two more pieces popped out of the toaster. Michael released – as quickly as he grabbed – them. They settled on the spreading board, layered in butter, and then slid onto fresh plates.

Scrambled egg stirred in the pan and then slid onto the pieces of toast; Michael exchanged the full plate with the empty one in Fred's hand, and then handed him a fork.

"Thanks."

Michael picked-up his own plate and cutlery, then walked to the large white table close to one of the elegantly dressed windows. Fred followed and sat down too. They ate their egg and toast together.

"Such a cheap date," Michael said.

"I never would have thought that I'd be sitting here having breakfast with you a year ago."

"Well, you might be having breakfast with me a few more times by the sound of things."

The toast crunched as the slightly burnt edge pierced between Fred's teeth, "What do you mean?"

"Oh, don't be cute; it's dumb," Michael said sipping his coffee.

A moment of interiority enchanted Fred: opportunity and its cautious cousin doubt pulled his gaze inward to consider Michael's comment - *had he just insinuated I could stay? How should I act so he doesn't take it back?*

"For a start, don't try to anticipate and control my intentions," if it weren't so cliché or cartoonish, Fred would have dropped his jaw at

Michael's mind-reading. "It'll never work: I know my own mind, and darling, I know you better than you know yourself."

"So, you're asking me to stay?"

Michael's eyebrows lifted above the cup of coffee tilted toward his lips, "well perhaps I underestimated your cheekiness, "'asking me to stay'". Michael imitated Fred's words.

"But seriously, you wouldn't mind if I stopped a few nights why I sort things?" Fred said in touch with his newfound hope – the drunken brain might not record experiences as effectively as the sober one, but a heart properly pumping is living memory. Fred spoke with expectation; his superiors, Ofsted inspectors, school leaders had throughout his career told him that he needed higher expectations, but it had taken a mini-meltdown and Michael's compassion for him to acquire it.

"Of course, but darling, I'll break it to you, it'll be a bit longer than a few nights. I want something from you in return."

Fred hadn't expected that, "What?" He said, his anxiety shooting upward in sync with the plethora of imagined perverted, kinky requests Michael was about to make.

"I'm dying."

Fred hadn't expected that either.

"Cancer." Michael got straight to the point eliminating the possibility that he was being dramatic. "The doctors said I have 6 months; that was 12 months ago." The mental arithmetic calculated in Fred's mind, "Yes – around the time I first met you. In fact, that's why I had to leave you that night. The sickness it used to come on at random. Now it's more the other way around: the good days are the more random ones, which statistically suggests that I'm overdue a downward turn."

"But you look fine," a lump wedged in Fred's throat as he scanned the apartment, for what he wasn't quite sure.

Michael, ever astute, caught the flickering movement of his eye. "There's equipment in the bedroom," he laughed as he pushed the remainder of the egg and toast to one side of his plate. "Fuck, my beautiful bedroom looks more like a hospital wing now."

Fred didn't know what to say.

"Don't worry, I'm not asking you to be living help," he summoned the restraint not to laugh hysterically at the thought of Fred simultaneously aghast and puzzled at the image of frozen bread. "Christ, I'd be better off with Walter Mitty or Joey Essex looking after me; no, that side of things is sorted – people come to the apartment for all that; no, I'm not requesting domestic prowess."

"But what can I do for…" Fred stumbled.

"For a dying old queen?" Michael's teeth shone in the sunlight now beaming through his beautiful windows.

Tears swelled in Fred's eyes. He didn't even know Michael that well, and he barely felt a tear, let alone shed one, at his own grandmother's funeral. It was bizarre – why did he care about this man? That lump clogged his throat. He wanted to speak, but he just didn't know what to say. Michael's greyish-green irises locked onto him, and Fred couldn't control himself. He lifted his palms to cover his face as his own eyes began to sob while his nostrils blasted shots of snotty hot air repeatedly out of his nose.

"Oh Christ, I'm sorry," Michael said rubbing Fred's bare shoulder; he hadn't put his top on yet.

"Don't apologise," Fred said beneath his hands, which continued to cover his crying face. "You're the one dying, and I'm fucking crying." Michael laughed, which caused Fred to also laugh into his concealed outpouring.

"I know it's difficult, but I want you to remove your hands," Michael said, his tone serious.

"I can't."

"As a dying man, the first part of what I want in exchange of you staying here is for you to remove your hands right now," his tone was jovial, but he meant what he said.

Fred's sobs stopped and his breathing attempted to regulate beneath his palms. Even though it was dark behind the skin of his tightly pressed unwrinkled fingers, his eyelids were closed. And although he knew this dying man, Michael, had asked him to look at him, superglue might as well have kept his hands to his face. He couldn't remove them.

In response, Michael placed his own hands onto them. Fred could feel a double layer of darkness, but the intimacy of having Michael's hands touch his own warmed his core. He hadn't realised he was cold. The superglue melted; his eyelids flickered upward, and cracks of light flittered between the crevices in both their hands. Fred, who considered himself ordinarily allergic to intimacy, soaked it in. Eventually, Michael withdrew his hands and so did Fred. Their greyish-green eyes mirrored one another as their hands rested together on the table; Michael's on top.

"I want you to do something important, Fred."

He nodded and with an open heart meant it.

"I need you to continue my story."

Fred didn't understand. He searched Michael's face for information.

"I lost him years ago," Michael tilted his head to a photograph of a handsome man wearing shorts and a brown vest on the side unit close to where they were sitting; he couldn't be more than early 20s. "I lost nearly everyone: AIDs. I was literally the only one of us, to not catch it. A larger group of happily smiling men all wearing shorts, huddled together in another photograph. "It was the early 90s – less than twenty years ago."

Tears now rolled down Fred's cheeks and dropped onto the table. He didn't attempt to conceal or wipe them away. They flowed uninterrupted. AIDs terrified Fred. He was too young to remember the tombstone adverts of the 80s, but he'd grown-up with their silent, omnipresent ghosts; the unspoken disappearance of thousands of young men was his childhood and adolescence; the hundreds of thousands of family members with holes at their dinner tables whom no teacher, aunt, uncle, brother, sister, neighbour, or friend acknowledged. Ghosts had been walking with Fred his entire life. He finally saw them, smiling back at him from the photograph on Michael's elegant glass unit.

"I need you to remember them when I'm gone."

Michael left the room to fetch several photo albums from a spare room. Their velvet covers rested onto the dining table and Michael's cancerous hands lifted the pages slowly. Athletic men with smiles as generous and as wickedly fun as that special sparky friend everybody deserves to have in their life, shone on every page. Bea's stupid horse teeth galloped into Fred's mind as the pictures imprinted themselves. He considered their fun, skimpy outfits; traced the way their arms wrapped around one another's shoulders; touched the blue of the summer sky that speckled above a London skyline in the background. "Where are they?" Fred asked with his finger laid on one of the pictures.

"Hampstead Heath," Michael said; sweet, too sweet, too bitter sweet[1] memories arrested his sentiment. His fingers continued moving through the album of these real men erased from history; the evidence of their lives gone, like the burning of their clothes incinerated in fires of shame. The wallpaper of their apartments bleached clean; their teacups smashed into pieces and sealed in protective lining before being discarded like industrial waste; their childhood bedrooms and photographs deleted from the family hard-drive; their ashes handled with plastic gloves and buried far away like dead batteries. The last page of the second album turned and the book closed. Michael's hand rested on the velvet casing.

Fred didn't know any older gay men, not really. He'd slept with a couple of men in their late thirties, maybe forties if they'd been honest to him about their age. "How old are you?" Fred asked.

"44 – I was born on April 1st 1965… born a fool…" Michael said and Fred smiled.

"How old are you?"

"26 – April 1st, 1984; guess we were both born fools."

---

[1] Christina Rossetti, *Echo*

"Really?" Michael was rarely surprised anymore.

"Yeh," Fred mustered the strength to ask Michael what he wanted him to actually do.

"Must be fate then."

"What must be?" Fred said.

"Our meeting…" before Michael could finish, Fred spoke,

"It wasn't fate – it was you lying about your age. You said you were 35 when I agreed to that date!"

"Yes, but if I remember rightly, you also lied: you said you were 32." Fred had forgotten about that. He did the arithmetic first…

"Yes, which means that you lied more," they smiled at each other and with facial expressions alone implied a truce. A peaceful silence settled on them like invisible flakes of warm snow. Michael moved his hand; it rested on top of Fred's. If Michael hadn't told him that he was dying of cancer and showed him two albums of dead friends, he would have pulled his hand away and scathed at Michael like some alley cat. He would have been lying if he was comfortable with Michael's hand on his; physical expressions of intimacy itched the receptors beneath his skin. Only intense intoxication gave him the power to ignore the electronic impulse to recoil, and even then it wasn't really proper power. It just tricked his system, created enough delay for the signal to reach his inebriated mind that by the time it did, he was already enjoying the physical sensation of the touch. "You know, I've never had sex – sober." Fred said.

Michael smiled, a gentle, small smile that conveyed gratitude rather than humour; a smile that said thank you for not being polite, for speaking plainly and truthfully. His eyes rested and Fred felt like he had to continue speaking as if he were sitting in a counsellor's office.

"I don't know why I said that," Michael just stared and waited for him to continue, "I think it's perhaps those men – your friends – they look so comfortable with each other. Comfortable being, you know," Michael's eyes narrowed and his lips scrunched,

"Go on…"

"you know, so… camp," the word came out of Fred's mouth as if it had been rolling around in a cauldron of dog poo, shame, and the smallest dose of intrigue. Fred had of course used the word before, but he was speaking nakedly honest in a way that was rare of him. He had had this conversation before; he'd argued about the problem of shame associated with language and the need of persecuted groups to reclaim labels that have been used to humiliate and suppress them: queer, nigger. But as this flickered through his mind, he recognised that the arguments had always been overly theoretical; that deep down, he hadn't been in tune with his affections. Now, as he felt Michael's hand, and thought of those men in the pictures, the language hurt him. It transported him into the prejudice, the insecurity, the hatred of the people looking and judging those men as they sashayed in the flesh.

Michael didn't react but waited for Fred in expectation.

"I don't know. Maybe I'm…" Fred tangled himself. He had become a bit of a knot. Michael rubbed Fred's hand, and then withdrew.

"We don't need to do it all in one go," Michael stood and walked to the mirror hanging on the back wall. His reflection straightened and poised, "hopefully, I've got a few more weeks, so with a bit of luck you'll be ready by then."

"Ready for what?"

"To remember them."

Michael made his apologies to Fred after that. Weakness had returned to claw him from the inside and he needed to lie down, "It was bound to come," he said. Secretly, he hoped to have a few more days of feeling good, but in honesty, he knew he had exceeded his quota by more than he could have imagined a year ago. The doctor's warned that he'd feel great for a few days before the very end; that it would be as if the cancer had miraculously disappeared, but that it would come back. Quickly. And with a definite ending. Michael's adam's apple rolled down his throat in the mirror as he swallowed. He looked at himself as a healthy, still handsome forty-four-year-old man and knew that it was the last time he was going to see himself that way. This was the end. He knew.

Fred didn't see any of what Michael saw in the mirror. With an aching heart, Michael turned away from his reflection; he made a promise to himself that he would not look again. He wanted to remember himself this way. "Fred, look at me."

"I am,"

"Really look," he left a few seconds for Fred to stare at him, "remember me looking like this."

Fred nodded. His impulse was to make a jibe – several inappropriate things became immediately available; it's always the way – but he didn't say them. He nodded with affection. He understood what Michael meant. "But there's plenty of time, you big drama queen. You can't get rid of me that quickly," this wasn't a jibe. Fred believed it. Michael smiled, a smile that said you're wrong, but God, I wish you were right. Fred didn't pick that up.

"I need a sleep, but we'll speak more later, ok. There's a spare key on the side," Michael indicated to the kitchen surface, "and there's a few empty draws in the dressing room if you need somewhere to store a few things," Michael began walking back to his bedroom.

"Michael," Fred said.

"Yes darling?"

"Thank you."

CHAPTER 11: Just because it feels important

The door of Michael's apartment closed without making a sound; Fred's one palm controlled the speed while his other hand wrapped and twisted the handle so that even the click was delicate. By the time he reached the end of the corridor, his careful stepping eased; the entire sole of his trainer pressed the floor, rather than just his tiptoes. Of course, he didn't need to tread so carefully, not even on the inside of the apartment, but the combination of Michael's vulnerability and generosity had altered Fred's disposition: he flipped from inept attempts of pragmatism to principle. It didn't matter whether there was a recipient of his consideration, he took the approach of being considerate regardless, his new default – automation; at least, this was the intention.

Outside the apartment, fancy Mayfair buildings surrounded him. Columns and external porches bordered those simple London front doors painted in a luxurious black evocative of downing street. Fred could envisage the Prime Minister standing at a podium in front of any of the entrances in both directions of the street. *Bloody hell,* he thought, *the apartment was fancy enough irrespective of wherever it was, but for the thing to be here, in the middle of Mayfair, well, it must be worth millions.* A feeling of shame nibbled upward along his arms. He wasn't sure if it was appropriate or tasteful to admire Michael's wealth given his cancerous condition and generosity. The topic just seemed a little taboo and so he put it out of his mind.

The horizons at each end of the street were equivalent: they both blended into more generic brick monied properties. The thing about the West End of London is that it doesn't matter which way you go, a tube station will always come along sooner or later. The street pivoted onto a thicker artery with the usual coffee shops, eateries and supermarkets repeating themselves behind endless bus stops: Starbucks, Pret-a-Manger, Nero, Leon, Sainsburys, Costa, Yo Sushi, Tesco Metro. Fred bought himself a large latte from one of the hipster independent coffee shops. The wad of cash pulled from the machine reminded him of last night's impulsivity; it glistened in the funky orange lamplight of the shop. He was so grateful he hadn't blown it. The notes nudged him to replay specific incidents about the previous evening. He thanked the barista and took his takeout coffee toward the comfy seats dotted along the glass window bordering the street. He sipped the extremely hot beverage and then placed the cup onto the small table. His phone lingered in the loose grip of his two hands. Messages from Nick, Heeta and Ryan scrawled the screen as Fred re-read them for the eighth time. Like a short story their tone escalated quickly; soft concern turned to alarm, which then turned to rage, before finally settling on an achingly painful indifference, the sound of numbness, that moment when they've run out of feelings.

Of course, he knew their relationship had not reached that stage; that one stupid, incredibly selfish night wouldn't have caused them to reject him. Fred had matured. Rather than linger in a state of self-pity and fantasy where he cast himself as the wretched sufferer who had slammed into the rocky-bottom of his life, alone and beyond hope, abandoned by his friends (justifiably); instead, he accepted that he'd been a dick and that his friends were more likely to be feeling furious and hurt by his ignoring them; hurt by his rejection and disbelief of them caring about him; hurt by his dismissiveness of their affection and support.

Fred stared at the responsibility lying before him, the grovelling he was going to have to do. Words stumbled together on his screen and then vanished. He struggled to string a sentence for any of them. The most difficult was Ryan. He knew he could smooth things over with Heeta and Nick. They knew him. They knew he could be a dick, *but Ryan doesn't know this side of me*, he thought. *Will he still want me?* He didn't know the answer, but it didn't scare him as much as he anticipated. Fred didn't want things to end; he wanted Ryan, but he also knew that he needed to stop pretending; he needed to allow Ryan to see him too; otherwise, it wasn't real.

He closed the text message to Heeta and Nick; he settled on a simple, '*I'm so, so sorry. On the way over. Will explain. What can I buy you to make up?*' He opened a clean message for Ryan and thought hard: '*Sorry about not responding. Got a lot to talk about if you still want to talk…*' He re-read the message too many times, over-analysed it and after deleting it several more times, he re-wrote the original and pressed send.

Ryan messaged back immediately, '*Of course I do! Where are you?*'

'*Some coffee shop in Mayfair…*' Fred sent this message without any consideration of how it might come across; about the suggestiveness of a small ellipsis. That's the problem with acting on principle – it reveals truth and truth can be unpleasant and unkind.

'*… Have you slept with somebody? …*'

But equally, it cuts out a whole lot of drama when the truth isn't filled with it, '*Ha! No. Thank God. It's a long story. Can we meet later?*'

'*Good. What are you doing now?*'

'*I need to go and grovel to Nick and Heeta – come over after?*'

Fred took another sip of his still boiling coffee. He couldn't believe how smoothly it had gone: Ryan was ok. He popped the lid from his coffee cup – the thing was never going to cool to a temperature that he could drink.

The phone laid on the table with the screen upward so that Fred could see when a message came through. His coffee cooled and half of the cup emptied, but no more messages appeared. Fred checked the signal; it was fine. The dregs of the coffee lingered in the cup which remained on the table. Fred left. Buses and taxis charged along the road as hordes of pedestrians clogged the pavement. The underground machine swished open and closed almost as quickly. Fred shot through holes in the earth. He shot under the Thames, and parts of south London. He made the necessary changes to overground trains at London Bridge station and eventually shot into Lewisham. He hoped Heeta or Nick would be home. He pulled his phone again to check for messages. He had sent a couple of apologies. One message asked if he could call; the latest said that he was going to call.

The rail track rumbled beneath as Fred walked across the overpass. The view of Lewisham's tower-blocks went unnoticed in the background. Heeta's name glowed in a thick bold font. Fred's finger hovered over it for a couple of seconds. He was nervous. He pushed her name and listened to the rings. It went to voicemail. After leaving the station, he tried again: voicemail. He tried Nick. He was over the apprehension now and pushed the call button without hesitation. He just wanted to speak to them regardless of how angry they were. By the time, he reached their street with its stack of cars wedged into every inch of road-pavement, he still hadn't heard from them. He called again, and this time mustered the courage to leave a voicemail telling them that he was almost at the flat, "I'm really, really sorry – please, please just pick-up and let me explain. I'll try again in five minutes and keep ringing until you answer, so you might as well pick-up even if it's just to tell me to fuck off."

At the flat, Heeta's little car rested between white vans. Fred's stuff squeezed against the windows – *it must have taken her ages to load everything,* Fred thought – his guilt rushing back. The intercom buzzed, a long drone of low expectation that became lower the longer it went on. A disappointed but not unexpected silence ate the sound as Fred removed his finger. He sat on the step, slightly to one side so that he didn't block the doorway.

"Fred," a voice called his name from above. He stood and moved back from the building a little so that he could see who had called him. Water poured down and smacked him in the face.

"What the fuck?" he said more out of instinct than injustice. Another blast hit him, and as he threw his arms up in protection, a third. "Ok, ok. I deserved…"

"Yes – you fucking do!" Heeta said. "You are one of the most selfish assholes I've ever met."

"I know, I've been a dick. I'm sorry."

A neighbour's net lifted and a giant perm sitting on top of an old lady's face stared out. Fred glanced and their eyes met briefly. He waited for a response. As droplets of water slid of his chin and cheeks, he realised that he would be waiting forever if he didn't continue speaking. "Look, I'm really sorry, Heeta. I was completely out of order and there is no excuse for leaving you like that."

"I wasn't bothered – well I was – about being left. What really fucked me off was sitting in a car with all your stuff until 8 at night, outside some shit hole flat, in some rough estate, wondering whether you've been killed, murdered; just because you couldn't be fucked to send a simple message; because you didn't have an ounce of decency to let me know that you were just having some selfish, existential crisis. Fine. I wouldn't have given a fuck – well I would because I'm your friend. But I wouldn't have sat waiting for hours, on my own, afraid, afraid of some wanna-be gangsters staring at me for hours on end, afraid that I've made some horrible mistake, afraid of getting fucking clamped and fined…" she burnt out.

"I'm sorry," Fred couldn't say anything else.

"Too late," she said, "I'm sorry too," she threw her car keys out of the flat window. "Get your stuff out of my car."

Fred wanted to say 'but I haven't got anywhere to put it', but he had the good sense to censor himself. He bent down and picked-up the keys from the gravel. He had no idea what he was going to do, but he honoured the affections that had arisen in him during his time with Michael. He dug into his (deeply buried) fortitude and grace and refused to appropriate this moment as his. For now, it didn't matter what he *was going* to do; it mattered that he respected Heeta's justified anger, her desire for him to remove his stuff from her car.

He unlocked the door and began moving boxes from the car to the patch of grass in front of the parking bays. More heads bobbed beneath and over nets in the windows of the building. Like a monk rotating prayer beads in his fingertips, Fred chanted to himself internally. *Keep going. Keep going. Keep going.* It didn't take long for him to remove his stuff. Fred closed each of the car doors except the driver's; through it, he leant into the car and pushed the locks manually. He then closed the last door and inserted the key to lock the final door externally. He didn't want the moment to end. He hoped that Heeta would have a change of heart as she watched him from the flat. He turned to look at her, but unlike every other resident, she wasn't watching him. She stood at the entrance of the building with her back toward him. He left his stuff on the grass verge and walked over to return her car keys.

As he got closer, she spoke, "I just need a bit of time Fred. We are still friends, but I can't look at you yet. It was cruel."

Fred's heart ached. Normally he would have fought, pleaded his case until she capitulated, but something had changed. Michael was with him. He was in a place that made him think beyond himself, beyond his own logistical dilemma of moving his crappy things; he was completely focused on Heeta, her feelings: her rage, her hurt, her pain. She needed time. He didn't challenge or burden her with his problems. He repeated her words, "It was cruel." He paused briefly and added, "you deserve better." He did not sound passive-aggressive or self-pitying. It was earnest and true – good.

"I'll call you. I promise. I just need some time," she said.

He placed the keys onto the step. She stretched her hand behind so that Fred could take it. He squeezed it with affection, "take as long as you need," he said, "and I really am sorry."

"I know."

He let go of her hand and walked toward his stuff on the verge; she walked back into the building. It was goodbye for now.

Five boxes and a guitar on a grass verge; that was Fred's life. His phone vibrated. As he pulled it from his pocket, Ryan's name occupied the screen. "Hey," Fred answered.

"Hey," a brief silence bounced between them: they were both providing the other with the gap to steer the conversation. Fred, in his new found zen, for once did not fill the space. Ryan eventually spoke, "So how much trouble are you in?"

"Oh, you know, I'm not quite suffocating, but the shit's almost at face-level."

"Disgusting. Where are you?"

"Outside Nick and Heeta's new place in Lewisham."

"Yeh – it's nice."

"You've seen it?"

"If you didn't realise you went completely off the radar last night – of course I've seen it. I went straight over when they called: we thought you'd been in some sort of accident. We were calling hospitals, police stations…" he paused for a second, "your parents."

"You called my parents?" It was the first time a flash of pre-zen Fred emerged.

"Fred, everybody was really worried. It wasn't like you just went off for a casual evening. You disappeared unexpectedly. It didn't make any sense. Heeta was literally packing your stuff and running an errand for you – when you didn't get back to her, we thought – well we thought the worst…"

The silence returned but this time it wasn't to give each other an opportunity to speak and steer the conversation. It was because neither of them had anything to say for the moment. Fred was ashamed and embarrassed. Ryan was re-living his fear of losing Fred.

"I love you," Ryan said. Fred did not expect it. He remained silent. Although he had been beyond certain for months that Ryan was going to ask him to move in with him, he'd never really thought about them loving each other, not properly. He'd fantasied about it, but that always involved some over the top romantic gesture: the words delivered at the top of the Eiffel tower avec an engagement ring. Something that would always happen later. He never really thought about how it would happen, how it would feel, in the present, in an ordinary everyday moment, especially one like this: a hangover, a state of shame, and semi-homelessness. But to Ryan, his calling hospital after hospital, asking them whether they'd received an a & e patient fitting Fred's description; this, not a trip up the Eiffel tower, made him recognise just how much he loved Fred. And he needed to tell him. Sickness had swirled and bubbled in his stomach every time a voice answered his calls. He had battled against the anticipation repeatedly, that each voice was going to respond in the affirmative; that they were going to tell him that they had received a patient fitting Fred's description, a cold, dead body, now lying in the morgue of their non-descript hospital. He had to tell Fred that he loved him before that ever happened.

To Fred though, Ryan's words made him think of Michael and the men from his velvet book. A punch to his gut struck emotionally. He covered his mouth with his hand and an ocean of sorrow rose behind his eyes. Ryan's "I love you," thickened the image of their faces, their red-lipped smiles, their joyful stretched out arms, their barely post-adolescent moustaches; their colourful bandanas; the smooth skin on their fingers; the hearts on their sleeves, literally, the lively, flamboyant shirts; their short shorts and trousers. Their spirits encircled him. How could he have this blissful love and honour their injustice by reawakening them within his own heart? They had not died, they had been erased; their existence scrubbed from history. He couldn't remember them and indulge his own gratification; the preservation of their pain became more important; he wanted to remember them more than he wanted his own happy ever after. And the two states seemed mutually exclusive: he couldn't have them both simultaneously. He told himself that he had to choose, and that choosing himself – choosing Ryan – was the wrong answer.

"Fred, I love you," Ryan repeated. "Live me with – I would have asked anyway if I'd known you needed to move out..." his tone was earnest. He meant what he said.

"I can't,"

That silence re-emerged, but no two silences are ever the same. Ryan waited for him to speak but couldn't bear the abyss forming between them, "Fred, I don't get it – what's wrong?"

Fred considered how to respond, but the scenario presented a calculation beyond the capabilities of his mind. Instead he spoke from the heart, "Ryan, I really like you, but I can't move in yet, and I can't say what you want me to say. It's not that I don't, it's just something happened last night and..."

"You slept with someone," Ryan cut in.

Fred responded with authority and compassion, "No. It's not about anyone else – well not like that. I stopped at Michael's."

"Michael who?" Ryan wasn't used to being so out of control.

"The older guy we bumped into in Soho a few weeks ago – you said he was one of the..."

"Queen Michael?" he cut-in again.

The casual adjective that he would have himself used a day ago to describe Michael evoked injury. "He's dying."

Ryan tried to respond, but he censored himself several times before replying. Nothing quite fit. He felt angry at Fred: he was opening-up to him, revealing his affections and proposing they move forward together, yet this person, the person he loved, was hiding behind somebody else's tragedy to deflect his own lack of affections. *Fucking coward,* he thought. He felt hurt at the thought of Fred not loving him back. His censure eventually yielded, "Just be fucking honest Fred, if you don't love me, then have the balls to tell me. It's obviously tragic if Michael's dying, but I don't see what that has to do with us."

"It's more complicated than that,"

"Fred, do you love me?"

To his surprise, he could answer easily, "Yes, of course, I do."

Ryan did not understand at all. He felt like Fred had plunged him into a giant puzzle, a maze in which he had been dropped into the centre by a God-like hand, and which had no exit. "I don't get it Fred. You do love me, but you don't want to say it, and you don't want to live with me?"

"Yes."

"Fred, you've got to give me something," his anger had melted to a plea.

Fred sat down on the grass verge beside his boxes, "Ryan, I do love you, but I can't…"

"You just said it,"

The smell of fresh cut grass accompanied Fred's inhalations; it was one of his favourite smells. He continued, "Ryan, I do, but I can't do the whole jumping up and down on the spot. I can't pretend that suddenly nothing else matters in the world because I love you."

Fred couldn't see it, but on the other end of the phone, Ryan smiled, a larger smile than he'd ever smiled in his life. It was all he needed.

"Ryan?"

"I'm here," his voice was deadpan. His happiness had created an overwhelming core of stability that played out in every part of him simultaneously. It deadlocked and jammed every emotion making him sound robotic, but nothing could be further from the truth. He felt intensely and indiscriminately.

"I know it isn't what you want to hear, but I…"

"Fred shut up."

Fred shut up. He loved Ryan and didn't want to upset him anymore than he thought he already had. He waited.

"I understand. I get it. I'm coming over, ok?"

"Ryan, I'm not sure…"

"Shut up. I'm coming over. You don't have to move in – I just want to know you're safe."

Ryan couldn't see, but now Fred smiled, a hearty, intimate smile, "ok," he said

"o.k."

They sat at either end of the phone without speaking but knowing that they were there for each other. They loved each other and they didn't need the Eiffel Tower, or a ring; Fred didn't need silk curtains blowing over a French patio door with Barry Manilow singing in the background. He didn't need anything. He had Ryan's love, and Ryan had his.

It didn't take long for Ryan to help Fred load his boxes into the car once he arrived, "You're sure about this?" he asked Fred climbing into the driver's seat.

The door shut and from inside the car, Fred replied, "Yeah – thank you. I can't quite explain why, but I need to be there. It feels important." Fred would have usually bent his head downward embarrassed by saying something so sentimental; something so open ended; something so lacking in logical self-interest and explicit rationale. Unbeknown to himself, Fred deified pragmatism and it had done his life a disservice. It stopped him saying the spiritual things he needed to say; it provoked him to censor and scorn his innate sentimentality, and of course it never worked. Like a Jack in the Box, he just became increasingly charged and his spring increasingly erratic and explosive like a damaged child. But something about Michael had healed him. He spoke those words – 'It feels important' – without pride or shame. The phrase became uncontroversial to him, it didn't require his convoluted justification. He could just feel and act upon it. He didn't need to become frustrated and ashamed in his inability to adequately explain, or as happened more often – explain away, his actions. He assigned meaning – 'it feels important' – and went with it, unshackled by the pressure of pseudo-scientific or bureau-corpocratic censorial etiquette. Fred was conscious of the change within him and he felt alive, unrestricted; happy. His shoulder twisted into the seat and his cheek pressed into the headrest. He gazed directly at Ryan and feeling like a Buddhist monk, he repeated himself, "did you do anything just because it felt important?"

Ryan pushed a lock of hair on Fred's forehead behind his ear, "you need a haircut." Fred allowed him to touch his hair and face; usually he would have flinched at the physical intimacy. "I came and sat down next to you, that day we met in SoHo. I had a dentist appointment, but I saw you and that empty chair beside you… I thought, this doesn't make any sense, but I've got to go and speak to him." Usually, Fred would have lightened the tone with a joke.

"You never said anything before."

"Well, you don't, do you?"

"Why not?"

Ryan laughed, "I don't know. We all do it, but you just don't talk about the reasons you do that stuff; the stuff you do just because…" Fred felt like he'd been missing out on a giant secret everybody had been in on; he felt like the world was a hypocrite – telling itself it behaved one way while secretly doing what it wanted. He had attempted to align his head and heart whereas the rest of the world seemed comfortable having theirs exist like a married couple who to the world appeared together but in private slept in separate bedrooms.

"But that's stupid," Fred said.

Ryan laughed again, "perhaps," he went to speak a few times, but the words took a little while to settle, "perhaps, you're meant to save that stuff – the sincerity – for the people you really like, special people,"

Fred's lips soured. He didn't like that comment, "But that's stupid." He wasn't quite sure why, but he felt something about what Ryan had said was wrong and that it was important for this – whatever it was – to not be wrong.

"Look I don't know," Ryan said, "I guess it's just the way I was raised: we were encouraged to follow our hearts, but I suppose… you know," he searched for the words to express himself, "but to do it quietly… of-the-record… I don't know, kind-of like carefully; like you shouldn't go around saying it too loud otherwise, it'll be taken away from you…"

"By who?"

"I don't know exactly… 'them'," Ryan searched to fill the empty pronoun with definition, "the people that want to control everything," he laughed implying a jovial humour motivated his language, but he meant what he was saying, and Fred knew it. Protectionism underpinned his thinking.

"Who are the people that want to control everything?" Fred asked. He'd never heard Ryan speak in this way. Ironically, it reminded him of himself – something he would say. But deep-down Fred had been raised to think of people as painfully free; an almost puritanical freedom rooted his midland upbringing. His conspiratorial rants reflected an adolescent rebellion against his own being, rather than a genuine expression of fresh values, self-consciously forged and imposed. Of course, people came together in the midlands; they acted in common, but unlike the north-north, it felt underpinned by ferocious, and often hot-headed, competitive willpower – no matter how much it hurt; no matter how unwanted, underdeveloped, or limiting; everyone was reduced to their own, inalienable self-control; collectives were only ever a borrowed pooling of willpower in pursuit of even riper spoils; they were not the deferential shields against exploitation as they were in the north-north. The pursuit of strength and the execution of desire for desire's sake was the true ubiquitous superglue uniting the ambitious people of Fred's feuding midland fiefdoms.

"I don't know what I'm really saying… I've never thought about it explicitly," Ryan said.

"But if somethings true, shouldn't you say it no matter what?" Fred said.

"It's not that simple,"

"Isn't it?"

"No," Ryan was firm now, and for the first time, they were becoming perceptively aware of their differences, the differences in where they were from; that the communities north of Watford Junction aren't indeed all the same. Fred wasn't *northern* in the way Ryan was northern. London had turned them into natural allies; they were the same by the fact that they weren't southerners, but their immigrant status was superficial. Their otherness didn't make them the same. Their communities were different.

"So, you don't think it's right to speak the truth?"

"Oh, come on Fred, that is such a loaded question. Reality is obviously more complicated… the whole world isn't always our friend. You've got to be careful…"

But to Fred this defensive sectarianism didn't sit right, "something just feels off," he said.

"Perhaps it is, but reality isn't perfect – weren't you the one telling me this?" Ryan attempted to soften the conversation by redirecting the focus back to their immediate, personal history.

Fred thought about Ryan's words. His posture remained in the exact same position, his cheek against the headrest, his body facing Ryan's in the passenger seat of his car. "You're right, I did," he said after a lengthy pause, but as he went to explain himself he stopped and reconsidered his position, "actually, no – I didn't suggest the world wasn't perfect. I wasn't really commenting on the state of reality. I said that I didn't want our love to isolate us... I didn't want to pretend everything was perfect and to separate ourselves from real life just because we're in love."

They both churned over Fred's words; they both asked themselves whether that was what Fred had said.

"Yeah exactly – so you said the world's not perfect,"

"You're missing the point I'm trying to make," Fred said. The engine of the car wasn't on but it was getting warm inside.

"I think you're missing my point," Ryan said.

"Not really. You're saying that you do care about doing the right thing, but only for the right people. That's cowardly."

"Fuck off, Fred."

"Correct me if I'm wrong."

Ryan twisted the key in the ignition and the engine fired into mechanical motion. "Fuck you. Perhaps it's better if you stop at Michael's for a few days."

Fred twisted his body forward. His seatbelt whipped across his chest and the buckle clipped into the socket. "It'll be more than a few days."

The car reversed out of the parking bay and then began to accelerate off Heeta and Nick's drive. "I need the address," Ryan said. The car stalled on the main road, but luckily there were no cars behind them yet.

"I don't know the address."

Ryan smirked,

"Fuck you," Fred said as he noticed Ryan's condescension.

"So, Mr Moralistic, how can I help drive you if you don't know where to go?"

"I know the road and building, just not the address, and you don't have to help if you don't want to. I don't need your charity," Fred was overplaying his hand here; he desperately needed Ryan to help him move; the thought of removing his stuff onto another grass verge was too much, but he'd slipped back into a deeper Fred – there was no way he was revealing his dependency – he'd rather cut his nose to smite his face.

"Fine. I'll just drive into the West end and circle around until you pick up a scent of his house," Ryan was being facetious but that was exactly what Fred wanted to do so he didn't say anything in response, and before long they were in that awkward place where the silence had become competitive.

Half an hour later, the Elephant and Castle shopping centre drifted past and Fred felt slightly smug that the plan had worked out. However, the crappy pub where he'd selfishly chosen to ignore Heeta's calls then drifted past too: he felt rotten. The evening whizzed through his mind, and the memory of that black velvet book with those free-spirited, generously smiling men, surfaced to the prime spot. It was the prompt he needed to bring him back out of himself, his stubbornly idealistic self-reliance. "I'm sorry," he said to Ryan.

"Dick,"

"I deserve that."

"Yes, you do," Ryan's words were firm, but the speed of his response implied his willingness to reconcile.

"This is why I want to stop with him."

Ryan broke his fixed gaze on the windscreen ahead of him for the first time since leaving Lewisham. He glanced at Fred for a brief second, his eyebrows scrunching. "You want to stop with Michael because you're a dick to everybody else?" His words were now playful, still a little scorned and truthful, but no longer motivated by a desire to express his own hurt.

"He had these friends. They died of AIDs. All of them."

Ryan went quiet. It might have been 2009, but the stigma was still intense. The word had its own power to induce fear. A terrifying fear of divine proportions, perhaps the sort of fear that deeply religious people experience when they contemplate the hell that they believe in so firmly. It had more power than mere death. It had the ability to erase and condemn the soul; to inscribe sentences in the afterlife, in each realm of Dante's nine hells.

"I think he wants to tell someone about them."

"Why?" Ryan re-found his voice. His question wasn't hostile; perhaps a little guarded, but there was sincere curiosity in it.

"I'm not sure exactly. It's what I was saying earlier though. He feels it's important for some reason, and I do too..." Fred's tone was less confident, less secure than earlier, but he still meant what he said. A short silence washed over them like a gentle wave rolling on a sandy shore. "Do you think I'm stupid?" Fred added.

"No." Ryan was as firm as he had been earlier. He didn't elaborate or justify himself. The word conveyed his conviction. It conveyed to Fred his unwavering feeling that it was somehow the right and a good, important thing to do, something bigger than either of them. But as the protective, guarded northerner, he had accurately self-identified as, he limited his articulation as if saying any more aloud would jeopardise the whole enterprise. Fred stretched his hand and laid it on Ryan's leg. Ryan placed his own hand onto Fred's. They drove into central London together in silence, their hands together apart from when Ryan moved it temporarily onto the gearstick in response to the traffic and roundabouts that required them to change speed. However, it always found its way back, regardless of whether it was for ten seconds or two minutes between each gearstick change. They were together again; together in the world and travelling to reclaim lost realities.

In central London, Ryan's Vauxhall passed beneath the screens of Piccadilly circus at least three times. Fred was trying to remember the general direction but lacked the commitment for firm decisions. The car eventually found its way through the grandiose maze of West End property.

Between a Porsche and an Aston Martin that mirrored the value of the apartments on the swanky street, Ryan pulled-up in his Vauxhall.

"Bloody hell, I never realised, he lived in a place like this," he said, "no wonder you want to move in."

Fred slapped his thigh.

"I'm joking," he said turning-off the ignition. "But seriously, Fred. Apartments along here must be millions. Michael must be worth a fortune."

Other than the general notion of being expensive, Fred had no concept of the real value of the buildings in the way that Ryan did. "Don't talk about money upstairs," he said to Ryan, "will you?"

"Not if you don't want me to,"

"It's just I don't want him to think that's why I'm staying because it isn't,"

"I was only joking; he won't think that,"

"I know, but money is funny. It makes people behave weird and I don't want that..." Fred was desperately earnest, "I want to be there for him – properly. I don't want him to think I'm only here because I'm expecting something."

Ryan nodded – he understood. "Come-on," he said opening his door onto the pavement that couldn't have been more expensive if it were literally made of gold, "let's get your stuff out." Boxes, half-Sellotaped, and looking rather desperate, crashed onto the slabs. The car looked so spacious when empty space returned. Fred's hand slid into his back pocket and felt for the key. As he took it out, and stretched his arm forward to reach the lock, Ryan noticed, "You've got a key?" It was more of a statement than a question.

Fred shrugged his shoulders as if it wasn't a big deal. Usually, he would have felt the need to explain such generosity; his staunch midland scepticism prompting an impulse to bury inconvenient facts in convoluted rationale that leads back to some sort of narrative of enlightened self-interest that bores listeners, who by the time they have followed the twisting logic, no longer care or remember the simple spirit of generosity bound to the act. But he didn't fight or indulge his impulse. Fred, instead, accepted as self-evident Michael's decision to give him a key: an unusual, unexpected, perhaps even objectively irrational; dumb act. But just allowing this interior mental response to play itself out without action or discursive elaboration, created the space for bodily emotion – one that was arguably more powerful than any intellectual understanding. Fred felt appreciation. He accepted he couldn't explain why Michael had trusted and been so kind to him; that there may be no objective reason; and so, he didn't try to find it. Instead, he felt gratitude and accepted that it was simply Michael's will, his choice, the way he wanted to live. Fred was finally embracing his forgotten, buried identity; he was learning to respect, rather than fight the midland reverence of the will, the spiritual dark matter that makes life endlessly possible and infinitely variable; that truth of human arbitrary willpower that enables life to be spent however the yielder so chooses; to love without reason; to act because it feels right; to give a key because it felt important; to trust when it seems reasonable to control.

The latch unclicked and the door opened.

Fred and Ryan ascended the staircase and walked across the corridor with boxes in their hands. The carboard brushed the fancy, immaculate paint of the communal walkway. Fred unlocked Michael's apartment and he and Ryan entered with his stuff.

"Fuck me," Ryan said, his promise to not mention money going completely out of the ten-foot bay windows stretching along the far side of the apartment. Michael sat on the sofa. The television was off. No radio played. He sat in silence, with light from the windows pouring onto his bald head. Boxes slammed onto the expensive wooden floor and Ryan strutted into the kitchen area, amazed at the elegance and size of the place; he hadn't seen Michael sitting on the sofa. It was all Fred could see.

"This place is amazing… it's fucking huge," Ryan didn't swear often, but today the language flowed liberally. His fingertips brushed the worksurface in a large semi-circle as he turned back to look at Fred, who just stood frozen by his boxes.

"It was a wig darling," Michael said without even tilting his head, yet alone turning or moving from the sofa. He could feel Fred's eyes on him.

"Oh shit, sorry Michael, I didn't see you there. This place is gorgeous," the bald head hadn't taken Ryan as quite a surprise. Fred had told him about the cancer and so it was what he had expected, but Fred's stomach ached. Michael hadn't looked like that this morning. He didn't even look that ill. He had transformed unfairly fast. Fred felt hurt, as if Michael had lied to him. And he felt sick at his own feelings: *'how are you making this about you?'* he thought to himself.

Ryan walked over and plonked himself beside Michael on the sofa. He leaned in to give him a hug, "you should have said something,"

"The last time I saw you, you had Madam to deal with," Michael said referring to Fred who was still stood frozen by the door. "I couldn't possibly burden you with my little problems."

Ryan took his hand and squeezed it, "You big queen."

Fred was irritated at Ryan's casual behaviour – how was he just sitting there speaking as if Michael wasn't bald, and visually, half the man he was this morning. His body seemed thinner; his face paler and malnourished beneath that hairless scalp. He hated himself, but he walked out of the apartment and used his fingers to push his cheeks upward in a successful attempt to stop himself crying. Hot puffs of breath shot out. His fingertips massaged the skin beneath his eyes like a pushy, erratic bodybuilder. He willed himself to not cry. Ryan ran over to the doorway, "What's wrong?" he said concerned.

"I can't,"

"Can't what?" Ryan's voice reduced to a whisper, "Come-on Fred, Michael's just over there…"

Fred inhaled a larger breath that pushed its way around his body, his head bobbed forward in small repetitive nods, "You're right. I'm sorry." He pulled himself together and entered the apartment. They walked over to the sofa and sat either side of Michael; they each took one of his hands and sat in silence beside him. The light shined on all three of them. Tears trickled down Fred's cheeks but he didn't try to hide them. He released his hand and leant his head on Michael's decaying chest; Michael pushed his fingertips through Fred's hair. Ryan tilted his own head so that it rested on

Michael's shoulder. The man with the cancer devouring him from within lovingly embraced two healthy adult men with long lives ahead of them. A warm, earnest smile stretched across his face and despite the light that had been flowing-in through those gorgeous windows, it was the first time, he looked like he had proper colour in his face. His mind was consumed with memories of his friends lying in the AIDs wards all those years ago, him as the healthy youngster climbing into bed to lie alongside their withering bodies, when almost everybody else wouldn't touch them without hazmat suits and a bottle of disinfectant. He closed his eyes and enjoyed the memories hoping that he would see them again soon. Fred somehow knew what was going through his mind. They sat on that sofa, still; peaceful, not needing words, for hours. They just sat and appreciated one another's existence, the gentle heat of the sunshine coming through the window, in a way that is only possible when faced with the imminent reality of an ending.

Late afternoon clouds darkened the room and without the light, the apartment became noticeably cooler. Hunger also struck Ryan and Fred's bellies like little drums; Michael hadn't truly felt proper hunger for quite a while, but he felt like he needed a little something, "Ok, ok. Come on gentlemen, time for food." Like a sensible mother, Michael was the one to put an end to a moment that had already passed. Life went on.

CHAPTER 12: First love

Michael died. It's how it happens with people you love: the moments with them feel eternal but when they go, those eternal moments are ground into flecks of powdered spice, as if some giant hand of God has reached into your mind, taken the substance of your memories, and used them in a pestle and mortar. The rich flavour of them remains; is intensified even. But the substance melts away like the softest piece of meat in the mouth. There is the sincerest desperation to hold onto it, but the yearning is futile. It goes quickly, quicker than we feel is appropriate. We're left with a horrid hole of guilt that attracts harmful narratives of human fickleness and accounts of personal unworthiness. The complexity of the deceased's life, the good and the bad, is distilled into one distinct flavour – one spice. It is the compromise our limited biology makes. We need to remember them, but in truth, their reality eludes us; and this truth is simply too painful for most of us to handle. The dead are not capable of existence in the container of another being's mind, no matter the depth of the love for them. They're gone. And so, we essentialise them as a way of keeping a part; our memories capture and presents a flavour as a substituted disguise of the whole. It helps us to feel as if they remain, at least for a while; it delays the brutal truth of separation.

Fred stared at Michael's cold body lying in the bed of machines. Darkness was slowly being evicted as slithers of sunlight worked their way into the bedroom. He died in the night. Fred sat on the yellow chair beside the bed, his bum perched on the end. He held Michael's hand and just sat there for a few minutes. He'd sat in that chair for countless hours over the last few weeks; he'd read entire novels aloud in a single day, in it. Michael had been too tired to stay awake and listen to the whole thing, but even when Fred's words trickled out of meaning – when they returned to the warm fuzzy soundwaves of our mother's and father's voices in infancy – he appreciated their presence. He was glad Fred was there, glad he wasn't alone, glad he was loved.

A multicoloured crochet blanket rested on the side of the armchair. Fred rested back in the chair and pulled the blanket over his body, only his hand stretched out, a symbolic gesture of connection to Michael's now vacant body. He couldn't do anything yet. As soon as he made the call, that'd be the end. He didn't want it to end. Stacks of novels returned his stares and indulged his hesitation. He picked up the book on the top of the pile – George Eliot, *Daniel Deronda*. He hadn't finished it. He opened it, scanned the page number, 422, and continued reading to Michael's dead corpse, from where he'd left off reading the night before to his lukewarm body...

"I wonder whether one oftener learns to love real objects through their representations, or the representations through the real objects,' he said after pointing out a lovely capital made by the curled leaves of greens, showing their reticulated under-side with the firm gradual swell of its central rib. 'When I was a little fellow these capitals taught me to observe, and delight in, the structure of leaves.'

'I suppose you can see every line of them with your eyes shut... You must love this place very much,' said Juliet Fenn, innocently, not thinking of inheritance. 'So many homes are like twenty others. But this is unique, and you seem to know every cranny of it. I daresay you could never love another home so well.'

'Oh I carry it with me,' said Deronda, quietly, being used to all possible thought of this kind. 'To most men their early home is no more than a memory of their early years, and I'm not sure but they have the best of it. The image is never marred. There's no disappointment in memory, and one's exaggerations are always on the good side.'"

Fred stopped reading. The thought of going home struck him hard as if his body had become the clock upon which its handles were thumping midnight upon itself with increasingly visceral pounds. He let go of Michael, and held the book in both hands. He flicked backward a couple of pages and re-read a couple of lines that had lingered with him before bed, the last time he'd seen Michael alive.

"'To delight in doing things because our fathers did them is good if it shuts out nothing better; it enlarges the range of affection – and affection is the broadest basis of good in life...

'I should have thought you cared most about ideas, knowledge, wisdom, and all that.'

'But to care about <u>them</u> is a sort of affection,' said Deronda, smiling at her naivete. 'Call it attachment, interest, willingness to bear a great deal for the sake of being with them and saving them from injury. Of course it makes a difference if the objects of interest are human beings; but generally in all deep affections the objects are a mixture – half persons and half ideas – sentiments and affections flow in together.'"

The book dropped from Fred's hands and the sound of a small collision filled the otherwise quiet room. The crochet blanket moved aside, and Fred stood. He leant over Michael and kissed his forehead. It was time. The last few weeks of Fred's life had been some of the simplest and also some of the most important. He knew, even in his shaken state, literally staring death in the face, that although Michael was gone, his affections for him would remain. That was enough for now. Enough for him to make the call to the hospital and allow reality to re-enter the apartment that had been held at bay during their enwombed existence in that apartment for the remaining days of Michael's earthly life. It was time. Time.

Ryan left work immediately to meet Fred. But the funeral home was efficient – perhaps there weren't many dead bodies for them to collect that morning – Michael was wheeled away beneath a black sheet without fuss or ceremony. It was complete so quickly. Fred felt like he had attended some sort of twisted shot gun wedding; he had signed the marriage certificate and then been abandoned at the alter: no partner, no congregation, no priest, no celebration, no future. An emotional day of expectation had been lifted upside down like a pair of ragged trousers, shaken mid-air until all its contents fell from the pockets. Emptiness and nothingness. He thought back to the funerals in Nuneaton, the ones he had internally judged; the scorn he had had for the lack of affection; the snobbery he had felt toward the lack of depth. In this moment, he developed a retrospective thankfulness for those funerals. They may not have been regal displays of sentiment swamping the streets of London in memory of some celebrity that had touched the lives of the masses, but people showed-up. There was an acknowledgement of the terrible loss, and a quiet recognition of the pain and suffering caused; a tender show of support and empathy to the bereaved that let them know they were not alone. Fred stood outside the building forty minutes later with Michael gone, and the world continued as if it were a normal day. People passed him along the street. Cars drifted up and down the road. Neighbours opened and closed their doors on their way to work as if it were the most normal of normal days. It wasn't. Fred was irrationally furious at them – at the world. Nobody was stopping. Nobody was affected by Michael's death, apart from him. Was this it – two unsentimental robots arriving like taxi drivers to collect a passenger for the airport? He stood on the pavement in devasting disappointment; he had no words. No fight. He walked. He needed to walk. He walked and walked and walked. Around and around. The sights and smells didn't compute. He walked without a destination, without anything. London might as well have been a blackhole. The vibrations of his phone eventually drew him out of himself. He answered it mechanically, but Ryan's compassion elicited some energy.

"I'm so sorry. You think you'll be ready, but you never are. Not really, no matter how much warning you have…"

Fred had nothing to say but he wanted Ryan to continue speaking.

"Are you there?" Ryan said after leaving a long silence.

"Yeah – I'm here…"

"Where's that?"

Fred looked around to try and work out where he was, "I must be close to Green Park because I can see the Ritz Hotel…"

"Ok wait by the entrance, I'm less than ten minutes away…" Ryan left a pause for Fred to confirm; when it didn't come, he pressed him, "Promise you'll wait for me?"

Fred nodded and then said into the phone, "promise." He meant it. The phones disconnected and tucked away into their respective pockets. The glitz of the hotel front dazzled like jewels peacocking their worth to passing traffic. The deep red of the awning flowed like lava above the main doors and beneath the increasingly hot sunshine. It was turning into one of those gorgeous summer London days where its entire 10 million inhabitants redirect their opportunistic, material pleasure-seeking into optimistic adoration for nature. Short tempered egomaniacs transformed into easy-going spiritual pilgrims. Its parks were already beginning to swell with people breakfasting on freshly cut lawns. By lunchtime, every green space would be populated with outdoor liquid lunches with spirits of every kind flowing into throwaway plastic cups: beers, alcopops, vodkas, gin and tonics. The entire city was rising to happiness.

Fred leaned against the glass panels of the hotel. Tourists took breakfast from inside while they watched people hurry past. Fred did the same from outside. Minutes melted away as quickly as the thousands of ice-creams would melt away later that afternoon. Ryan reached out his arm and laid his flat palm onto Fred's window-pressed shoulder.

"Hey – you ok?"

Fred nodded his head a little - the walk had eased his anger. Although his mind responded with a dose of guilt, the sunshine had also drawn out a little happiness. "It's so weird. I was crazy mad less than ten minutes ago; I just couldn't cope with the nothingness of it all… the poof! He's gone. Move-on. You know?" He read Ryan's face, and picked-up the scent that he should continue speaking. "I mean, it's stupid. I know there wouldn't be a funeral the same day. And obviously, that his family weren't interested. But… until you're standing there… with literally nobody…" he covered his mouth with his hand and tensed his facial muscles. Ryan placed his hand onto his other shoulder and they looked at each other squarely. Fred held his breath instinctively; he choked his body of oxygen in the attempt to disable it from reacting, and of course, the body protested as it would in such a scenario; his shoulders jittered and jutted while his face spluttered like a junkie in cold turkey. He moved his hand and sucked breath like a swimmer after a deep plunge. In full view of the guests breakfasting inside the ritz, Ryan pulled his hands together on the other side of Fred's head, their faces radiated heat into one another; their noses brushed liked Eskimos. Ryan's deep red lips pressed onto Fred's and stayed there as London churned: cups of tea continued to lift and tilt into mouths inside the hotel; pieces of toast continued to crunch; the circular doors continued to spin, the taxis continued to breast-stroke behind front-crawling double decker buses; pedestrians continued listening to their iPods; commuters continued checking their watches; waitresses continued laying cutlery; pigeons continued cooing; grass continued growing; thin clouds continued dissipating; endless blue sky continued stretching into the universe. The world continued but Fred and Ryan stayed still in the longest, most perfect kiss imaginable, a kiss that would have made Michael proud, a kiss that would have spread joy across every one of those men's faces, a kiss that took both of them way beyond themselves, a kiss of kisses, a kiss of kings and queens; their kiss.

Ryan softened the grip of his hands and although physical space increased between their bodies, their souls were bound for life. They would never be apart again, not in the way it matters. They smiled generosity and thanks at one another. They did Michael and his friends proud. They turned to be aside one another and walked hand-in-hand, fearlessly, along Piccadilly.

As they reached the end of the street, Fred stood beneath the screens and stopped to speak to Ryan so that he could see his face at the same time, "I need to go home."

Ryan nodded. He thought he understood – it was only logical that Fred felt the need to see his family. "I understand."

"I mean, permanently," this, Ryan did not expect. He felt like a baseball had torpedoed through the sky and slammed into his chest.

"Not the physical place," Fred elaborated, "I mean emotionally... I want to stop running away and embrace who I am. I want to live with you, Ryan. I love you. I want us to start a proper life; for us to have a proper home; roots, a place where we're known and where we know people; a place where we aren't hiding; permanence; history; belonging."

Ryan's heartbeat returned, "You are a dick."

They smiled at each other and laughed. Fred hadn't intentionally meant to mislead Ryan, but the state of terror that thundered across Ryan's face let him realise the effect of his words pretty quickly... "I guess I know how you feel about moving to the Midlands now though..." Fred said laughing.

"I don't care where we live, as long as it's together," Ryan said in earnest.

"Me neither, but I kind of hope that you'd prefer to stick in London, at least for now?"

"I thought you just said you wanted to stay in one place for ever," Ryan teased Fred with a literal interpretation of his hearty speech.

"I didn't mean…"

"I know!" Ryan cut-off Fred's attempt to explain himself by placing his hand across Fred's mouth to stop him speaking. "I was joking. I agree with everything you said. It doesn't matter if we live in twenty-five different towns, or one; wherever we go, we go proudly; together."

People walking past stared at Ryan's hand silencing Fred. They scrunched their eyebrows and delivered disapproving stares; he removed his hand and they laughed. "So, what now – do you want me to come to Michael's? … We can pack up some of your stuff and move it over to mine?" Ryan said.

"No. Today's the first time I've left the apartment properly in weeks; I can't go back for a few days. It's selfish but I need a bit of time…" he left a short pause. He knew what he wanted to say but was building himself up. It was one thing to declare his new found pride, and another to take his boyfriend home to meet the family. "I think I do actually have to go back to Nuneaton. I have things to clear up… people think I've disappeared… again…" he paused; he still hadn't said what he needed, "… will you come with me?"

Ryan smiled, "Nah, not really my scene…" he teased before telling Fred that he would love to meet his family.

"Ok…" Fred felt like confetti… excited and joyful, but also a bit anxious of mess. "Well I should probably…"

Ryan replaced his hand across Fred's mouth. "Don't explain though. It'll be fine. Let us meet each other without you trying to control all our responses. We'll either like each other or we won't. It doesn't really matter does it?" he smiled wickedly, "we're family after all."

Fred laughed into Ryan's hand; he considered it such an alien thought, Ryan and his family – as family. Fred became aware of one of the simplest truths that evades children the world over: the fallacy of blood – genetics – as the defining feature of a family. Despite American T.V telling him otherwise – *Friends* – Fred had understood family as the people you are biologically bound to; the people you are stuck to just because of a shared gene pool. He told himself otherwise, but he never felt the plunging, hopeless attachment to friends in the way he did his siblings, cousins, parents. But he had not really thought properly about the truth of it all… that the heart of every family is not those feelings of oppressive uniformity and obligation; that obsession with a common gene pool and blind obedient deference; indeed, quite the opposite… save in situations of incest, a healthy diversity of genes is the source of any secure bonding. Difference, not sameness, is the secret sauce that enables life to proliferate. Children take time to appreciate that; but as they learn the truth of who their parents are; that they did not begin life together; that they are not attached by innate wiring, but by choice, commitment, interest, and love. It is in this moment that they properly understand the nature of family, the nuclei magnets orbiting invisibly within their parents. Fred's distance from his family, his going out into the world to find somebody to love, to care about more than he cared for himself; his separation, his risk; all these things had, ironically, been the only way for him to properly go home as a man. Fred stared at Ryan standing beneath the screens of Piccadilly Square, and he realised this. Ryan was not a barrier or an adjunct to his family, he was a blessing, a rare bridge, who made it possible for Fred to re-know his family. Ryan was a crossing from Fred's otherwise island life. He was dumbstruck. His fear and anxiety dissipated on the spot. The fallacy of risk disappeared. There was none. He could jump on a train and return to see them, but deep down he knew there would be a metaphorical ocean between them without Ryan – he may have threatened Fred's fragile mental construct of the family – his expectation of perfection, the need for idyllic relationships and the total absence of conflict. But he also knew, looking into Ryan's real eyes, slightly irritated by the London fumes exacerbating them with its unusually high London temperatures, and knew that he needed Ryan. He knew Ryan was his means of going home for the first time as an adult; he was going home and he would be able to see his parents, his family; to know them properly; to empathise with their love; their choices, commitments, and continued willingness to be together. He was not going to honour abstract obligations imposed by a gene pool or pay deference to notions of biological tribute; he was going to see real people. He was going to see his family.

"Shall we go back to mine so you can shower?" Ryan said.

"No. Let's go now…" Fred stared at Ryan with joyous enthusiasm.

"Now?" Ryan liked to plan things.

"Yeah, it's only an hour from Euston."

"But what about your family – won't they need notice?"

"What for?"

Ryan stuttered, "I don't know… work… to make beds?"

"No. We don't need to worry about that sort of stuff. I'll give my mum a call to let her know. She'll be happy we're coming." Fred never gave much warning when he went home; like a Cat, he would turn-up randomly and people would make the effort to come and see him. He didn't really think about them having schedules, or the time it would take out of their lives.

"Have they even heard of me?"

"Yeah of course – Nick told them about you at my gran's funeral."

"Nick?"

"Yeah – people kept asking if he was my boyfriend, so he had to tell them about you."

"Jesus Fred, 'had to tell them'… I sound like some shameful ogre."

"Well, you'll exceed expectations then… really, I've done you a favour."

"Thanks," Ryan said.

"Oh, come on – you know what I'm like, and wasn't you the one that just told me to not control…"

For the third time, Ryan placed his hand on Fred's mouth. "ok, ok," Ryan knew Fred was correct; he was being honest, and that's what he had asked for. He could feel Fred's smug smile beneath his hand; it drew a happy smile of defeat from Ryan; the kind that is genuinely pleasant because the game had been far more enjoyable than the outcome. "Come-on then, let's go and see what kind of place is responsible for releasing you into the world."

Fred licked his fingers before Ryan's hand peeled back.

"Yuck!"

"You deserved it."

The set off for Euston station. The underground was already sweaty; it would be unbearable in a few more hours. After purchasing tickets, and a rubbish baguette with chewy bread, they alighted one of Richard Branson's vibrantly red horizontal shuttles. There were plenty of seats and cool air blasted through the air conditioning units – it was going to be a pleasant journey. They sat opposite one another, across a small table.

"Reminds me of heading back to Manchester," Ryan said… "In fact, I think the train used to stop at Nuneaton… did you come to London much before we met? Perhaps we travelled on the same train without knowing it…"

"Not much… nights out mostly… and…"

"and what?"

"Well, you know."

"No Fred. That's why I asked," Ryan said laughing.

"You know, to meet people," they had spoken a little about past experiences, but neither Fred nor Ryan had had any serious relationships so the conversations had been brief.

"Oh yeah?" Ryan said interested.

Fred felt awkward. He was not sure on the etiquette – was he supposed to tell Ryan about those parts of his past? He nodded and waited to see whether Ryan would press him further.

"Oh for God sake, Fred – come on, there's obviously a story there," Ryan took from the brown paper wrapper, the half of his baguette that he had not yet eaten. The chewy bread tore in his teeth; he was hungry, for both the baguette and to hear Fred's story… "is this the first guy you ever met?"

"Yeah," Fred's mood sobered. This story weighed heavy in him. He had begun to share it – he had told Nick and Heeta, but they were friends; it felt odd – somehow risky – to share it with Ryan.

"At this rate, you might just about get through the prelude by the time we arrive," Ryan said taking another bite of his baguette.

Fred censured his head, and followed his heart. He loved Ryan – *'you're meant to share everything with the person you love',* he told himself and so began to share the story of his first love, a painful, irrational, unrequited love with a man that was cruel.

"I was sitting in class – sixth form – so like over ten years ago now –" Fred began, "and my phone vibrated. I hoped it was him," he said "him" as if it took a huge reserve of his energy to do so. "There were only a few minutes left until the bell went, but I could hardly wait to find-out what the message said. I ran my pencil back over the notes I'd made in my organised pad; I made the letters thicker, and the bullet points rounded to twice the size they had originally been. I looked at the clock on the classroom wall and my heart fluttered around the augmenting flick of the hand as it moved from second to second." Fred paused, and looked out of the window. Euston station began to separate from him as the train propelled. Fred did not yet realise, but his decision to tell Ryan his story, was allowing him to let go of it, a story that was sub-consciously, still defining him, ten years on. Ryan was surprised at Fred's seriousness – he knew the story was important and so he listened without commentary. His back pressed into the chair, and he remained in complete listening mode. Fred continued,

"The smile on my face was uncontainable. I knew people noticed, but it just made my smile bigger. I pulled my gaze back into my notebook and continued pencilling over the letters, waiting for the bell to ring. After it did, my friend asked as she packed her things away: "what are you smiling at?" She never expected a response… nobody did. I was secretive back then. People just accepted I was a bit weird; they didn't challenge my privacy and I never felt awkward about being private." Ryan considered that person – it wasn't the verbose Fred he knew, the Fred who became uncomfortable with keeping information about the colour and size of his shit, secret. Ryan did not articulate his thoughts; he was intrigued about what had changed Fred so fundamentally.

"I told her that I would see her tomorrow without making eye contact. My attention remained forcibly on the pencilling of the letters. I was making it obvious that I was staying in the classroom for a while; that I wanted to be left alone so that I could look at my phone in privacy. She, the teacher, and the rest of the class left. Only then, in that boxed classroom, did I pull my phone from my jean-pocket and nervously stare at the red-framed screen. I closed my eyes and let my desire pulse for a couple of seconds." Fred paused, his re-telling was not just re-telling; it was re-living. He took several deep breaths and smiled imitating the smile across his face in that room ten years ago.

"Before I checked the message, I opened my eyes, and breathed consciously. I told myself there was a possibility that the message might not be him, as if it would cushion my disappointment if it wasn't," The Fred on the train sitting opposite Ryan laughed at the naïve, younger Fred.

"I then read it. I flipped open my phone and checked the message. It was him - *'Come see me tonight, sexy,'* it read... My eyes darted at the doorway to ensure nobody was lingering in the corridor; my teeth were on full display. My fingertips punched a response and I pressed send before I could take it back: *'What's your address?'*"

"I bit the nail of my thumb and pondered the thought of meeting a man, a real man, a man existing in real life. Real flesh. I felt positively sick in that exciting way children do at Theme-parks," Train-Fred said this sentence more as a narrator, aware of the separation between the character Fred and Ryan sitting opposite him. He returned to his telling,

"*'Clapham.'* That's all he wrote back. I didn't appreciate what that meant. To me, those 7 letters didn't refer to a south London urban sprawl of terraced houses and amenieties. It became the pin-point location of his house – my new home – the place my heart emigrated to, there and then, on the spot. It was for real. I knew I couldn't say that I would go unless I meant it. He would think I was a kid otherwise." Fred said this, still from the perspective of the younger Fred; ten years later, still raw.

"*'What time shall I get there?'* I text him back. I had committed. I was going. He responded straight away: *'Seven.'* I couldn't believe it. I pulled my hands to cover my face, but I swear if there was anybody else in the room they would still be able to see my smile." Even though Fred knew how it ended, he imitated that euphoric smile on the train in front of Ryan. The pain that came and lingered to his immediate present, had not crushed his capacity to empathise and incubate that naïve, wonderfully naïve, teenage passion and blindingly optimistic, crushing hope.

"I laughed into my palms and squeezed my eyelids as tight as was physically possible. 'I'm actually going to do this!' I said aloud. After all the months of late night phone calls; after the hours of back and forth messaging on MSN; after the endless texting, paranoia and stomach-wrenching fear, I accepted that I was finally doing this. *'See you then.'* I typed and closed my little red, flip-phone. I shoved my notes and pencil case in my bag and strutted out of the classroom feeling like a model..." Fred was slim now, but at that time, he had starved himself to be about the size of a model.

"I unlocked my bike and cycled home beneath a pure blue sky feeling like a bird on first flight. I was ecstatic that I barely felt the crisp water as I showered and dressed before I was properly dry. I wore a plain blue t-shirt without any pattern or collar and tossed-on a pair of ordinary jeans. I hadn't really learnt anything about clothes back then. Before I joined the sky outside, I forced myself to be serious for a moment; to have a word with myself. I insisted that it was important to take precautions; to apply a bit of reason," Fred chuckled to his former self.

"I scattered coded diary excerpts into draws around my bedroom; I had invented my own alphabet so that I could keep a journal without the worry of anybody finding it by accident and knowing what I'd written." Ryan laughed at this part of the story – this was the first proper bit of Fred that he really recognised in the story. Fred laughed too and then continued.

"I left enough coded notes and clues for the police, with a bit of effort, to be able to work out where I had gone in case this guy turned out to be a murderer or was going to sell me into slavery; but not enough for any causal snooping family member to find out where I had gone in case I had to come back."

"That was it. After that, I could let my heart flutter freely. I was going to London, to meet a real man. Although, actually I did do one more thing - en route to the train station with nothing but my phone and wallet, I sent the girl from the classroom a text message to tell her that I was going to meet a lady in London. I made clear that I was only telling her so that she could alert people in case I never came back. She urged me not to go, but I interpreted her words as joyous and playful; she wasn't one to harp-on; it was why I liked her. She let me be."

"I bought my ticket. I would be in London in just over an hour." Fred looked out of the train window, the train that was catapulting him back to the place from where he left that day. London had already faded into the background, and green rolling fields filled the view. He continued.

"I was desperate to text and call him, to say that I was really coming, but I didn't. I told myself it would be a surprise – a grown-up surprise – selectively ignoring the reality that I had told him I would be there at 7. The people on the train must have thought I was a lunatic: I smirked like a stoner who had just found God and been reborn, for the entire journey. I ignored them, and pretended to look out of the window at the green fields, but my mind was filled with ideas and questions: living with him; would I be the talk of the town because of my elopement? I was so excited at the prospect of being town gossip. My head played movie trailers of my own life."

"The train eventually began to roll into Euston. I imagined him stood inside each of the apartment windows towering beside the station. I wondered what his house would look like?"

"I departed the train with pride, pretending that I had returned rather than arrived. I wanted the other people to think that I was a native Londoner; after all I would be soon." Ryan thought of his own meeting with Fred, the back and forth they'd had about Fred being a Londoner.

"While I queued for an Oyster card, I succumbed to the temptation and text him. I expressed how complicated the tube was. Stupid. I regretted it immediately. I was excited at the complexity, the vastness of London; but I had presented myself as some wuss. *'It's easy. Just take the Northern Line.'* He text back though, and I was relieved that I hadn't cocked it up. I thought to myself that, at least he knows I'm here now, and also overanalysed the message, of course," Train-Fred smiled a conscious smile at Ryan, emphasising his self-awareness. Ryan smiled back.

"I concluded that he had helped me, and decided that was a good sign. I bleeped my new Oyster card on the machine and strutted through the barrier as if I did it all the time. The escalators took me down, and exaggerated the new depths of feeling I had. I felt courageous for the first time in my life. It was love at first sight – with London. I knew there and then that it was going to be my home one day. I applied a straight face to blend in with the people, but a small smirk couldn't help but shine through, just a little.

"I took the wrong Northern line. Instead of jotting straight down to Clapham, the tube bent me eastward for a voyeur beneath the edge of the city. The train also stopped for 10 minutes, which worried me a bit: I didn't want him to think I wasn't coming; but mostly, I couldn't help enjoying watching everybody pull exasperated faces and shuffle around one another – it was another opportunity to pretend I was a native; that this sort of thing happened every day. I scowled and subtly shook my head; I exaggerated the lack of space and discomfort on the little wedge that I perched on.

"Another hour later, I arrived at Clapham North station. I climbed the stairs out of the station, and kept speed with the masses of people exiting. I took my Oyster card and bleeped out of the barrier. For the first time, I felt proper anxiety. He could be here, looking at me. I felt exposed. I left the station anyway. I re-joined the still blue sky, chillier, but still warm. As I started walking along the street, I thought to myself that he better not kick me out: I was only wearing my plain t-shirt.

"I took out my phone and called him. I felt sick that no words would come-out when he answered. It was one thing talking on the phone in the middle of an empty park at 10.30 in the evening, and something else entirely when you're around so many people – speaking to a man in broad daylight who lived close by."

"He directed me along the high-street to one of the side streets where he lived. The place was so busy: I remember being amazed at the amount of people walking in and out of blockbuster, thinking of how, literally nobody, used our blockbuster, especially not on a Monday evening. I remember what it felt like for the first time to see people sitting drinking coffee in the street, in the evening. I was in love and scared stiff at the same time. The reality of this man being a crazy paedophile hit me outside that blockbuster. I had thought in abstract about being killed, murdered – you heard about it – young boys meeting people of the internet, never coming back, but until you are two minutes away from meeting the man, the risk is abstract. It was only standing there on that Monday afternoon, that I felt it all – visceral and gumptious simultaneously."

"I walk along the side street and appreciate that he lived in one of the terraced houses. My feet carried me along the path involuntarily. I was glad I didn't wear a jacket; otherwise I might have been tempted to stop and think, which would have stopped me moving forward. The chill pushed me onward. I told myself I had to just do it, I counted down the house numbers and arrived. I had arrived."

"I pressed the bell and waited like a boy about to piss himself. The door opened as if in a slow motion movie; the gap widened between it and the frame at an increasingly painful speed. My eyes fixated on the floor and it was his jeans that I saw first. My eyes crawled up his leg, over his torso, his broad shoulders, his perfect lips and nose, and they finally rested on his eyes. It felt like love at first sight – again. It hadn't occurred to me though how young I would look next to him – and short. I felt so embarrassed. He was a beautiful man with his own apartment, a strong independent man, and despite my London adventure, I was catapulted back into the firm position of boy, a short, unexperienced, naïve boy.

Ryan stared at Fred, gripped by the story, "what happened?"

Fred felt finished though – his energy sapped, "we had a great time. I stopped the night. We slept together. Everything was perfect; to me, anyway. We woke-up the next morning, I watched him iron his shirt. I felt like a man like I'd graduated or something. We walked to the station together, but the platform was so busy. I'd never seen trains so packed: the tube doors closed with him on the inside and me lingering on the congested platform. I wasn't able to get on. We waved goodbye. And that was the last time I saw him. The image of him standing on the other side of the tube door in his beautiful suit, looking down at me through the small window." Fred stopped himself from saying that, that window had imprinted itself onto his very core and that as the train began to move along the platform, it felt as if his heart had been dragged along with it.

"I stood there in the midst of the commuters and watched the train bob against the side of a platform that was impossibly becoming even more congested; the fast-moving train burrowed into the depths of a black, endless tunnel."

Ryan felt so sad for Fred. He went to say something but wasn't quite sure what to say.

Fred wasn't sure if it was the right thing to be telling Ryan all of this, but his heart told him that it was and so he continued while looking out at the green fields, "I felt like a Rockstar – that life would never be the same again – but of course, life was exactly the same, and I just sort of spiralled downward from there. I called and called and called. He never answered. I missed lessons to sit in the computer room, staring at the little icon that showed he was online… I waited for hours with my icon showing that I was also online, just in case he decided to chat to me. He never did. Or once or twice, he dangled a vacuous, 'hey – hope you are well', but nothing. I bombed class, failed to get into the university course I wanted, and so ended-up training to be a teacher at the local comprehensive."

"I went back to London loads more times; each time the doors of the underground opened and shut, I would imagine him climbing into the train and standing beside me, his arm easily stretching up so that his fingers could wrap around the handle dangling from the train's roof and beneath where his biceps would be, the slight sag of his neatly ironed city shirt would droop just ever so softly that the material would rest on the edge of my cheek, to just that extent that it wouldn't come across as rude to the other passengers, but to me, I'd know that it was his way of making a public connection," Fred was letting it all out to Ryan.

"A heaviness protested within my chest since that day; before I moved to London, before I met you, I felt like I was dying a little bit more each day. Resentment slowly turned to hatred. I started to hate the place; it was like he awakened some dormant force that had been sleeping in the very depth of my being, until that day of my life. He awoke a hunger and took away my peace. I felt like some demonic dragon with ferocious claws that tore away and cannibalised my own insides, but over time I think I turned into that dragon. I lost myself. I took the heaviness clutching to my organs and tossed it epically away. In the fantasy of being that dragon, I lost my vulnerability – my peace. I became power itself; I hated the idea of feeling weak; I tore-up my roots, my connections, my belonging, and flew away. But it has been fantasy. I'm not a dragon.

Ryan laughed, a heart-filled, supportive, kind laugh. He held out his hand and Fred took it. "So, the point of this story is to tell me that you don't want to be a dragon any longer."

Fred laughed. He laughed, and laughed and laughed. That story had shaped him, made him paranoid that a life of unrequited love awaited him, that his chance of happiness had gone; that he would never be properly capable of love again. But it all dissipated in the sharing of his story. He had rediscovered his humanity. He could feel the soft beat of his own heart and appreciate that Ryan's beated in the same way; so too, his mother's, father's, siblings'; Nick's, Heeta's, Bea's. A rush of love for the real people in his life flooded his entire being. He let go of the cruelty inflicted by that man and stopped trying to imitate his power. Fred had taken his first step on the metaphorical road of Damascus – he was going home with Ryan and he was ready to love his friends and family.

The End

Acknowledgments

Thank you to Debbie, Adam, and Arron for reading, commenting, and humouring my writing throughout the bleak opening months of 2021. Your interest and enthusiasm kept me going – writing can be a lonely process, but you always made it social – your GIFs, messages and calls were wonderful (especially anything to do with Bea's horse teeth) ... and your casting projections were fascinating - let's see whether Hollywood agrees ... ⍰

Thank you to all the staff and colleagues from school(s!) (I do like to move around). My characterisations of teaching are exaggerated: (adult) school life is wonderful, and I urge anybody thinking about teaching, to do it. The camaraderie and piss-ups aren't exaggerated ... if you don't believe me, find the teachers' watering hole and visit it at the end of term!

And, finally, thank you to Nuneaton and its wonderful inhabitants. It's a funny old place, but a special funny old place that is in my heart. There is nowhere else I would have rather been raised ... except maybe Bali...

About the Author

Mark James Birkett is a full-time writer of fiction novels. Finding Fred is his first novel. He is 33 and lives with his husband and dog (Max) in Salisbury, UK. He has been a successful teacher and school leader — and despite some of his characterisations of school life — loved working in education. He greatly admires the work of compassionate teachers throughout the world.

If you enjoyed Finding Fred, What About Nick? is also available. Mark is working on his third novel, Eve's Brook, which will hopefully be available by Christmas 2021. Each novel is a standalone story, but the characters and settings intersect.

If you enjoyed the book, please leave a review on amazon & Goodreads. New authors depend on ratings, so please leave a stared review (or written comment!).

You can follow Mark on Instagram & Facebook @mjbirkett123

Printed in Great Britain
by Amazon